"There are two alternatives," Jim said. "We all stay . . . and die. Or one goes for help."

Gerry nodded. "You go on, Jim."

"I can't leave you here," he protested. "David will probably go berserk from thirst—and you can't handle him."

"You have to do it," she said. "It's the rule of the bush: Two stay and one goes on. And I won't leave David behind."

Jim got up slowly. Their eyes met in farewell and he turned away. . . .

NOBODY READS JUST *ONE* LUCY WALKER!

The Other Girl
Heaven Is Here
The Distant Hills
Sweet and Faraway
The Call of the Pines
Come Home, Dear
Love in a Cloud
Follow Your Star
Home at Sundown
Reaching for the Stars
A Man Called Masters
The Stranger from the North
The River Is Down
The One Who Kisses
The Man from Outback
Down in the Forest
The Moonshiner
Wife to Order
The Ranger in the Hills
Shining River
Six for Heaven
The Gone-away Man
Kingdom of the Heart
The Loving Heart
Master of Ransome
Joyday for Jodi
The Bell Branch
The Mountain That Went To The Sea
Ribbons In Her Hair
Monday In Summer
Pepper Tree Bay
Girl Alone

The Stranger from the North

Lucy Walker

BEAGLE BOOKS • NEW YORK

Published by arrangement with the author and
the author's agent, Paul R. Reynolds, Inc.

First printing: March 1971
Second printing: June 1971
Third printing: November 1971
Fourth printing: August 1972
Fifth printing: October 1973

Printed in the United States of America

BEAGLE BOOKS, INC.
201 East 50 Street, New York, NY 10022

CHAPTER ONE

GERRY MEREDITH swung herself off her horse with a beautiful movement. She had put her left hand on to the pommel of the saddle and it took all her weight as she swung away from the right stirrup, making a beautiful arc in the air, and it was as rhythmical as music. Bill Seddon, the head stockman, liked watching Gerry dismount from a horse. He knew nothing of rhythm or music but he knew that Gerry was a pretty sight.

Even on the ground, in her faded and worn jeans, a small tear in her blue shirt and a lot of dust on her face and in her hair, Gerry was a pretty sight to Bill. The thick-set middle-aged stockman was the last of the staff to remain on Yandoo Station and, though he would never have admitted it, he remained for Gerry's sake.

There wasn't a great deal of Gerry. She was only two inches over five feet but her firm little chin and the way she tossed her hair out of the way of those blue eyes would make anyone believe there was a lot more to her than just inches. Bill Seddon, for instance, knew that the light in Gerry's eyes was a brave light for she had a lot of trouble on her young shoulders. Sometimes she had a hint of rueful laughter in those eyes and occasionally an imp of mischief. Her troubles didn't get her down.

At the moment her hair might be called sandy rather than fair for there was a certain amount of red and brown desert sand clinging to it.

In spite of being tired, wind-blown and dusty Gerry had a smile of greeting for the stockman. It took some of the weight off Bill's own shoulders. The girl had been out since the crack of dawn hunting up stray bullocks feeding on the edge of the scrub. She must be tired but there was a lot of fight in her still.

It was four o'clock and a bright autumn day. Everywhere the grass was shooting green after the receding of the waters since the Wet. Along the edge of the boundary fence was a strip of wildflowers making a carpet of rioting colours. When the Dry had really set in there'd be nothing but brown stubble there; at the moment the earth was smiling.

"Hallo, Bill, still at it?" Gerry asked as she looked at the bits and pieces of the bore that Bill had dismantled.

5

"Day after to-morrow I'll have the mill fixed," said Bill. "I've only got to get the lead into the trough and a new plug and she'll be right. Howzit up in the bullock paddock?"

He always addressed Gerry as a fellow stockman these days though her small slight figure barely looked its nineteen years of age. She did a man's work and he gave her a man's tribute.

"Another lot of thirty," Gerry said, wiping her arm over her dusty face. "All cleanskins. If we can run them down here, Bill, we can brand them and let them feed."

Gerry had half turned away from him and she lifted her head and stared into the distance.

"I can see dust," she said. "Or maybe it's only a willy willy."

The stockman pulled his hat down to shade his eyes as he looked into the north. His native offsider did the same thing.

"One fella whiteman and boy come along black-fella," the native said. "Him got five six horses."

It had never ceased to be a wonder to Gerry that the natives always knew how many people were coming and with what sized plant long before they could possibly see anything.

"Someone's coming all right," Bill Seddon said.

"I wish I could think it was someone coming to give us a hand," Gerry said. "What are the chances it will be a stockman looking for work, Bill?"

Bill shook his head and went on with the business of fitting parts of the bore engine together. He did not say that far and wide the itinerant stockmen knew that Yandoo was on its uppers and therefore not a good place to look for work.

Gerry's father had died five years before. Her mother, Mrs. Meredith, had carried on the station with the old hands until a serious illness had overtaken her. Gerry had been at boarding school and had known nothing of the plight into which the station had fallen. She knew her aunt, Mrs. Sylvester, and her cousin, Lulu Sylvester, had gone to stay on Yandoo but had not realised it was to attend to her failing mother. As neither Mrs. Sylvester nor Lulu knew anything about running a station the place had fallen from bad to worse.

When Gerry had come home from boarding school in Sydney she was aghast at what she found. The stockmen were leaving one at a time and the natives, except Johnny, had gone walkabout and not returned. The book-keeper was the last to go after he had written to Mrs. Meredith's bank and told them they had better look into affairs. The drought and then a fire which had wiped out the new grasses last year left no possibility of the overdraft being reduced.

The bank immediately sent a man down to inspect Yandoo. As a result of his repo' t at headquarters the bank had informed Mrs. Meredith they were sending a man down from the north to take over the managership of Yandoo in order to see if something could be salvaged for the shareholders. They regretted it would probably be some considerable time before he could get down to Yandoo. There were so many rivers in flood and he would have to cross them with all his gear. It would take time. In the meantime if they could get some temporary help——

Though Mrs. Meredith and Gerry knew that a manager might save Yandoo for them it was a terrible blow to their pride. They told no one in the district that the bank had taken this action. The Merediths had been a proud family and they dreaded fellow station-owners knowing that the bank had taken over.

All this had happened two months ago and almost daily Gerry waited to hear who this new manager might be and when he would be coming.

In the meantime she and Bill Seddon, the one faithful stockman, worked themselves thin trying to keep things going.

They leaned against the broad trunk of another old tree and watched the dust cloud that was bringing the stranger towards them.

Bill Seddon's eyes were screwed up as he looked into the distance.

"He's got those horses fanned out loose in front of him," he said. "That means they aren't wild horses. They're his own plant. The native's riding behind again . . . with the pack. Looks like three packhorses."

"That's a big plant," said Gerry ruefully. "It means he expects to be weeks on the track. It doesn't look like a wandering stockman looking for a job, does it?"

She felt childishly disappointed. Quite apart from desperately needing help she would have liked to have some kind of a front to show when the man the bank was sending down from the north got to Yandoo. He could be weeks coming yet. The bank had said the man they were sending was coming down from the fringe of Arnhem Land. That meant many rivers to cross and the Wet had been heavy. All the rivers in the north had been running a banker.

Gerry had mixed feelings about the new manager. Time and again she found herself saying, "How soon will he come? What will he be like?"

Then her little jaw would stiffen and she would tell herself she wasn't going to let any new manager take Yandoo from her. She wasn't going to be bossed about by a manager.

Then at other times, when another bore broke down, or when riding through the scrub she would see tracks of cattle that had got away, she would almost cry to herself, "Why doesn't he come?"

Her greatest prayer was that two or three repentant stockmen would turn up and help Bill Seddon and herself get things somewhat into shape before the manager came. If only that could happen they . . . she and Bill . . . would have the upper hand. They would be in control, as it were.

She sipped her tea and watched the dust cloud materialise into two men, a boy and eight horses. If only they would stop and work on Yandoo for a week or two. Perhaps a month.

Bill got up slowly and walked in his curious horseman's gait over to the wire boundary fence. He leaned on it and rolled himself a cigarette. He watched the stranger from under the brim of his ancient broad-brimmed hat. Johnny, the native, did not stir, but he took everything in. He knew the native travelling with the white man was from farther north than his own country.

"Him come from edge of desert, that one," he said quietly. "Him mighty good tracker, that fella. Horse-breaker too, mine tink."

Neither Bill nor Gerry asked him how he knew. The native bush lore was too intricate for them.

Gerry joined the stockman by the fence. She stood leaning against it, her hands one on top of the other resting on the straining post. She looked hopefully at the stranger.

He looked like a stockman, and yet he didn't. He rode a horse the one and only way a stockman rides a horse; his back slightly curved and his foot hanging long in the stirrup. Yet there was more to him than just that. He'd be a tall man because his back was long and that stallion he was riding would be quite sixteen hands. His khaki clothes were in good repair and they weren't dust laden. Either he hadn't come so very far to-day or he kept a good camp, washing things as he went. His Stetson hat, broad of brim, was a good one. The harness on his horse was shining and well-kept, and so was

8

that on his native's and the boy's horses. His face was free from too much dust so maybe he had had a wash-up not too many miles back. He looked strong and sure of himself. He might be somewhere between thirty and forty.

His horse had dropped from a jog to a walk now as he neared the fence and the waiting trio. His eyes which had just been dark pools in a sun-browned face could be seen now. They might be a dark blue . . . yes, that was what they were. They were summing up what he saw in front of him.

"He's a hard man, this one," Bill said out of the corner of his mouth to Gerry. "Knows his own mind."

"Yes, I think so too," Gerry said, also out of the corner of her mouth like Bill.

"He's come a long way," Bill said. "He's spruced up but look at those horses. They've been on the track weeks."

"He doesn't look the kind that would take orders easily," Gerry said. "What do you say, Bill? Do we offer him a job?"

Yet something about the man stirred her. He was strong and good-looking in a tough sun-burned way. There was a personal magnetism about him that was hard to define. Perhaps it was his eyes. They were hard, clear and compelling.

"We'll offer him the courtesy of billy tea," Bill said quietly. "Then we'll see how he makes out."

Looking at the stranger, Gerry had a queer feeling that it would be he who saw who was making out.

He was near enough now to salute them. He lifted one hand. Bill and Gerry lifted a hand each.

"G'day," Bill said. "You come far?"

"This side of the Yeebong Creek since morning," the stranger said.

The old stockman smiled. He knew what that answer meant. The man was going to tell just so much of himself, and no more. There is a tradition in the outback that you don't ask a man who he is or where he comes from if he doesn't volunteer the information. But his voice was good. It was vibrant and there was a note of authority in it.

Gerry dropped her hands from the fence post and let them slide down the sides of her jeans. Suddenly she was conscious of her sandy wind-blown hair and of the fact that her face hadn't been washed since early morning and she had been in the sun and the dust ever since. For some extraordinary reason she thought of the fine peppering of freckles on the bridge of her nose. Oddly, she wished the stranger would think well of her.

9

This man was hard and lean and strong. He was bronzed and there was a great power in the fine bone structure of his face and in the intent eyes that expressed little but missed nothing.

He drawled his words in a way that gave him time to consider Gerry and Bill just as they were considering him. His eyes flicked away from their faces and with a quick glance took in the trough rusted from lack of use; the broken parts of the bore engine lying in the shade of the tree; the fence but newly mended and held together here and there by old rusted strands of wire.

He pulled in the corners of his mouth and then reached in his pocket for the makings of a cigarette. He had not dismounted. He sat his high saddle easily, one leg hanging out of its stirrup as if he might dismount any time now but had not made up his mind about it yet.

Gerry felt, in some oblique way, he knew about the wattle striplings used to tighten up slacking fence-wire miles away and about the cattle running wild in the scrub; in fact that one glance, ice-edged, had sufficed; and that he knew all that was to be known about a station just held together by bits and pieces of makeshift machinery and wire.

This strange feeling she had as she looked at him had a touch of trepidation in it, almost as if intuitively she knew he was going to have some great impact on her life: or on Yandoo. Yet how could this be? He was a stranger, and perhaps only passing through. Little lights seemed to dance about in the back of her mind like signals on a railway line. They were lights that said: Look out! Look out!

She flushed and her small rounded chin tilted up a little. Her head was high on her slender young throat.

"You just passing through?" she asked in a regular bushman's way. She knew she looked like a hired hand.

The stranger looked at her and seemed in that one direct glance to take in the dust in her hair and the freckles on her nose.

"Is that tea you've got in that billy?" he asked. He still drawled, and had not answered her question.

"We were thinking of asking you to come through the wire and take a swig," the old stockman said. "You got your own mug, I suppose."

The man nearly smiled. His mouth showed fine white teeth in his bronzed face but his eyes still appraised and gave nothing away. He swung off his horse in a manner that was even more rhythmical than Gerry's. He threw the reins across the fence post and ducked down to climb through the fence wires. When he stood up straight he was just beside Gerry and he was very tall.

"This is Yandoo," he said. It was a statement and not a question. Of course the man would know where he was. Yandoo would be on every pastoral map of Australia, the whole seven hundred and fifty thousand acres of it.

Then without waiting for Gerry's comment he turned to the boy, sitting slack on his horse the way the older man had been doing a few minutes before.

"Come on down, Simon. Here's tea," he said abruptly.

Simon came down off his horse with a sliding movement, ducked to get through the wire fence and came to where Gerry and the stranger stood. He walked with an exaggerated stockman's roll.

The tension was suddenly relaxed because of the boy. Gerry smiled and an imp of laughter danced in her eyes. Then quickly she shut it out. She saw at once she must take Simon as seriously as he took himself. He was perhaps eight or ten years old, thin, sun-browned, and now when he took off a Stetson, probably inherited from the older man, his brown hair was straight and sun-bleached. His blue eyes appraised the camp fire and the boiling billy.

"Good idea," he said laconically.

Again Gerry had to hide the desire to laugh.

"You have your own mug, I suppose," she said in the same tone of voice in which Bill Seddon had asked the stranger this question.

Simon swung his snake belt around and unhitched his mug.

Gerry's eyes sought the stranger's, but there was no smile in his eyes. He took Simon quite as seriously as the boy took himself.

"Your son?" Gerry asked.

"No. Just travelling along with me."

So, Gerry thought. Don't ask questions because you won't get answers.

Bill Seddon turned to his own native stockman. "Johnny," he said, "you give that blackfella one bit your damper. You fetch billy for that one fella."

"Okay, Boss."

The stranger looked at Bill Seddon. He had taken off his Stetson hat and his hair was very black. It was thick too and didn't look as if it was full of sand. He was very attractive.

11

Gerry could see that even hardened old Bill Seddon was impressed.

"You the boss round here?" the stranger said to the stockman.

"No, I am," said Gerry, lifting her head. "I'm Geraldine Meredith of Yandoo Station. . . ."

The man looked as if this amused him but not enough to make him smile.

"Geraldine," he said. "That's a big name for a not so big person."

Gerry flushed.

"I . . . that is I and my family own this station. Your stock map would tell you that, Mister. . . . We haven't got your name yet, have we, Mister . . . ?"

"Jim Conrad," the man said. His eyebrows moved a fraction of an inch. "How do you do, Miss Meredith?"

Gerry's hand was both dusty and sticky but she had to hold it out and find it lost in his hand. It was iron strong. Her heart more than her hand tingled as he stood looking down at her. His blue eyes were hard, yet very intelligent.

"This is my head stockman," Gerry said, gravely turning to Bill Seddon.

She was certain there was a hint of amusement in the man's eyes. It was almost as if he had said, "*Your* head stockman indeed? What is a small two by six-inch piece of timber like you doing with a head stockman all your own?" Gerry suddenly felt smaller than her five foot two.

Jim Conrad said, "Glad to meet you, Bill. I'm generally called Jim." He untied his mug from his belt. "That tea certainly looks good," he added.

Johnny, the native stockman, had taken billy tea outside the fence to the other native. Gerry and Bill Seddon and the stranger sat down in the shade of the tree. Gerry leaned against it.

This man was very important to himself, she thought. Whoever he was, he was on the move and that meant he might take a job. Yet somehow he didn't look the kind of person to whom one offered a job. But she and Bill were desperate for help.

"Those colts have got a touch of Arab, I see," said Bill Seddon, eyeing Jim Conrad's horses with admiration.

Jim Conrad looked at him sharply.

"You know good horseflesh?" he said.

"You bet I do," said Bill. "We've got Arab stock on Yandoo —when we can find 'em."

Gerry looked at Bill crossly but if Jim Conrad heard him he made no sign.

"If you're good with horses we can do with some help on Yandoo," Gerry said, trying to hide her anxiety.

His glance went back to her. Gerry thought her offer had probably surprised him. He was a proud man. They wanted his help and it might have been better tactics if she had let Bill Seddon do the offering.

"What do you think, Bill?" she said, as if deferring to the stockman.

"We could do with a hand to muster up the horses to begin with," Bill said. "Then when we've got a few fresh young 'uns broke in we could do with a hand with the cattle. Things are a bit short on Yandoo at present." He was almost pleading.

"So I heard," Jim Conrad said.

Yes, of course he would have heard. Every station he had passed through south of the big river would have told him how Yandoo stood. You can't hide anything in a country like this. Every stockman on the stock routes carried the gossip from station to station. If Jim Conrad was going to stay they wouldn't be able to hide the state of affairs from him.

"Things will be looking up soon," Gerry said as matter-of-factly as she could. "We've got a new manager coming in shortly. He's a very reliable man and will recruit more staff."

Jim Conrad was looking at her intently now. There was a fleeting ironic smile at the back of his eyes. It was gone as quickly as it came.

Until this minute Gerry had half-hated that unseen manager. His appointment had been a sign of defeat. Every thought of that manager had been a sword in Gerry's heart.

"A very reliable man," Gerry repeated, breaking off a twig from a fallen branch near her and whisking away the flies. She did not look at Jim Conrad any more and she hoped her words didn't sound like a plea. "A friend of the family, of course, otherwise we wouldn't dream of appointing him. A first-class man with stock of any kind . . ."

She looked up. Jim Conrad had leaned forward and run his fingers through his hair. It was quite a minute before he turned and looked at Gerry.

"Quite a paragon," he said.

Gerry flushed.

"Do you want to stay?" she asked, meeting his eyes with a challenge in her own.

"Well, now that you come to mention it . . ."

Gerry jumped up. She should have left it to Bill. Oh, if only she could afford to do without him! She went quickly across to her horse and loosed the reins from the broken branch of the tree.

"Bill will give you the details," she said. "He'll show you the track to the quarters." She was battling with tears behind her eyes.

Jim Conrad had got up and he came across to her horse in a leisurely way. Gerry swung herself up in the saddle. Jim put his hand on the horse's cheek strap.

"Who taught you to mount a horse that way?" he asked.

"I did," said Gerry. "We had a black stockman who used to do it. I learned from him."

Gerry had mounted from in front of the left foreleg by turning the stirrup and then swinging right round, making three-quarters of a circle in the air.

Jim Conrad still held the cheek strap.

"I think I'll come up to the homestead."

"I'm not going up to the homestead," Gerry said, still very much on her dignity. Though she was pleased that he had noticed and knew the unusualness of her way of mounting she felt there was something vaguely condescending in Jim Conrad's manner. "I have work to do. Here on Yandoo we have to work by moonlight too. Bill Seddon will give you directions."

"Listen, young lady . . ." Jim Conrad began. His eyes were flint hard now.

Gerry's back stiffened. She pulled on her right rein and swung her horse round.

"If you can mend the fence after you, you can bring your horse plant through the wires," she said. "The boy can come up to the homestead, if you like. He looks as if he needs feeding up."

"He was trying to high-hat me," Gerry told herself. "He thought coming on to Yandoo was an amusing thing to do."

Let him wait till he saw for himself what work on Yandoo meant. The fact that the place was in pieces didn't mean she and Bill Seddon were letting it get that way. It had been that way when she had come back from boarding school a year ago. Well, this new hand would have to battle too. He'd earn every penny of his wages.

14

Wages!

Gerry reined in her horse.

The bank would have to pay his wages, of course, and maybe the bank would wait until the new manager had formally taken Jim Conrad on before they agreed as to how much he would get. No one would work for the minimum Arbitration wage on Yandoo. He would have to do two men's work and by moonlight as well as daylight. He'd expect more. Quite a lot more probably.

Oh dear! How did she handle this one?

Suddenly her heart misgave her. They wanted extra help so badly but how did one cope with help that too obviously had a will of his own? And that boy! Oh, dear, she'd ridden away without saying good-bye to him. And he was such a funny, thin, lonely-looking little boy!

Jim Conrad did as Gerry had suggested. He cut the wire fence with pliers and led his team through. Then meticulously he and his native mended where they had cut with new wire which he uncoiled from one of the packhorses. When the job was done the fence was in a better condition than before he cut it.

He swung himself up in his saddle.

"I'll see you later," he said to Bill Seddon. "Come on, Simon."

"Keep left of the main homestead track and you'll see the quarters," Bill advised in a friendly voice.

"I'll see you later," Jim Conrad said again. "At the homestead."

Bill Seddon lifted his battered old hat and scratched his head as he watched the horseman ride up the homestead track.

"He ain't no ordinary hired hand," he confided to Johnny. All the same he felt a lightening of his own load. The man had that effect on him.

In the saddling paddock Jim left his native to unsaddle for him. He had turned the spares and the packhorses into a small stockyard. The boy sat down in the shade of a big gum tree.

Jim let himself through the small wicket gate and walked with a firm stride up to the homestead. His eyes did not appear to look around but he took everything in, including Lulu Sylvester sitting on the veranda. She was very pretty, stretched there in an old canvas chair, doing nothing.

He stepped up on to the veranda and took off his hat. Lulu sat up.

"Oh!" she said in surprise. This was the best thing that had come through the garden gate since she had arrived with her mother on Yandoo eighteen months ago. He was tall and handsome and had an air about him that challenged her interest.

"Are you another Miss Meredith?" Jim asked.

Lulu shook her bright golden head. Her blue eyes were paler than the girl's down there at the boundary and her skin was better cared for. So were the long pink polished nails of her hands. In fact she was altogether very well cared for in comparison with the other one, Jim noticed. She didn't work in the sun, that was why.

"I'm Lulu Sylvester, Gerry's cousin. Who are you and where did you strike Gerry?"

Jim didn't answer the first question. He concentrated on the last.

"On a horse about ten miles back." Suddenly he smiled. "She's just hired me."

"You?"

Lulu stood up in order to demonstrate her surprise. She was taller than Gerry and a year or two older. Her figure was so good Jim Conrad couldn't help thinking about it. Lulu laughed. She knew he knew she was pretty.

"That must have amused you," she said. "Gerry's only a kid. She can't hire or fire anyone. And I bet she looked as if she had the whole of central Australia in her hair and on her clothes."

"I think Mrs. Meredith is the head of this firm," Jim Conrad said levelly. "I'd like to see her, please."

Lulu considered.

"She's an invalid," she said. "I think you had better see my mother."

"Mrs. Meredith please," Jim said.

He meant it. Lulu looked at him in surprise. Even if Aunt Mabel was on her death-bed this man was going to see her.

"Well . . . if you insist . . ."

A thin frail voice came through the open french window, a few yards farther along the veranda.

"Who is that, Lulu? Does someone want me?"

"Well . . . yes, Aunt," Lulu said reluctantly.

She was still looking at Jim. He had turned away and was leaning on the balustrade of the veranda looking out over the neglected garden. He turned his head. Goodness, she thought, he's good-looking! Her heart rose.

"Just tell her Jim Conrad's here," he said. "She'll see me."

Lulu went to the door and spoke to her aunt. Then she turned.

"You can come in," she said. She stood aside to let him pass and she smiled up at him. "I'll tell Mother you're here. She'll make you some tea."

Jim Conrad went into the room. It was a big square room furnished partly as a living-room and partly as a bedroom. A thin pale woman was lying on a sofa.

"Mrs. Meredith? I'm Jim Conrad."

Mrs. Meredith did her best to smile.

"Are you the man who's come to take Yandoo away from us?"

"No," he said. "I'm the one who's come to give it back to you. That is, if you will let me." He pulled up a chair.

In the kitchen Mrs. Sylvester, a slight nervous woman with greying hair, was making tea.

"I don't know who he is, Mother," Lulu said. "But he's attractive. In fact he's marvellous."

"Don't be foolish, Lulu," her mother said. "You shouldn't bother about anyone who can't afford to keep you."

"One doesn't have to *marry* a man just because he's interesting," Lulu replied crossly.

They had to wait quite a while for the kettle to boil on the slow wood stove and before the tea had had time to draw in the teapot they heard firm footsteps coming out of Mrs. Meredith's room. The footsteps crossed the passage. He had obviously gone into the office.

"Go and see what he is doing," Mrs. Sylvester said anxiously. "He must be looking for something. What a strange man! Walking about in the house like that!"

He was looking for paper and pen and ink. By the time Lulu had come to offer her assistance he had found them.

"It's all right," he said. "I've found what I wanted. I'll need you in a minute."

"Need me?" Lulu was taken aback. The man was behaving as if he belonged in the house . . . as if he owned it.

Jim smiled at her.

"I won't be long," he said and strode through the door, across the passage back into Mrs. Meredith's room. He closed the door behind him.

Lulu went back into the kitchen.

"Well, I never did," she said. "He's taken possession of the place. I think you'd better come and meet him, Mother."

"I'm coming, dear," Mrs. Sylvester said. "I can't help wishing he had taken possession of the place. Or anyone else for that matter. I can't leave Mabel . . . but I can't stand this place much longer. It's the climate . . . and I do miss my bridge."

For once Lulu said nothing. She went into the passage and opened her aunt's door for her mother to pass through with the tea tray.

Jim Conrad was standing by Mrs. Meredith's sofa. The latter was just writing something . . . her signature on a piece of paper. Jim Conrad looked up.

"How do you do?" he said rapidly. "You are Mrs. Sylvester? Would you mind witnessing this signature for me?" His hard blue eyes turned to Lulu. "Your aunt tells me you are twenty-one. You could counter-sign, please."

"Excuse me if I say I feel faintly breathless," said Lulu with a laugh.

Mrs. Sylvester put the tray on the small table.

"How do you do?" she said formally. "I suppose you are a friend of Mabel's? So few come to visit now, and she does appreciate it."

"Yes, I am a friend," Jim said. "I am just completing some business for Mrs. Meredith. Now would you mind signing just here, and you, Miss Sylvester . . . here."

"What am I signing?" Mrs. Sylvester asked, bewildered.

"You are witnessing Mrs. Meredith's signature, that is all. Just here, please. And put the date, will you?"

He was doing everything in such a business-like way and so rapidly Mrs. Sylvester did not have time to think. Oh, well, Mabel was ailing and failing but at least she had her wits about her. Few though the visitors were to Yandoo those who did come nearly always had something to be signed. Cheques for deferred payment mostly. Mrs. Sylvester, for her sister's sake, hoped this wasn't too big a one. If only that station manager appointed by the bank would come! Her sister, Mrs. Meredith, would perhaps give up her last tenuous hold on Yandoo and let them all go back to the safe cosiness of the city house.

Mrs. Sylvester signed and then Lulu followed suit, leaving a small blot where she had meant to put a full stop.

"Just like me," she said. She looked up at Jim Conrad contritely. "I never did have a head for business."

Jim Conrad waved the paper in the hot air streaming in through the french window. When he thought the blot sufficiently dry he read the paper, then folded it and put it in his pocket. He turned again to the group on the other side of the room.

"I'm sorry I didn't introduce myself, Mrs. Sylvester," he said. "I'm Jim Conrad. I've just been contracted by Mrs. Meredith. I'm here to straighten things up and I'd like to begin at once."

Mrs. Sylvester looked up from the teapot which she now had tilted effectively over a cup and saucer. The spout moved a fraction of an inch and tea flowed into the saucer instead of the cup.

"Oh, dear," she said.

"Contracted?" said Lulu. "But there's a manager coming, isn't there? What have you been taken on as? An overseer or something? And you ought to know . . ."

"Lulu!" Mrs. Meredith interrupted. She was sitting up now. Her head was high and she had a proud look on her mouth and in her tired eyes.

Lulu shrugged.

"Of course, Aunt being unwell, she found it necessary to appoint a manager. . . ." Her voice trailed away. She didn't want to get mixed up in the business of Yandoo. She wanted this man to talk about other things. Any kind of things as long as he would look at her with eyes that said he saw her and saw that she was attractive. His eyes had looked at her that way when he had stepped up on the veranda.

Jim Conrad sat down and accepted a cup of tea from Mrs. Sylvester, who said anxiously, "Of course my sister is never very well."

"When did you last see a doctor, Mrs. Meredith?" Jim asked.

"I should think it would be quite two years ago. He couldn't do anything for me. I believe there is a new man at the air-base now but my trouble is quite incurable, you know."

"I don't know," said Jim. "And I don't think anything is incurable." He said it so pleasantly no one in the room thought he was contradicting Mrs. Meredith, which is what he was doing. They thought he was making cheerful conversation with the sick woman.

19

When he had finished his tea, which he had taken for politeness's sake, he stood up abruptly.

"I think I'll begin with the office," he said. "If I send my man down to the native quarters will he get a meal at sundown, Mrs. Sylvester? Can you feed the boy up here?"

"The boy?" The three women looked at him with startled eyes.

"He goes along with me," Jim Conrad said.

"Oh . . ." Lulu's voice was breathless with disappointment. "Your boy? Are you a married man?"

Jim Conrad's eyes fixed themselves on Lulu's face.

"I'm not married, Miss Sylvester. Simon is on a working holiday. He goes along with me. He's my nephew. Simon Conrad."

"Do you mean he's on holiday from school?" Mrs. Sylvester asked, perplexed.

"On holiday from his own home. It got blown down in a cyclone last March." Jim Conrad let his words fall like stones in a still pond.

"So you're sort of . . . ?" Lulu said hopefully.

"So I'm looking after him. Yes."

"Doesn't he miss his schooling?" Mrs. Sylvester said in a worried voice.

"He's getting it. With me. One day he might own a station. He's learning the hard way."

The two ladies said "Oh" rather helplessly. Lulu's eyes brightened. He was really tough, this man. It was all most exciting. She even envied Simon though she had not yet seen him.

"Bill Seddon, the stockman, cooks for himself and Johnny," Mrs. Sylvester said at length. "But they never come in till all hours."

"Could my man Dinny get something from the kitchen then? We could make other arrangements to-morrow. Simon will eat with me."

Mrs. Sylvester was at a loss.

"Well, I . . . well, I suppose so." She turned to her sister. "Mabel dear, what is Mr. Conrad to do exactly? I mean what position did you give him?"

"She gave me power of attorney, Mrs. Sylvester," Jim said quietly. "Over all her affairs. That is to say, I am in charge now. In the homestead as well as out on the run."

Lulu was sitting upright, her blue eyes wide and a look of mixed wonder and admiration in her face.

"You are a fast worker, Mr. Conrad. Or do I call you Jim?"

"Jim, I think. If I weren't a fast worker, Miss Sylvester, this place would fall apart before we had a hope of salvaging it."

Then he smiled again. His smile was disarming. His eyes had a small light in them and his mouth showed creases at the corners and his white teeth shone in his sunburnt face. Mrs. Meredith's shoulders relaxed and she leaned back against her pillow. Mrs. Sylvester sighed. Lulu's heart missed several beats.

"I hope it won't upset that manager when he comes," Mrs. Sylvester said lamely and because she had to say something.

"I believe he's a friend of the family. And a very reliable fellow to boot," Jim said and his eyes met Mrs. Meredith's. Something passed between them.

Mrs. Sylvester straightened her shoulders and held her head up.

"Of course," she said. "My sister wouldn't dream of appointing anyone she didn't approve of in *every way*."

Jim Conrad stood up.

"If you'll excuse me," he said. "I'll see Simon and my native, and then get to work on the office right away. Does the transceiver set work?"

Mrs. Sylvester nodded.

"Oh, yes," she said. "*That* works."

"Shall I show you?" asked Lulu eagerly.

"No, thank you, Miss Lulu, I learn quickest by finding my own way about." But his smile was once again disarming.

Lulu's eyes sparkled. He *was* attractive!

He went out of the room by the french window and they heard him cross the veranda and jump down to the ground instead of taking the three steps one at a time. He was already in charge, and they felt it.

The three women looked at one another again.

"You see, I knew his father . . ." Mrs. Meredith said evasively. "It's so much more satisfactory than a manager sent by the bank."

"Oh . . . if you knew his father . . ." said Mrs. Sylvester in a voice that said that the man had been personally recommended by the Queen. "What a strange man! Just a little bossy, I thought at first. But good manners . . . the way he passed the cake . . ."

"What does 'attorney' mean?" asked Lulu.

Again they all looked at one another.

"Get the dictionary, dear," her mother said.

CHAPTER TWO

IT WAS NINE o'clock when Gerry came in. Anyone listening could have heard her tired footsteps ascending the three veranda steps and crossing the short distance to the french window in her mother's room.

Mrs. Meredith was in bed now.

"Gerry, darling," she said in her small frail voice. "You really should take a bath. You're very dusty."

"I know, Mother. I wanted to see how you were. I'll have one later. It's been so hot to-day. The real heat will be on us any time now. And I've got news. We've got someone to help us."

"Oh, have you, darling? How splendid. Now we ought to be able to manage very nicely. The Wet ought to be over altogether except farther north and perhaps you can get the mustering done."

Gerry leaned on the end of her mother's bed. The dust streaked her face so that, in the dim light, they might have been tear stains.

"Well . . . some of it . . ." she said guardedly. How much had her mother got out of touch that she didn't remember it took a team of at least ten men to run a muster, even without the cattle in the scrub!

"Oh, and yes . . . Gerry dear. When you go inside you'll meet a man. Quite a nice man. He's going to take charge for me. I knew his father. I mean I think your father knew his father . . ."

Gerry's back stiffened.

"A man? What man? What is his name? What does he look like?"

"He knows all about cattle, dear. He'll be able to teach you some things about the run. His name is Conrad. Yes, Jim Conrad."

Jim Conrad.

Gerry was so tired yet she summoned up the energy to be surprised and even worried.

"Oh, *Mother!* What could he teach me I don't know? I was years at school but years before that I was *here*. And all this year. What have you *done*? This man has taken advantage of you."

So that was why there had been no sign of Jim Conrad down at the quarters. He had come up and installed himself in the homestead. He had taken advantage of her mother's gullibility and her aunt's innocence. He must have known her mother was ill and out of touch.

Her weariness dropped a little from her in the face of this invasion. How was she, Gerry, to work out there on the run and at the same time stand guardian angel over everyone inside the homestead?

If only that manager would come!

All along the fringe of the desert the grass was springing after the heavy Wet and it was wonderful feeding land for the cattle. Even a small mob mustered and drafted and put out to fatten would bring in money.

If that manager would only come he would handle this disturbing Jim Conrad and help them to salvage some of the cattle before it was too wild for any buyer to contemplate handling.

"I'll go and see him, Mother," she said. She walked towards the door leading into the passage.

"And darling, do have a bath first. He wouldn't be a bit impressed with you like *that*."

Impressed? Who was worrying about impressing Jim Conrad? Yet there was a delicate fluttering in her heart: a faint uplift of spirits.

In the passage Gerry stopped. The light was on in the office and the door was closed. But through it Gerry could hear voices. Lulu's voice and that of Jim Conrad.

Gerry let her hands drop to her sides. She hadn't any doubt that Jim Conrad knew all about horses and cattle. He would soon learn that Lulu knew nothing. He wasn't a fool.

She turned away and went on down the passage to the kitchen. She turned on the light and went over to the stove. She stooped and took her dinner from the oven.

Aunt Sally was, thank God, a good cook. There were lots of things Mrs. Sylvester could not do and was not interested in doing but cooking was her saving grace. Gerry had never eaten roast beef the way Aunt Sally could cook it. And Gerry was very hungry.

As she lifted her fork she heard Jim Conrad coming down the passage. She knew it was Jim because of the firm heavy tread. She went on eating, but her heart did very queer things inside her breast. Jim stood in the doorway and looked at her.

"You've met me before," Gerry said, meeting his eyes. "You remember . . . Geraldine Meredith."

"Why are you eating your dinner here, at this hour, and alone?" he asked. There was anger in his voice.

Gerry looked up again and her eyes flashed.

"Why are you here to see me eating it here, at this hour, alone . . . Mr. Conrad?" Some silly thing inside her made her defy his note of authority.

He took three steps into the kitchen, swung round another bentwood chair and sat down.

"Because I happen to be in charge now," he said. "So I'm afraid there's a lot of questions I have to ask."

Gerry went on eating. She must have palpitations, surely. Palpitations came when one was over-tired. It must be that.

"You don't understand," Gerry said gravely. "My mother is hardly fit to put anyone in charge. Besides . . ."

He nodded. "I know. You've got a manager coming. A very reliable fellow . . . you told me. A friend of the family."

Was there a note of irony in his voice? Gerry looked up.

"That's right," she said. She moved a pleasant morsel of well-chewed beef to the other side of her mouth. "A very fine man. A very well-mannered man. He will take charge of the *staff*."

"Until then," Jim Conrad said quietly, "I'll take charge of it. How do I rank you, Miss Gerry? Are you staff or family? Are you on the pay-roll or do you do all that you do for love?"

Gerry flushed angrily. She spoke very quietly in spite of the flush and the tilt of her proud little head.

"You mind your own business," she said and was aghast she could so easily be so rude.

"It is my business. You see, I now have power of attorney. Do you know what that is, Miss Gerry?" He allowed himself a smile. "Miss Lulu looked it up in a dictionary in case you are in doubt."

Gerry ignored this.

"And who gave you power of attorney?"

"Your mother. It's all signed and witnessed here." He tapped his coat pocket.

"My mother is not able . . ."

His eyes challenged her across the table.

"Are you prepared legally and categorically to state your mother is incapable . . . mentally . . . of using her judgment?"

24

Gerry jumped up. She put both hands on the table and leaned forward.

"Mr. Conrad. Jim Conrad. How dare you . . . ?"

"Exactly," he said. "This paper gives me my authority, until you or someone else disputes it. And there's only one way to dispute it. . . ."

Gerry knew what he meant. They were caught. They were all caught in a trap. To take his power from him they would have to pillory Mrs. Meredith.

Gerry's face went quite white.

"Now sit down, Gerry, and listen to me."

Gerry sat down, not because he had ordered her to do so but because she suddenly felt weak. Oh, if only that manager would come . . . and rescue them.

"That's better," Jim Conrad said. "Here, I'll get you a glass of water."

He went to the refrigerator, another thing he had thankfully found that did work. He brought her a jug of water and poured some into a glass for her. Then he sat down opposite her again.

He spoke quietly yet there was an inflexible strength implied in the very quietness. And there was inflexible will in his eyes. Gerry knew before he said another word that he was too strong for her. He had trapped them and his will was like iron bars to a prison ward.

"Now listen to me, carefully," he said. "I'm a good cattleman and I've good backing. You've nothing to fear from me. I've already been on the transceiver set to Ruloo Station. Someone's got to help pull you out of this mess and I'm the man to do it. Your mother can hold her head up as far as the district is concerned with a personally appointed attorney. It sounds better than a 'manager,' doesn't it? And your mother is going to see a doctor. Ruloo Station has already been in touch with the flying doctor. He can land there, though he can't land here. The manager is bringing him over."

Gerry was bewildered. How much was he in charge already?

"Mother won't see a doctor," she said. "It isn't any good. They can't do anything for her."

Jim Conrad took out the makings of a cigarette and slowly rolled one. He pushed the stray ends of tobacco in with a match and lit it. He blew out a thin spiral of smoke.

"Rubbish!" he said.

Gerry was speechless.

Jim stood up and went towards the door. He turned round. "And your mother will see a doctor whether she wants to or not. I say what goes on here. And, by the way, I intend to get Bill Seddon to take me for some inspection work to-morrow."

Now Gerry was on her feet. She came quickly round the table and stood in front of him.

"If you take Bill Seddon off the fences and the bore at the Ten Mile we'll never get a mob of cattle quietened down to feed. And what's more . . . where Bill goes, I go."

Jim Conrad looked down from his height and considered her. Gerry's blue eyes met his unflinchingly. A small smile eased itself round the corners of Jim's mouth.

"You can come if you like," he said, and he went out the door.

"If I like?" Gerry stared at the empty doorway. Was she dreaming? Had all this really happened? How many hours had he been on the station?

She went back to the table and picked up her empty plate. She took it over to the sink. As she rinsed it she caught sight of herself in the little mirror hanging at the side of the pot rack. Her heart sank.

"As if a man like that would take any notice of *me*," she said sadly.

She dried the plate and knife and fork and put them away. She folded away the little tablecloth and then went back to the pocket mirror. She shook her head at the reflection she saw there.

"Such a dirty face . . ." she said. She didn't know that the droop of that mouth was for the benefit of the reflection. If she had smiled at herself and held her head up she would have seen that she was very young, and very gallant.

She walked around the veranda and saw the boy Simon lying, his arms flung out on either side of him, on top of an old iron bedstead. The moonlight flooded his face and he slept silently and peacefully, in the clothes he had worn all day.

Gerry sat down on the side of the boy's bed and looked at him. He was very young, he had come a long way and, like hers, his face was streaked with dust.

Poor, thin little boy, she thought. To-morrow she would tell him to bath before he went to bed. Maybe they could cut down a pair of her father's pyjamas.

To-morrow . . .

Well, maybe she could put up with Jim Conrad for a little

while if he could be of real help on Yandoo, and if she could have a little time to feed this boy up.

She wondered why he was thin. He didn't look frail. He looked wiry and his skin was firm and tough. All the same a child always needed good food. . . .

It was several days before the flying doctor could arrange to call at Yandoo Station. He would land on Ruloo and the manager of that station would drive him across to Yandoo.

In the meantime Jim Conrad with Bill Seddon and Gerry made tours of inspection around the homestead.

The stockman had quickly succumbed to Jim's authority.

"He knows what he's talking about," he told Gerry. "And Mrs. Meredith sent me a message to do what he tells me. I'm only a stockman. I've got to take orders."

It was quite clear Bill Seddon was almost falling over himself to please Jim Conrad. What a power the newcomer seemed to have over everyone! Gerry, looking very serious, nodded her head.

"I think he can do a lot to help us," she said gravely. "I just don't want any trouble with the bank. After all, the bank inspector had mentioned in his report only 'temporary' help."

"You leave it be, young 'un. No bank's goin' to quarrel if a few hundred head of cattle's salvaged for the sales when the buyer comes around."

That was sense and Gerry knew it.

She made a silent third to the party that inspected the harness room, the smithy, the saddling paddock and the stock in the bullock paddock. Her anxiety lay in the fact she knew her mother was a sick woman and did not now have her hands on the management of the station. Yet from both love and loyalty she, Gerry, could not bring herself to dispute her mother's decision. When all was said and done how much did she know of the management herself? Her mother had never taken the girl into her confidence on the financial side.

Jim's all-seeing eye did a lot to win Gerry's confidence in the first two days but on the third something happened that brought back the worried crease to her forehead.

She had ridden with Bill, their own native and Jim Conrad's native out to the Ten Mile Bore where Jim Conrad had first come into Yandoo Station. With the help of the two natives Bill was able to finish putting the bore to rights.

When, in the evening, Gerry had ridden back to the homestead, she found Lulu waiting for her on the veranda.

27

"You'll never guess who turned up to-day," Lulu said from her chair on the veranda.

She had on a pale corn-coloured cotton dress with blue binding to the neckline and sleeves. The touch of blue deepened the colour in Lulu's eyes and made her even more attractive than usual. She looked so cool and refreshed that Gerry felt all the more jaded by comparison.

"Not the flying doctor?" Gerry asked anxiously.

"Better. Pierce and Redmond."

Pierce and Redmond had been two of Yandoo's stockmen who had left them after the fire burnt out the grasses last season.

"And willing and ready to work," Lulu added. "The word must have gone up the stock routes that Jim Conrad is putting things right here."

Gerry had mixed feelings at this news. She was delighted that the hands were returning. That meant the station might soon get in humming order again. But somehow it was hurtful to her pride that it was the presence of a man like Jim Conrad that had won back the confidence of the stockmen in Yandoo.

Nevertheless it was good news and after a minute's reflection Gerry's spirits rose.

"Where are they?" she said. "Down at the quarters?"

Lulu shrugged.

"They rode in here at midday and had a session with the boss in the office. Then they rode out in the direction of the creek. Perhaps they're going to camp down there . . . or have gone back along the stock route to get their gear."

Gerry's back stiffened a little at Lulu's reference to Jim Conrad as the "boss" but she said nothing.

At that moment Simon came round the veranda.

"Hallo, Simon," Gerry said. "Have you had your dinner?"

"Yes, thank you, and it was a good 'un. Yours is in the oven, Gerry. Say, when are you going to come home on time for meals? My mother used to say if we weren't in on time we didn't get any."

"How often did you go without, Simon?" Gerry asked.

"Oh, plenty often, I suppose."

"I suppose so too," Gerry added. "Where's your uncle, Simon? And do you know if there are two stockmen down at the quarters?"

"My uncle's in the office, and if you mean the two stockmen who came in at lunch-time, my uncle's turned them away."

28

Gerry had taken a step as if to go around the veranda to the office but now she stood still.

"What do you mean? Turned them away?"

"Sent them flying. Said they weren't any good anyway."

"Weren't any good?"

She stood looking down at the small boy.

"But . . ." She broke off. "Simon dear," she said in a different voice, "don't you forget to have a bath, will you?"

"Look, Gerry," Simon said wearily, "a fellow can always bath in a waterhole . . . if he's lucky enough to come by one at sundown."

"But in a homestead he gets under the shower every night."

"You know what's wrong with this station, Gerry?" Simon said wearily. "Too many bosses."

Gerry smiled.

"But it's okay to have the kind of boss in the kitchen who can cook a big roast dinner every night, isn't it?"

"Well, you've got something there."

"Then have a bath like a good fellow. You'll get more respect from Bill Seddon that way."

"Okay," Simon said, affecting the stockman's slow drawl. "But I don't know what's the good. It all gets on again to-morrow."

"I don't know why you bother with him," Lulu said. "Kids like being dirty, don't they, Simon?"

"Well . . . some of the time," Simon said.

Gerry knew that Simon in his hesitating answer was being a little loyal to herself. Her heart warmed to him.

"I'll see you by and by, Simon," she said. "How would you like to put my dinner out for me? But put a cloth on the table first, won't you?"

"Cloths and baths!" said Simon. "What's a stockman coming to these days?"

Gerry laughed. Then remembering that Jim Conrad had sent away two of Yandoo's best old-time stockmen, she went round the veranda to the office.

The door was wide open and Jim Conrad was sitting behind the paper-littered table. His legs were sprawled out under it and his head was bent to see something close-written that was on the table before him.

Gerry stood in the doorway.

He looked up, then slowly drew his feet in and stood up.

"Have you had your dinner, Gerry?" he asked. His unsmiling face looked stern in the poor light shed from the overhead bracket.

"Simon's getting it for me," she said. She took a few steps forward and stood looking at him across the table.

"Did Pierce and Redmond come back to work?" she asked steadily.

"They said so. I didn't give them the opportunity to put their intentions into operation."

"You didn't . . . you didn't send them away? Why? They were two of the best horsemen on the place. We're nearly crazy for help, you know that."

"Not that kind of help."

Gerry was upset.

"How do you know? They've worked here for years."

"They didn't work here when they were most needed. You know what kind of animal it is that leaves a sinking ship, Gerry?"

Gerry's face went white.

"Yandoo was not sinking," she said. "Bill and I had done a lot. We'll do a lot more . . ."

Jim looked down at the paper on the desk. Then he lifted his head up again. He put his hands in his pockets and looked very hard at the young girl standing across the table from him.

Gerry no longer cared about the dust on her face and in her clothes, or the freckles on the bridge of her nose. What was Jim Conrad doing to them all?

"I'm sure of it," he said with an edge of irony in his voice. "In the meantime you'd better get your dinner, Gerry. You need it."

This was how she herself talked to Simon. She thought Simon's pretensions to being a stockman were amusing and really what he needed most was a good feed. She treated him as the child he was. That was what Jim Conrad was doing to her. Treating her as a child who amused herself being important out on the run but who really needed feeding up.

She had no idea how to treat Jim Conrad now. She couldn't very well say "How dare you?" because he had dared and would continue to dare. She knew that very well. And she couldn't say she was not to be treated as a child because it would be admitting that was what he was doing.

He noticed her hesitation, and he took a cigarette from the box on the table and lit it.

"Handling men is a man's business, Gerry," he said. "You'd

better leave it to me." His words were a command and not a suggestion. They fell like the cold strokes of a lash on the air.

"With no men on the place?" Gerry asked.

He seemed to tower over her even though the table was between them. She thought perhaps that cold set look on his face meant he disliked her. Well, it was a pity but she couldn't help that. Yandoo was *her* station, not Jim Conrad's. At least it was hers and the bank's and one or two outside shareholders' until someone took it from them all. Could that possibly be what Jim Conrad was trying to do? Where had he come from? Who was he?

In the painful silence that followed Gerry's question Jim picked up a paper-knife and beat a tattoo on the desk. Jim Conrad was not even bothering to answer her. Then Lulu appeared in the doorway.

Jim looked over Gerry's head.

"Well, Lulu?" he said. His face relaxed and he looked amused. "Have you come to render your services? There's quite a pile of correspondence here."

Gerry turned on her heel and went out of the office. Somehow, beside Lulu she was at a greater disadvantage. Lulu was so bathed and fresh and attractive. Besides, she would give in to Jim Conrad on every point. And that was the kind of thing he liked!

Gerry went down to the kitchen. Simon had put out the cloth with a knife and fork on it. He was standing by the oven and when she appeared he stooped and lifted her plate out.

"What you need, Gerry," said Simon, "is a good feed."

CHAPTER THREE

ON THE DAY the flying doctor came to see Mrs. Meredith Aunt Sally Sylvester had cooked a superb lunch. There was grilled steak with salads, crisp new-made bread rolls and sliced oranges and cream.

Jim Conrad listened exclusively to Lulu because Lulu talked exclusively to him. Mrs. Sylvester was pleased with Lulu because of her good social manners and she wished that Gerry would be a little more gracious. Gerry was so very silent. It would be a good thing if the doctor ordered Mabel back to Sydney and something could be done about dressing up Gerry. Finding Lulu a suitable husband wouldn't be such a problem in Sydney. She, Mrs. Sylvester, would have to do something about Gerry too. What a good thing it was, she thought, that young jackaroo David Randall had left with the other stockmen. It was quite clear Gerry might have lost her heart to him. Too foolish, since neither of them had any money. Anyhow the young fellow had seen the writing on the wall and had gone to better prospects.

Meantime Mrs. Sylvester was very impressed with this new man Mabel had had the wit to install to see them over the bad period. She liked the way he listened to her, his head a shade on one side, his eyes intently on hers. No one, not even Lulu, ever listened to Mrs. Sylvester. It touched her and pleased her immensely to receive Jim's grave attention.

"At least he has the good manners to listen," she thought.

She did notice he gave each person this concentrated attention. Yes, he was a clever man. He was taking every little detail in, and saying nothing himself.

After lunch Gerry went in to see her mother.

No one had told Mrs. Meredith the doctor was coming. Gerry did not like to deceive her mother yet she knew the news would have upset the invalid very much. Mrs. Meredith was convinced no one could cure her and had refused any kind of medical assistance. The very idea had distressed her in the past.

Gerry tidied her mother's room and settled her for her afternoon rest. Though Gerry had not been in the homestead in the day-time for many months, Mrs. Meredith did not notice there was anything unusual about the day. Gerry could not bear to disturb her peace of mind and when she saw her mother was dozing off she went quietly outside.

When the dust cloud of the Ruloo manager's car could be seen in the distance Gerry went down to the saddling yard and sat on a cross-piece of the fence and watched the horses.

Jim Conrad had taken everything out of her hands and she could not bring herself to join the party up there at the homestead waiting for the doctor. Everyone was sort of deferring to Jim Conrad, and it was *her* mother.

An hour later, after the doctor, Jim Conrad and Mrs. Sylvester had had a discussion in the office, the doctor and Mrs. Sylvester went into see Mrs. Meredith. Lulu, freshly bathed and dressed in the corn-coloured dress with the blue trimming, was sitting on the veranda and she noticed the doctor was smiling and looking sanguine even before he had seen the invalid.

Jim Conrad came out of the office, nodded his head and smiled at her briefly as he left the veranda and walked down to the garden fence. He stood there gazing thoughtfully out over the plain. Lulu wondered whether she would join him or not.

Already he had told her she could help him in the office and though she had not particularly wanted to mind any of Yandoo's affairs her former secretarial training came to her assistance. Moreover, she liked being useful to Jim Conrad. There was something about him that commanded attention and Lulu found it pleasant to respond to him.

Down there at the garden fence his back made him seem unapproachable. Besides, Lulu had had a little experience of men in Sydney and she knew it was infinitely more beguiling to let them make the advances . . . even if it was only to a little desultory conversation.

While she was thinking thus the Ruloo manager came out of the main homestead door and he in his turn stood looking across the garden at Jim Conrad.

He took out his pipe and packed it.

He glanced at Lulu.

"The doctor thinks your aunt can be cured with these modern medicines that have come on the market these last few years. I suppose that pleases you, young lady," he said.

Lulu looked up at him and smiled.

"It pleases me very much," she said. "It will please Gerry better. It is rather hard to believe . . ."

He struck a match and lit his pipe.

"One of the things that pleases me about this occasion," said the manager of Ruloo, "is the opportunity of meeting Jim Conrad. I've heard of him for years but never dreamed I'd meet him on Yandoo."

"Heard of him?" said Lulu, looking up with interest. "Is he that well-known?"

"Well-known?" The man looked at Lulu in frank astonishment. "He's one of the big names in the cattle industry. Got an interest in half a dozen stations in Queensland alone."

Lulu sat up.

"Then what's he doing working on Yandoo like a hired hand?" she asked, round-eyed.

"Hired hand!" The Ruloo manager took his pipe out of his

mouth and stared at Lulu. "Young lady, you take another look at that man. He doesn't get hired. He buys in. There isn't a station north of the twenty-sixth parallel he couldn't put to rights. That's his line . . . and he's nearly always got an interest."

Lulu sat back.

"Oh . . . I see," she said.

The Ruloo manager came and sat down beside her.

"Great name in cattle," he said. "There's nothing he won't take on. Nothing he won't do. Quite a legend on the stock routes is Jim Conrad."

"I wonder if that is why the stockmen began coming back?"

"You bet that's why."

He sat back, drawing on his pipe and gazing contentedly at Jim Conrad's back where he stood looking over the plain at the end of the garden.

Lulu sat silent. Now was not the moment to show that here on Yandoo no one had known anything about him.

"Mind you," the man added reflectively, "he looks after Jim Conrad too. He'll turn a station inside out and upside down and leave it in tip-top working order. But he always rides away with a sizeable share of it in his pocket."

"Why doesn't he . . . why doesn't he stay put on one?" Lulu asked wonderingly.

"When one of these station-owners' daughters catches him he'll stay put," the manager laughed at Lulu teasingly. "Up to date he's loved them and left them, I'm afraid."

"Yes . . ." said Lulu slowly and thoughtfully. "He's very attractive. I suppose he would be a man of 'affaires.'"

"There's been many a young lady who has lost her heart, I'm told. You'd better be careful, Miss Lulu." He was still teasing.

Lulu turned her head to look again at Jim Conrad standing at the foot of the garden. There was an eager light in her own eyes which she was anxious to hide from the manager of Ruloo.

Presently Gerry left the top rail of the horse yard and walked along the fence of the paddock towards the creek. During the Wet the billabong around the creek elbow had run a banker. Now the waters had receded a little, leaving a green velvet carpet of grass heavily dotted with tiny star-faced wild flowers.

It was very lovely. When Yandoo wore this smiling face

after the Wet Gerry's heart had always lifted. The spring-time in her own heart matched the soft gaiety of the between-seasons in the outback. Even now, though her heart was anxious for her mother, there seemed somehow sunshine and all its sparkling life around her, and in her too.

Here and there were shadows. Strange, but that was just how she felt these last few days . . . as if one minute she was almost dancing like the motes in the shafts of light and the next she was walking sombrely in the shadows.

She sat on the roots of a great old red gum and looked across the water. The ducks were there already and now the pelicans and the moorhens were coming home in their ordered ranks. Where had they been out there in that desert?

In her thoughts Gerry passed out of the sunlight into the shadow again as she wondered what they were doing up there at the homestead.

Why, she wondered, had she come away down here by herself while earth-shaking decisions were being made about her own and much loved mother?

Had she run away from anxiety or from the fear of showing to someone like Jim Conrad how deep that anxiety was? Jim Conrad would scorn a person who could not take a blow un-flinching.

She had tended to absent herself from the homestead even more than usual. It was something to do with the cosiness of Lulu and her proprietorial attitude to the affairs of the office and Jim Conrad. Even Aunt Sally hung on every word Jim Conrad uttered as if a very Daniel had come to judgment.

Only Gerry herself defected from this attitude of the devotee. It gave him ideas about himself. No wonder he was so lofty, confident and unapproachable. Even Bill Seddon was a victim of his charm.

Charm! Gerry pulled herself up with a start as the word came unbidden to her mind.

A man who walked in and took possession of somebody else's station the way Jim Conrad had done couldn't have *charm*. Nobody who was autocratic, domineering and swept people aside as Jim Conrad swept people aside had *charm*.

He was a ruthless, a selfish man and Gerry's quite proper feelings about her own rights on Yandoo were quite properly hurt.

Or was it just because she was young and felt Jim disregarded her when really she knew so much about the

35

station than anyone except Bill Seddon? Jim Conrad always asked his questions of Bill Seddon, occasionally of Lulu. Never of Gerry.

Then Gerry, sitting there by the billabong, while the birds came home for the night, took herself to task.

Her mother, and Yandoo, were the most important things. She must stop thinking about Jim Conrad as a man. She must just think that Yandoo, even in a few days, was beginning to breathe and live again. It was slowly coming to life. What did it matter that this life blood stemmed from a powerful personality who was clearly already master of all situations there? It was not the man that mattered. It was the station.

Funny how, sitting here, she felt he was even waving a magic wand over her mother and that he would tell the doctor to cure her mother. And that that was just what the doctor would do.

Gerry heard a "Coo-ee" and turned to look up the track towards the homestead. Simon was coming down it on an old bicycle he had patched up.

"They're looking everywhere for you, Gerry," he said. "Why are you sitting down here all by yourself?"

Gerry smiled ruefully at the small sandy-haired boy.

"Somebody's got to be sick, and the doctor come, for me to have time to sit and look at the billabong, Simon," she said. "Soon it will dry back and most of the birds will go."

"Where do you reckon they'll go?"

Gerry shook her head.

"That's something no one's ever been able to find out. Where do they go each day? How far have they come from their birthplace to Yeebong Creek?" She stopped suddenly. Then after a pause went on. "Simon, why are they looking for me?"

"Aw, don't look so scared, Gerry. Your mother's going to be all right, I reckon. I saw the doctor laughing when he came out of Mrs. Meredith's room and Mrs. Sylvester was crying and then said she was crying because she was happy. Gerry, why do women cry?"

Gerry was nearly crying herself but she forced back her tears.

"I guess it's because they're weak, after all."

"You aren't weak. My uncle Jim Conrad reckons you're game as Ned Kelly."

Ned Kelly was the Robin Hood of Australian bush-ranging days. A kind of legendary hero.

36

Gerry looked at Simon in astonishment.

"Did he say that?"

"Yep. He said it when you were riding off before daylight the other morning to go down to the bore with Bill Seddon."

"Oh, is that all. There's nothing game about riding out for a day's work."

"Maybe it's because Lulu's too frightened to get on a horse."

They had neared the homestead turn-off now and Gerry could see Jim Conrad and the doctor coming towards her. The doctor was doing the talking and as Simon had said, he was smiling as if well pleased with himself. Gerry could not help her heart beating a little faster at the sight of Jim. Even though he was cold and aloof there was something strong and attractive about him.

When still some yards away the doctor lifted a hand in greeting to Gerry.

"Good news, Miss Meredith," he said.

Jim Conrad looked at her closely. His tone was cold, even severe, when he spoke.

"Why did you go away, Gerry? We expected you to be the first to hear the good news."

"Maybe I was running away from bad news," Gerry replied, looking at him gravely. "Maybe I was just running away."

"Oh, come, Miss Meredith," said the doctor. He was a young man and perhaps impatient of a girl who wanted to sit alone by a billabong while a verdict of life or death was being passed on her mother. He wouldn't understand. . . .

"Dr. Cranston's diagnosis of your mother's ailment was quite correct," he went on. "Your mother suffers from a blood deficiency but modern drugs discovered in the last few years can rectify that."

"Do you mean my mother is going to get *well*?" Gerry was incredulous.

"Certainly. It's quite simple. Just a matter of tablets. Of course she will always have to take them but that's easier, you know, than insulin injections the diabetics have to take. Of course she will have to have some intensive treatment first to build her up."

"You mean . . . you mean she will actually become well again? Like me and Aunt Sally, and ordinary people?"

The doctor smiled.

"Certainly . . . if she obeys instructions. I'm afraid I'll have

37

to send her to hospital for a few weeks for early treatment. Your aunt tells me she has a house in Sydney. I think Mrs. Meredith should be under a specialist's care in Sydney for a few months. But that's routine re-establishment. It just takes time."

Gerry dragged her eyes away from the doctor's face and looked at Jim Conrad. He had turned aside and was breaking a twig from a tree to examine it. There was no help there. Neither he, nor the doctor, would ever understand the deep surge of emotion that suddenly made Gerry feel a little rocky on her feet.

What had she done these last few years? How remiss had she been not doing this thing Jim Conrad had done . . . force a doctor on her mother?

She just hadn't known.

The doctor went on talking technicalities but Gerry did not hear him. She could not sort out her thoughts. There was a curious stabbing joy mixing itself up with remorse.

It was Simon's touch on her arm that brought the swimming world to a standstill.

"Gee, Gerry," he said, "you've gone all white."

Jim turned and gave her one of those quick diagnostic looks that meant he was seeing all but saying nothing.

"You know," Simon went on, "what you want? A good feed."

Suddenly Gerry laughed. Simon, for all his tender years, had a nice wit. He took Gerry's own words and turned them back on herself and his tone of voice was exactly hers. He was a born mimic. She had said, "You need a good feed" to Simon so often in the first three days of his stay on Yandoo that the boy thought food was Gerry's antidote to all hardship.

"Simon," she said, looking down, "Aunt Sally made a raspberry sponge with cream filling for the doctor's afternoon tea. Do you suppose they've left us some?"

The doctor had been looking at Gerry with a professional eye. Now he smiled.

"Left you some?" he said with assumed indignation. "I haven't had any myself. We've been looking for you."

They all turned to go back to the homestead.

"And now, young lady, just tell me why you went down to that creek at the time of my arrival? Have you been worrying?" he asked.

Jim Conrad was walking the other side of her and Simon

was pedalling his bike ahead of them. Gerry looked quickly at Jim.

"Yes, I've been worrying," she said. "About a lot of things. Mr. Conrad wouldn't understand that."

Jim glanced down at her.

"Mr. Conrad understands more than you think," he said shortly. He lifted his glance to the doctor on the other side of Gerry. "I think you might prescribe a holiday to Sydney for Miss Gerry. She should accompany her mother."

Gerry stopped short and stood gazing hard at Jim.

"Go to Sydney?" she said. "Aunt Sally and Lulu will go with Mother. I have to stay here and look after Yandoo whether I like it or not. Someone has got to look after the station."

"I'm looking after Yandoo whether you're here or not, Gerry." He had dropped the "Miss" again. "You need that break and without your mother and aunt you cannot stay here."

"Cannot stay in my own home? Not look after Yandoo? Mr. Conrad, what do you think I've been doing for a year?"

The eyes of the two men met over Gerry's head. She had the awful feeling of having the ground cut from under her feet. She looked from one face to the other.

"Oh no you don't," she said desperately. "You don't hatch up any plots to get rid of me. There's the shareholders . . . and the bank . . . and all the cattle in the scrub . . . and no stockmen . . ." She was almost breathless. She turned to the doctor. "You see, Mr. Conrad . . . Jim Conrad turned away my stockmen. Bill Seddon and I have to do it all . . ."

She broke off. She couldn't talk to the doctor about the domestic affairs of Yandoo. Besides, Jim Conrad had brought him here and by that action had undoubtedly saved her mother's life.

She felt helpless. Again it was Simon who saved the situation. He had turned his bike and let it coast back down the track towards them.

"Hey, Gerry," he said, "what about afternoon tea and that raspberry cake?" He got off his bike and considered Gerry's face. "You know what, Gerry. You need a . . ."

"All right, Simon. I'll come with you. We'll leave the men to talk to themselves."

She went up the tracks, keeping pace with the boy who was running his bike to make the incline easier going. As

39

she went, her spirits rose in spite of the decision about her own future that Jim Conrad was trying to make. How would her mother have taken the news? Would the shock have upset her? But it would be only temporary, surely? And if her mother wanted her to go to Sydney that would be different, of course.

On the other hand there was Yandoo. Someone from the Meredith family would have to be here when that manager arrived. Besides, why should they leave everything to Jim Conrad? He knew his business . . . that was clear. But he was a stranger, wasn't he? He could possibly have sent for the doctor not only to save Mrs. Meredith's life but to get rid of them all, to leave him in absolute power here.

She must stay. Whatever came . . . however her mother felt . . . she must stay. Her mother would be in good hands with Aunt Sally and Lulu.

If only she'd had a brother or an uncle . . . or something. Someone to care for Yandoo while she took her mother to Sydney. How different would everything be then.

"You're awful quiet, Gerry," Simon said.

"So would you be if you knew the face of the world was about to be changed, Simon. One has to prepare for it."

"What do you mean . . . 'face of the world'?"

"Well, our world's the homestead, and Yandoo. The homestead is old and shabby. We'll have to jack it up ready for Mother when she comes back healthy and well. If we could get men to work the out-station and the run we could build a better garden. We could make it look so lovely. Shrubs . . . and flowers . . . the way it used to be . . ."

Gerry was out of the shadows and walking in the sunshine again. Her world shone bravely and her heart was suddenly as full of gay plans as it was of hope.

"I reckon I could give you a hand at that," Simon said.

"I think you could, if you were here long enough."

"Oh, I'll be here long enough. When my Uncle Jim Conrad gets his teeth into a station he never lets go till it's just a hundred per cent jake."

"So he's been on other stations? I mean other than that one where the cyclone did all the damage and where your parents live?"

"You bet. He's always got his eye out for a bite into another station. My dad reckons he'll be like Kidman one day. Own all the raking stations in the State. That's why I'm sticking with him. I'm going to get one of those stations for myself one day."

Gerry listened but said nothing to the boy. For a moment she felt a chill at Simon's words but then she had remembered the bank and the manager who would come. Thank God, now, for that manager.

She was quite certain now she was not going to leave Yandoo . . . not even if her mother asked her. All her mother's fortune was wrapped up in Yandoo and Gerry must save it for her. She couldn't tell her mother any of this, but she would do what her conscience told her was right to do. She would stay on Yandoo. And guard it. Yes, guard it. What did any of them know of the real Jim Conrad?

Lulu's reaction to the intelligence that Jim Conrad was a big man in the cattle industry with vested interests in a number of stations was quite different from Gerry's.

She had thought Jim an unusual and attractive man from the first. Now she was delighted to know he was, in addition, a man of substance. Moreover, Lulu felt that Jim drew the best out of her. When she had left school she had done a secretarial course. She was a very able girl and had done the course easily and competently. The trouble was she just didn't like the work very much and when her mother had had to go to Yandoo Station to look after Mrs. Meredith Lulu had willingly thrown up her job and looked forward to a life of leisure and excitement on a big cattle-station. Her disappointment at finding Yandoo run-down and the homestead shabby had been incalculable.

The jackaroo, David Randall, might have been interesting except that he was young and without property. He was one of those jackaroos who were learning station management in order to take a post in a pastoral company in the city. He was not a station-owner's son learning his business on another station-owner's property as was the custom amongst the squat-tocracy.

Also he spent most of his time outside . . . and that was in Gerry's line of country. Anyhow he too had left when things got bad at the time the book-keeper went.

Jim Conrad had commandeered Lulu's services in the office. Oddly enough, probably because Jim Conrad praised her work and thanked her for it, she began to take an interest in it. That is to say she had begun to take an interest in doing the kind of work that meant Jim Conrad would look up and say:

"That's fine, Lulu. You've covered a lot of ground to-day. Between us we'll get this mess cleared up in a fortnight."

She was waiting now for the doctor and Jim Conrad to come up to the homestead for afternoon tea. She had gone to her room and changed into yet another dress. It was a very pretty one she had had sent up from Sydney, and then been disappointed because there was no occasion on which to wear it effectively. It had tantalised her hanging there in the cupboard. It was a pink and white polished cotton dress with a tight-fitting bodice and just enough flare in the skirt to give it a swing.

She saw Gerry and the boy Simon come through the gate and go round to the bicycle shed. No one, she thought, would ever divorce Gerry from those jeans and a shirt blouse! To-day, thank goodness, since she hadn't been out on the run they were still fresh and free from dust.

Gerry's slight figure was pretty and Lulu would have done a lot with it if it had been hers. However, it was just as well, as things were, that Gerry did have such a passion for Yandoo and for cattle work. She wouldn't want to leave Yandoo. That gave Lulu a chance to stay on for a while— just to find out what sort of a man was under Jim Conrad's austere surface.

"Gerry's bound to stay here," she had said to her mother. "I think I'd better stay awhile to keep her company. Even Gerry needs someone to see to the meals in the homestead."

Mrs. Sylvester had got over the immediate relief that her sister would get well and that now she could go back to Sydney. She was putting the tea things on a tray and brought out the large raspberry sponge she had cooked that morning. She had whipped up the cream and as she now spread it on top of the cake she shook her head.

"Lulu, you've never taken an interest in cooking," she said.

"You've never let me, Mother. The kitchen is always full of you, and too many cooks not only spoil the broth, they get under one another's feet and irritate one another. Anyhow, I think I owe it to Gerry to stay. It would be just too selfish for us all to leave her."

"Gerry should come with us to Sydney. Her mother will be quite all right in my care. But all the same . . ."

"She'll never leave Yandoo, Mother, and for goodness' sake don't try to persuade her. All you'll get will be trouble. Be-

42

sides, I think she ought to stay on Yandoo. After all, Jim Conrad is a stranger. Whatever money Aunt Mabel's got left is in this place. It would be disastrous if she lost it."

Mrs. Sylvester finished creaming the cake and looked up at her daughter. There was puzzlement and uncertainty in her eyes.

"Would you really stay, Lulu? But you've been so bored."

"Oh, only for a few weeks till that manager comes. A few more weeks won't matter."

"I'm beginning to be uncertain about that manager. I can't understand why we haven't heard from him."

"Gerry said it can take months for a man, with his gear, to get down from the north across those rivers."

"I don't understand why he doesn't come by aeroplane."

"Oh, it seems that that sort of person always brings his own string of horses. Seems as if a stockman always works best with his own horses. And they bring them rather than truck them."

"Well . . . I don't know. I'll have to think about it. I don't know what Mabel wants. It's so hard to get anything out of her at all at present. She's lost all interest . . ."

Lulu knew that familiar waver in her mother's voice. She smiled to herself as she took the loaded tea tray out on to the veranda. She set the tray on the table and walked to the steps. Gerry and Simon had gone round the side of the house but Jim Conrad and the doctor were walking up the path towards her. She was conscious she made an attractive figure standing there at the head of the steps and that both Jim Conrad and the doctor knew it. There is nothing more pleasant for one girl than to share the admiration of two men. Jim Conrad's mask did not deceive Lulu. Any man on a lonely outback station will respond to the allure of a pretty girl.

"Perfect timing," she said with a laugh. "The tea is just ready and on the table."

"It's a pleasant occasion," the doctor said as he took a chair. "Nothing nicer than to give a patient a future. Where, by the way, is Miss Meredith?"

"She went round the side," Lulu said as she took up the teapot. "But I can hear her voice in her mother's room. My mother's just taken in Aunt Mabel's tea so we will go on, if you don't mind."

By the time Gerry and Mrs. Sylvester joined them Lulu had settled the affairs of Yandoo Station.

"Gerry and I are staying on for a few weeks to look after

43

you," she said to Jim Conrad. "Now don't get that distant look. Every man likes to come home to a good meal . . . and it's all decided. Mother and Aunt Mabel insist."

Jim Conrad leaned forward and took a piece of the raspberry cream cake.

"There must have been some very quick decisions," he said.

"They're made," Lulu said airily, then smiled sweetly. "Please promise you will let us stay."

It was at that moment Mrs. Sylvester and Gerry came out on to the veranda. Gerry had washed and combed her hair and put on a touch of lipstick. Suddenly she didn't look quite so young and defenceless. The doctor gave her a quick appraising look.

"I don't think you need any doctoring up after your shock, Miss Meredith," he said. "In fact, you are beginning to look as if you've already had a tonic."

"Of course she has," said Lulu. "And she knows Aunt Mabel will be in the best possible hands with Mother, don't you, Gerry?"

She poured tea for her mother who had a vaguely puzzled look as Lulu passed it to her. There had been a transformation in Lulu's dress and in her manner. Her mother could not quite understand it.

Lulu went chattering on before anyone could say anything.

"Raspberry cake, Gerry? You can afford it. You're all skin and bone really. And you will stick up for me against Jim about staying on Yandoo, won't you? We've simply got to stay and look after him, haven't we?"

Gerry was startled now. Jim Conrad looked at her with one faintly raised eyebrow.

"I think Mr. Conrad can look after himself, Lulu," she said quietly. "It's Yandoo that needs the attention. Since the would-be stockmen have been sent away it means Bill Seddon and I have much to do."

Jim took another bite of cake.

"I don't know anyone the length of the overland stock route who calls me 'Mr. Conrad,' " he said caustically.

At that moment the manager of Ruloo Station joined them.

"Just been looking round the engine room, Jim," he said. "I'll send a man over for you by the end of the week. He's a first-class mechanic and should fix that up for you in two days. Can you put him down at the quarters?"

"Can do," said Jim.

"You see?" said Lulu triumphantly. "Another man to be

44

fed. Of course you need women on Yandoo and don't you protest, Jim. We're staying, aren't we, Gerry?"

"If you will stay with me I'll be very grateful, Lulu," Gerry said. "Do you mind if I salvage some of that raspberry cake for Simon? He went out to feed Jim's dogs." This time she forgot to call him "Mr. Conrad."

At that moment Simon came round the veranda and Gerry handed him the cake plate.

"Hurry up, Simon," she said with a smile. "I'm having to defend your share."

Simon took an enormous bite which left both raspberry and cream on his cheeks, before he said thank you.

"Is the fight over yet?" he said.

"Oh, dear," said Mrs. Sylvester. "Who's fighting, Simon?"

"Gerry and Uncle Jim Conrad will fight because he can't stand women around ever . . . and she'll want to stay."

"He'll stand this pair," said Lulu with a laugh. "He'll have to stand them because we're staying."

"Dear . . ." said Mrs. Sylvester, "do you think it will be quite proper? What do you think, Doctor?"

"Well, that's up to Jim Conrad," he said with a smile.

Jim had been watching Gerry's face as she handed Simon the cake. When Simon had opened his mouth to take that big bite Gerry had opened her mouth too as if it were she herself who was taking the bite. There was something sympathetic in her eye as she watched Simon. Jim looked thoughtful for a moment. Then he turned to Lulu.

"If you will stay, Lulu, then I think it will be all right for Gerry to remain here until we staff the place. In the meantime I'll move down to the book-keeper's room in the store."

Gerry said nothing but Lulu's face fell.

"But what about your meals? You must look after your food, you know."

"Are you going to cook my meals, Lulu?" Jim said. "In that case I'll come up to the homestead for them."

"You know what," said Simon, taking the last piece of cake. "People round here are always talking about food. Me and Uncle Jim can scrounge for ourselves. We been doing it for months, haven't we?"

"That's a man's way of doing it, Simon," Jim said with a touch of sarcasm. "Now the women want to soften us up. Go and clean your teeth after that cake, young feller. There isn't a dentist for six hundred miles."

He stood up abruptly and turned to the doctor.

"I expect you want to be getting off. I'll drive Mrs. Meredith and Mrs. Sylvester over to Ruloo to-morrow and from there they can take a plane out."

He had put a period to the afternoon tea party but more than that he was again acting as if his decisions alone ruled the comings and goings on Yandoo.

Gerry's heart dropped a little. It seemed so safe here in this rather large gathering. When they were all gone, including her mother and her Aunt Sally, she would be left alone with Lulu to try and sort out whether Jim Conrad's presence on Yandoo had a sinister motive or whether he would really help build it up.

CHAPTER FOUR

TWO DAYS LATER the invalid and her sister were gone and Jim Conrad's things had been moved down to the room in the store. Even this gesture on Jim's part made Gerry angry. It was a public rebuff and just too absurd. As if anyone for a thousand square miles cared where Jim Conrad slept. Besides, it made him all the more a stranger . . . someone of whom one was not quite certain.

Lulu, quite incredibly, was a different person. She was up early in the morning and as soon as breakfast was over ensconced herself in the office. Gerry, who knew nothing of office or secretarial work could see, even in an inexperienced way, the neat and orderly way Lulu was going about the business of putting the paper work of Yandoo to rights. Gerry could also see that Lulu's competence was a relief to Jim Conrad. For that, at least, Gerry was pleased. She felt Lulu had some kind of ulterior motive but she couldn't imagine what it was. Lulu, she was certain, would be too ambitious to be seriously interested in an unknown quantity like Jim Conrad.

The two girls had never been close to one another so Gerry did not miss Lulu's companionship now that the latter devoted all her time to the office and Jim Conrad.

For three days after her mother's departure Gerry remained in the homestead going through her mother's things and spring cleaning the invalid's room. In all that time she hardly spoke to Jim. He had been away two days, one going and one coming, when Mrs. Meredith had been taken to Ruloo. When he had returned he had come up to the homestead and gone into the office with Lulu. There they had remained, only interrupted at midday when Lulu had come out, cut some sandwiches and made tea. She had taken them back into the office.

"Sorry to leave you alone, old thing," she said over her shoulder to Gerry. "But we've got yards and yards of work to do here. Heavens, that old book-keeper of yours was lazy, Gerry. I can't understand why you had to go off horse-riding every day when so much work needed doing."

Gerry might have retorted by saying Lulu herself had been on Yandoo nearly eighteen months and had done nothing about the office work then. It did not occur to Gerry to do so. She was just thankful there was one more person on the station to give a hand now.

Lulu's words about the book-keeper, however, set up a new train of thought. If he was as lazy as all that, what sort of a mess would his rooms be in down at the store? Common decency demanded that she see if Jim Conrad's accommodation was adequate. She would have done that for stockmen down at the quarters.

After she and Simon had had a sandwich lunch in the kitchen she walked with the boy down to the store.

Heavens, how depleted the shelves were!

She turned the handle of the door into the sleeping quarters. The floorboards were swept and scrubbed spotless. Jim's bed was made up as carefully as a hospital bed, his gear was stacked methodically in one corner. On the dressing-table there was a leather wallet that held a brush and comb outfit, and that was all.

"Goodness," said Gerry. "It's as clean as a monk's cell."

"So it ought to be," Simon said. "Dinny did it. Dinny 'ud get a stockwhip cracked at him if he didn't do things tidy. My uncle can't stand a mess. My dad used to say Uncle Jim was a pain in the neck he was so tidy. All the same that's why he let me go with my uncle. The homestead was down in the cyclone and there wasn't room down at the quarters for everyone and my dad said if I went with Uncle Jim I'd learn how to run a station good and proper."

"Good and proper? What do you mean 'good and proper,' Simon?" Gerry said reprovingly.

"Beginning at the smallest detail," Simon said in a voice that was so obviously his uncle's that Gerry had to smile.

"You like to do everything that your uncle does, don't you, Simon? And the way he does it too. . . ."

"He's a pretty good bloke even if you don't like him," said Simon defensively.

"Who said I didn't like him?" asked Gerry absently as she glanced once more round the room and then went out, shutting the door behind her.

"You don't have to tell me, I just know. Same as I know what Uncle Jim's thinking."

"What is he thinking?" Gerry asked, startled.

"He's thinking Yandoo is a pretty good wicket. You know what, Gerry?" Simon affected a stockman's drawl again. "We might just buy up a bit of this place and stop here a bit. We kinda like the look of the grasses and judging by the way those gums are flowering heavily down by the billabong it's going to be a good season. We could run a mob in that gully back of the creek, feed 'em up and turn a pretty penny in one season."

Who was Simon imitating now? The only possible person could be Jim Conrad.

"Simon . . ." Gerry began. Then she stopped. A heavy quick tread was coming down the dirt track outside the store. Gerry leaned against the counter and watched the doorway with fascinated eyes. Jim's shadow fell across the patch of sunlight and then he came in.

He stopped short when he saw the boy and the girl.

"Did you want something, Gerry?" he asked abruptly.

"Yes . . ." she said slowly and feeling she was assuming a courage she didn't have. "I want to know who you are? Why you have come to Yandoo?" Her eyes were big with the effort of attempting this showdown with Jim Conrad.

Jim's eyes dropped to Simon's face.

"You young devil," he said, as if he guessed Simon had been talking too much. "I'll wallop the backside off you if I catch you playing at being big fella stockman. Get up to the harness room and clean up that horse gear of yours. If I find so much as two inches of rein unpolished I'll make you clean the harness for the whole plant."

To Gerry's amazement Simon took no offence at Jim's tone.

"Okay, boss!" he said and he rolled out of the store doorway like a veteran horseman.

Gerry's eyes met Jim's.

"You shouldn't speak to a boy that way," she said.

"It's language he understands."

"Like cracking a stockwhip? Is that how you get Dinny to clean your rooms so perfectly?"

"Look, Gerry . . ." Jim's voice had a forced patience in it. "I'll handle my staff my way."

"And my staff you just send away?"

"With the toe end of my boot, if necessary. I'll get staff for Yandoo when I'm ready. And do you still want to know what I'm doing on Yandoo?"

"Yes I do."

"Cleaning the raking place up. Now you go about your work, Gerry, and I'll go about mine. Between us we might get something done."

Gerry flushed.

"Look, Mr. Conrad . . ."

"Jim Conrad."

"All right then. Jim Conrad. Yandoo Station belongs mostly to the Merediths and it doesn't belong to you. And it never will."

Jim's face was frozen in a cold smile.

"What's left of it might belong to the Merediths, Gerry, if we do something practical about it . . . now."

"Such as running a mob of cattle into the gully behind the creek for fattening up?"

"Exactly. I'll be out on the job to-morrow."

"Then so will I," said Gerry.

She moved to pass Jim, who was still only a few feet inside the doorway. As she reached the door he spoke again.

"Lulu tells me you know a jackaroo called David Randall?"

Gerry jerked up her head.

"He's on his way back here. Dinny told me he's twenty miles back on the route."

"And are you thinking of turning him away with the toe of your boot?"

"I don't know. I'll look him over first."

When Jim had told Lulu up in the office that his native Dinny had told him who was coming along the track Lulu had looked up and smiled.

"Oh, that's Gerry's boy friend," she said. "You'd better not turn *him* away."

Gerry was in the doorway now. Suddenly the stiffness went out of her back. She couldn't fight Jim any more. He was too strong for her. And supposing he really was salvaging Yandoo? Supposing Simon was wrong? After all, he was only

49

a child and he did love to aggrandise himself and his uncle.

Jim's voice behind her was unexpectedly quiet. It startled the girl.

"Gerry?" he said. "Would you like David Randall to stay?"

"Yes," she nodded. "Yes. I'd like him to stay."

"Very well. If he's looking for a job I'll give it to him."

"Thank you."

As Gerry walked up to the homestead she realised she had thanked Jim for employing a member of her staff on her station. She shook her head. She supposed that soon she would be asking him for instructions for herself.

"Please Jim, may I go out on the run to-morrow? Please, Jim, may I visit the Ten Mile Bore and see how it's working?"

How easy it would be if one could do just that! If someone sort of took over and she didn't have to worry any more. When that manager came . . .

Supposing she wrote to him, care of the bank. It would get to him. Letters were passed on from mailman to mailman. Somewhere up the country he was working his way down across the rivers and from station to station up there the words would be known as to whereabouts he was now. A drover, a passing stockman would take the letter out with the mail.

Gerry's spirits rose.

She would write to the manager, not to-night, because she was too tired and their own mail wouldn't be going out until the mechanic lent by Ruloo Station to fix the engine returned to Ruloo. She didn't know his name yet . . . but the bank would know. She would write to the Manager of Yandoo Station, care of the bank.

Gerry went to bed early. To-morrow she would work out on the run with Bill Seddon. The bore at the Ten Mile was working and he and Johnny and Jim Conrad's native had fixed the fences right through the sand dune country as far as the spur of the ranges.

Gerry woke in the morning to a multitude of sounds. Some heavy rain, perhaps the last whisker of the Wet, had fallen in the night but although the stars were only just fading Gerry knew it would be a fine cloudless day. The air was heavy with the sweet pungent odour of rain on gravel, grass and fallen gum leaves. Kookaburras on the rail of the horse paddock were filling the morning with the sounds of their laughter.

But more, on the side veranda outside the office door there were sounds of men's boots and men's voices.

It was like Gerry's childhood days when the men each day came up to the office for her father to give them instructions for the day's work. While she dressed in her working clothes and before she had seen anyone Gerry felt the atmosphere of activity, even impending excitement.

She went hurriedly to the kitchen to make herself some breakfast. Tea, and thick doorsteps of bread and butter and jam was all Gerry ever had time for in the mornings.

To her surprise the kitchen light was on, the fire was crackling in the stove and quite definitely the kettle was boiling.

Simon sat at the table occupying himself with a large bowl of cereal.

"Simon! Did you light the fire? I generally use the primus at this hour."

"Uncle Jim said, 'Light the fire, you young tike. Get your breakfast, get Gerry's breakfast and get out here at break-neck speed. And don't wear those raking spurs, you're on the calves to-day'."

Gerry knew Simon was taking off his uncle, word for word.

"What goes on?" Gerry asked as she poured boiling water from the kettle into the teapot. "Who's out there, Simon, with your uncle?"

"Stockmen. Whole bunch of them came riding in to the quarters late last night."

"Is there a man called David Randall there, Simon?"

"Nope. Uncle Jim called his name but he didn't show up. One of the stockmen said he struck him camped down back along the track. His horse had cast a shoe. Said he wasn't hurrying any."

"Oh!" Gerry felt deflated. If David was taking his time it wouldn't impress Jim Conrad.

"You know what?" Simon said. "You'd better eat quick. My uncle's just about got the team worked out and he'll get mad at you if you're late."

"Is that so?" said Gerry, torn between curiosity and indignation.

All the same she did hurry. She had a feeling that life was ebbing back into the station. Things were moving, and if there was a bunch of stockmen and Jim Conrad was going to work them on the place only good could come of that.

She swallowed her breakfast hurriedly. On her way out she

51

paused at Lulu's door but her cousin was still wrapt in sleep. Gerry thought there was no point in waking her and she passed hurriedly on to the side veranda door.

The first morning light was streaming across the homestead yard. Under the box trees at the far end were six saddled horses, geared and equipped for work. On the gravel square below the veranda were three stockmen. They were all strangers to Gerry.

Jim Conrad was standing outside the office door, a work sheet clipped to a wooden board in his hand. He was noting letters and figures down as he spoke.

"All right, you three . . . you're on as from midnight. You'll ride with me. We'll draft out all the scrubbers we can find along the edge of the plain and herd them down to the crossing. If we've enough and they handle well we'll get them over the creek by to-night." He looked up and saw Gerry. He went on in exactly the same voice in which he had been speaking to the stockmen. "Bill Seddon says you're accustomed to sleeping out on a muster, Gerry. He's taken your sleeping gear out with the rest of the plant in the truck. He and the two natives then move on to the Number Three Bore to fix the pumping rod and get it going. You're coming with me."

He bent his head and wrote again on his tally board. Gerry was so surprised she was nearly in a state of shock.

"Would you explain what it's all about . . ." she began hesitantly.

"I'm sorry, I haven't time. We've got to get going. If we wait till the sun's up the cattle feeding on the plain will dodge back into the scrub. You ready, Simon? Then get cracking. You ride on. The little wiry fellow will give you your orders."

Gerry had taken a deep breath which gave her time to adjust herself to the pace at which Jim was doing things. If a muster team had arrived on Yandoo overnight then time was the essence of the contract, she knew that. Her heart beat rapidly. Yandoo was humming again.

She didn't know what this man Jim Conrad was doing here, or why. All she knew was that life was leaping in the green grass and men were riding out over Yandoo plains again.

She pulled her felt hat on her windswept curls.

"But Lulu!" she said. "We should tell Lulu, if we're sleeping out. She is still asleep."

Jim looked up over his tally board. Unexpectedly there was a smile in his eyes.

"Leave Lulu to her beauty sleep," he said quite gently. "Bill

Seddon and two of the men will be in at the quarters to-night. I've left a note on the office table for her."

He turned into the office. Before Gerry had had time to pull on her old leather half-gloves he was outside again, pulling the veranda door shut behind him. His Stetson hat was pulled down over his brow and he carried his stockwhip. Gerry noticed he wore high-heeled stock boots. They were well-cleaned and his spurs shone. Jim Conrad never missed a detail in orderliness.

Gerry looked at him with a puzzled brow. He stopped beside her.

"Are you worrying about leaving Lulu?" he asked. "You needn't you know. I'll do all that."

"How can you when you're out on the run?"

"I can always have a mind here and a swinging right arm out there," he said enigmatically.

Yes, Gerry thought. He wouldn't forget about Lulu. She was very valuable to him with all that book-keeping work. And maybe he liked her company in spite of what Simon had said about his uncle not being able to stand women round the place.

As Gerry crossed the yard to the box trees where her own horse Mandy was standing saddled, she remembered how extra pretty and well-groomed Lulu had looked the last three days. And she'd been doing quite well in the kitchen for someone who had always avoided those regions before.

Simon was standing, the reins of his own horse looped over his arm.

"You ready by any chance?" he drawled. Simon was being the veteran stockman again. Gerry hid a smile.

"Okay, mate," she said.

Simon loosed the reins from his arm and smacked his horse into a run. Then as the horse passed him he twisted the left stirrup with his hand and swung up into the saddle from in front of the left foreleg. Gerry's way of mounting.

In a second she was on her own horse and after him. Half-way down the flat she overtook him and with a quick flanking movement of her horse cut him off. Both mounts came to a standstill.

"Who said you could mount a horse like that?" Gerry asked severely.

"Like what?" said Simon innocently. "I just got up on the raking horse, that's all!"

53

"That's all!" scoffed Gerry. "You've been watching me and you copied me."

"Could be the other way round," Simon said with a tired shrug.

"I'll wallop the backside off you," began Gerry.

"Who's copying Uncle Jim now?" shrieked Simon. He dug his heels into his horse and set off at a mad gallop in the direction of the blue gums down towards the creek.

Jim rode his horse up beside Gerry.

"Who's copying Uncle Jim?" he queried. He was looking at Gerry curiously. Obviously he thought the by-play and friendship between Gerry and Simon was a matter for wonder.

"Not me," said Gerry firmly. "And unless we have to pelt madly along the track after the team would you tell me who those men are and what we are doing this morning?"

"I sent word out along the stock route the day after I got here that I wanted a mustering team. That's what I got. They'll do."

"The day after . . . .?" said Gerry incredulously.

"Yes, the day after I got here. I don't waste time, even when I'm working in the office."

"I didn't think you were wasting time," Gerry said thoughtfully.

"I had some co-operation there." Then he added mockingly, "Charming co-operation." He meant, of course, Lulu.

There was a long pause, then he looked at her with eyes that held that disturbing and faintly ironic smile.

"You'll have some co-operation yourself when we get in, Gerry. By that time David Randall ought to have made up his mind to arrive."

Gerry touched Mandy with the handle of her stockwhip.

"Hurray!" she said over her shoulder. "Someone to talk to at last."

CHAPTER FIVE

IT WAS GREY DAWN when Jim and Gerry caught up with the three new stockmen waiting bunched under the cover of trees at the western end of the scrub belt. Simon was sitting his horse a few yards away from them. The silent immobility of their figures warned Jim they had sighted the cattle.

They were like six ghost figures as they all met. The small

wiry man pointed with the crop end of his stock-whip. Jim kept his two dogs at heel. They stood, quivering with anticipation, their ears pricked and their tails stiff, longing for the word that would put them in action.

Jim nodded.

"All right," he said briefly to a tall, dark-skinned man. "You move in the scrub and see if you can find the track in. Head them out into the plain when they begin to move."

To the wiry man who was apparently someone in whom Jim had confidence he said, "You take the creek bed and head off the east end. Take Simon with you. As soon as they're moving I'll take the leaders and when we've got them out in the plain I'll turn them." He turned to Gerry. "You wait till they're moving and ride this wing. When we turn them you follow the stream clock-wise."

Gerry nodded. It was no sinecure that Jim had given her. She would have to prevent the mob breaking past her or heading back into the scrub after making a half circle on the fringe of the plain.

Sometime later there was a crashing in the scrub and the thrashing and cracking of a stockwhip. The cattle turned, faced the plain and began to run. A minute later they were streaming out, well into the open.

Both Jim's dogs looked at him longingly.

"Not yet," he said. "They're still too near. the scrub."

A stockwhip cracked from the east side of the mob.

"*Right*!" shouted Jim.

His horse, and that of the third of the stockmen seemed to spring off the earth. In a second they were racing with the pace of wind on the wing towards the cattle. Gerry moved out quietly from the trees and galloped her horse a hundred yards behind Jim.

Jim raced round behind the mob, passed the stockman on the other side, and headed the cattle. They turned west and Gerry cracked her stockwhip. The dogs, who understood perfectly what they were to do, remained dead still in the path of the cattle. The leaders saw the dogs and swerved inwards a few yards. Jim was racing with incredible speed around the far side; he passed right round the two sides of the mob now.

Gerry knew her timing had to be perfect.

As the mob, still turning inwards to avoid the dogs, came level with her, she dug in her heels and it was Mandy's turn to spring into action. She raced in the same direction as the mob, keeping them turned inwards away from the scrub.

55

Minutes later the cattle were racing in a circle, the leaders with their nose to the laggards. The outside circle of stockmen closed in, still racing, still shouting, still cracking the whips.

Jim stepped up the pace and now everything in the world was racing round and round in a circle.

Gerry knew the cattle were safe now. The stockmen would race them round in that circle till the cattle came to a bewildered and exhausted stop, discovering they were going nowhere in a circle. They would be bunched and ready to be handled.

Mandy was the fastest horse on Yandoo.

"Ata, ata, ata!" Gerry shouted in Mandy's ear.

The mare lengthened her stride. A few minutes later she had overtaken one stockman; then on in the mad circle and overtaken the next.

Round on the vast circle, outside the stockmen, Gerry raced. She stood up in her stirrups and Mandy's tail streamed out behind her.

Jim was just giving the signal to ease the pace when Gerry raced past on the outside of his wing.

Seconds later she heard the pounding of hooves behind her. Some almost hilarious madness possessed her. Not since her father had died had she raced madly with someone else like this . . . the blood of a race of stockmen singing through her veins.

She dug her heel into Mandy. Whoever it was would have to have a very fast horse to overtake her.

The very earth seemed to shake with the galloping horses. The horse behind Gerry was overtaking her.

Suddenly excitement and joyousness gave way to a little thrill of fear. The other horse was riding too near her. He must be only inches away on her left side. That was dangerous. If they collided at this pace . . .

She must keep Mandy's head steady. Six inches to the left and anything could happen.

The other rider was beside her now. The horses were shoulder to shoulder, the rider's leg jamming her own against Mandy's side. Then it was inches in front and an arm shot out. Jim Conrad leaned sideways as he galloped and caught Mandy's cheek strap. In two minutes he had brought both horses, nostrils distended, their sides heaving, to a standstill.

This had never happened to Gerry or Mandy before.

Jim's brows were thunderous, his eyes under them cold with anger.

Gerry spoke first, astonishment and perplexity in her voice.

"Why did you do that?" She had thrown her head back just as Mandy, nervous under the iron hand holding her, was rearing backwards.

"Who told you to overtake one man, let alone the whole team?" Jim demanded. "Who gave you permission to circle the muster at that pace?"

The horses were still now and Jim released Mandy. The mare moved back a pace.

"Well . . ." said Gerry, at a loss. "I just wanted to do it. I felt like it. It wouldn't cause the cattle to stampede. They were circled and under control . . ."

"I give orders to the team," Jim said sharply. "You ride where I tell you, or you're out."

Before she could answer he had ridden away and was giving the small wiry man instructions to head some leaders out of the mob in the direction of the cattle track across the plain.

"Turn them at the bend of the creek," he said. "Feed them into the rain gully beyond the turn-off."

Gerry wheeled Mandy and rode after Jim. She felt deflated but apart from this she wanted to tell Jim why she knew this particular mob of cattle would not stampede. She had broken rules by her mad gallop but the cattle in this part of the scrub had been handled before. She had handled them, alone, except for Mandy or Sultan and the dogs. Every time she had passed by early in the morning she had chased the strays to get them used to the sound and feel of a horseman and the snapping of a dog's teeth at their hocks.

As she rode up he turned his head and glanced at her.

"You follow the tail," he said curtly. "And stay on the tail. Leave Simon to bring up the calves if they lag."

"Jim . . ."

"Yes?"

"I'm sorry but . . ."

"Don't do that again. If one of the men had done it I'd have sacked him on the spot. I'll see you later."

He wheeled his horse and rode back along the track. Gerry looked after him. She supposed that was how Jim Conrad got things done his way. Do as you're told or get the sack! But what made men come willingly to work for him? Or perhaps they didn't yet know what manner of man he was.

57

On this point Gerry was mistaken as she found out at the camp fire that night. Every one of the new stockmen knew Jim Conrad. They'd either worked for him or knew of him.

Gerry was too loyal a person to begin asking questions or to complain about Jim's terse treatment of herself. Actually she knew the other men knew Jim had spoken to her about that run of hers and her pride was a little hurt. Gerry knew that few stockmen respected a show-off and she suddenly felt afraid that that was what they all thought . . . or at least that Jim thought she was. She could never explain the terrible depression of inactivity that had settled on Yandoo previously and the wonderful exhilaration of seeing the station in action again. Her pride wouldn't let her explain that either.

Gerry found Simon a pleasant comfort to her. In spite of the boy's longing to be a great stockman and his tendency to emulate anything a stockman said or did, it was to Gerry he attached himself when they made camp.

"I'll unroll your swag, Gerry," he volunteered. "Let you and me sleep over by that log. When the wind rises it will blow the fire smoke over us and we won't get eaten alive with mosquitoes."

"All right, Simon. Give me your tin plate and I'll get your tucker for you. A big helping, huh?"

"Look, Gerry," Simon said wearily. "You can't get your mind off food, can you? What's wrong with being skinny? Less weight for my crooked legs to carry."

Simon's legs weren't crooked yet but if he spent his boyhood on a horse the way these stockmen must have done they'd be well bowed by the time he was twenty. The boy could affect a good roll when he walked but with the stockmen it was natural.

Bill Seddon had earlier in the day set up their camp gear for them and then driven off with the natives to attend to the broken pump at Number Three Bore. Towards late afternoon he had driven back to hear what the day's tally was and if the camp had everything it needed.

Gerry walked down to the creek bank with him. Simon had not forgotten his fishing line. He was already hauling in the morrow's breakfast.

"Bill . . ." Gerry asked tentatively. "Why is Jim driving those cattle into that gully? I can't understand why he doesn't use a drafting paddock. The fences are all right, aren't they?"

Bill shook his head,

"I shouldn't worry, Gerry. He knows what he's doing, if ever a man does. Tell you the truth I ain't never seen anyone organise a muster at his pace. And he can pick the good stuff from the bad stuff with his eye, at a hundred yards."

"But why that gully? There's only a creek pool at the bottom for water. It could dry out in days if the heat really strikes us. It could any day now."

"He probably aims to move 'em before then, Gerry. He's just not a man you can ask questions. He just don't answer 'em, if you do."

"There's a cattle pad out, the other end of that gully," Gerry said uneasily. "And Bill . . ." Her voice was even more hesitant. "We don't know any of these men, do we?"

"No, but I guess I can tell yellow from black and white, and there's no yellow streaks in the hearts of those men. They're just crack stockmen working for a wage, Gerry. If I was you I'd just trust 'em. And Jim Conrad too. He's on the level."

Gerry looked at Bill.

"You like him, don't you, Bill?"

"I like a feller that can work the way he works, and knows what he's doin'. An' I like a feller that looks you straight in the eye the way he does. An' your Ma knew about him, or your Dad used to, or somethin'. Don't you worry, Miss Gerry. You take it from me he's square and on the level."

"I can't help believing that too, in a way, Bill. It's just so odd the way he walked in and took over and within a few days was running the place as if he owned it." She smiled ruefully. "Do you know he's got me down on the wage list as G. Meredith at stockman's casual rates? I'm not even Geraldine Meredith of Yandoo Station any more."

Bill laughed.

"He's just seeing you get some pocket money, Miss Gerry. Get some tucker and a good night's sleep. You'll feel different to-morrow when you see how he handles them men and them cattle. Meantime I gotta drive the boss up to the homestead . . . so I'd better get trackin' or he'll be taking a bite at me."

The stockman moved back to the camp where Jim Conrad was detailing the work for the men in the morning. A few minutes later Gerry saw him drive away in the cabin seat of the truck with Bill. He had given her, Gerry, no specific job for the morrow, and he hadn't said good-bye.

All this happened before the camp meal. Simon had been the only one to comment on Jim's departure.

"You know, some things about my uncle make me tired,"

59

he said to Gerry wearily. "Going up to the homestead to look after Lulu! Wouldn't you think he'd get some sense?"

"He's quite right, Simon," Gerry said reprovingly. "After all, Lulu is alone in that homestead."

"There's women alone in every homestead from the Gulf to Lake Eyre. I reckon he just likes Lulu. All those pretty dresses . . ."

"Simon," said Gerry in her best admonitory manner, "I think you're plain jealous."

"Well, aren't you?"

Gerry looked at the small boy indignantly.

"Of whom, and why?"

"Aw . . . I don't know. All those pretty dresses. And you know what? I kinda like my uncle when he smiles, and he only smiles when he talks to Lulu . . . worse luck."

"Let's stop talking about your uncle and Lulu."

"Okay, if it makes you snappy, Gerry. How about coming fishing with me to-night? I can lend you a line. Fix you a rod too, if you like."

"All right, Simon. I'd like to do that."

In fact Gerry was not an expert fisherman but she did love to sit at night on the creek bank when the moon came filtering through the branches of the gum trees. She liked the smell of the night air on the fallen leaves, and she liked the stillness of the creek water under starlight. Fishing with a good companion like Simon meant peace and solitude. Besides, the stockmen would want to tell their usual yarns around the fire and a girl's presence would restrict them.

The men had settled round the camp fire, their cigarettes alight and one of them with a concertina, when Gerry and Simon picked their way down the cattle pad to the creek. Before tea Simon had located two good perches and in his quaint, rather old-fashioned way he settled Gerry down, fixed her line on the end of a fine green sapling rod and moved a dozen yards away to his own perch.

"There's a stump behind you to lean on, Gerry," he said. "And if you get your line tangled just sing out. I'll fix it."

Something about Simon warmed Gerry's heart. There was one creature in the world who thought about her comfort. Strange that it should be a thin little boy out of the north who owned Jim Conrad for an uncle.

She sat in somnolent peace and let her line dangle in the

water. From the occasional splash she heard farther up the bank she knew Simon was catching fish. Gerry would have liked a bite or two just to keep up her prestige with the boy, but for the rest of it she was content to sit and watch the reflection of the stars in the water and listen to the soft tones of the concertina at the camp behind her. She knew her bait was water-logged and would lie on the bottom. Presently she would haul in and re-bait just so she wouldn't go up to the camp empty-handed.

Simon stole down the bank towards her.

"How you doin', Gerry?"

"Fine. I haven't caught a fish yet but I like sitting here."

Simon hauled in and re-baited for her.

"You gotta re-bait, Gerry. We haven't any floats and the fish won't bite on the bottom."

"All right, Simon. I'll do just what I'm told. You're the expert."

"I'll say!" said Simon. "I caught five this afternoon and four since tea."

"Well, go back and catch some more, like a good boy. I just want to sit and think."

"Think?" said Simon with astonishment. "What's the good of thinking? That won't catch you anything."

He went back to his own perch between the two roots of the giant gum. He was clearly puzzled at the ways of girls. They went fishing and didn't try to catch fish.

It was the tinkle of horse-bells, the muted concertina, the still clear night with its stars and silent water that Gerry was enjoying.

Sometime later—was it one hour or two hours?—she heard the rhythmical cantering of a horse coming down the track from the homestead.

She heard a man's voice at the camp fire and the quiet muted tones of men answering. Then presently the heavy boots of a horseman coming down to the creek edge. She looked up and saw the dark shadow of Jim Conrad standing behind her. She knew it was Jim by his height and some extra sense that told her none of the other stockmen would have come unannounced to the creek bank.

He stood in silence for a minute then sat down beside her.

"How's the fishing?" he asked casually.

"You'd better ask Simon," Gerry said quietly. "He's the only one catching anything."

"Here, let me haul in your line."

Jim took the rod from her hand and flicked the line out of the water. He coiled in the line carefully.

"You haven't any bait on," he said. "Don't tell me you don't know how to fish, Gerry."

"I wasn't really trying," she said. "Simon is catching enough." She must speak calmly as if nothing had happened this morning.

Jim let the rod and line lie on the ground. He hunched his knees up, took out the makings of a cigarette and began to roll one. When he had finished he handed it to Gerry to lick the paper down. Then he poked in the tobacco with a match and gave it back to her.

"Yours," he said. He too was calm.

Gerry hardly ever smoked but now seemed quite a good time to have a home-made cigarette.

Jim lit it for her. In the flame of the match she could see his eyes, dark pools with the fire from the match giving them a flickering light.

Then he rolled himself a cigarette.

What was this all about? Gerry wondered. Peace-making because he had spoken to her this morning as if she was what he had put her down on the tally board . . . no more than a hired hand employed on casual rates?

"Why do you fish without trying to fish?" Jim asked curiously.

This did not sound like a peace-making overture to Gerry.

"Well . . ." Gerry said hesitantly, "if I just came down here and sat, Simon and the men might think it peculiar whereas there's nothing peculiar about fishing, even if you don't catch any, is there?"

"What is peculiar about just sitting?"

"Do you ever just sit?" Gerry asked in surprise.

"Sometimes I sit," Jim said dryly. "And sometimes I sit and think."

"Oh!" Gerry was at a loss. For one who was as brilliantly active as Jim Conrad this was a strange statement and quite a new aspect of his personality.

"Anyone who has never just sat by a camp fire or a creek bank on an Australian night has missed something in life," Jim added softly. "In the northern hemisphere they say 'See Naples and die.' Same sentiment."

Inexplicably Gerry's heart, which had been just a little leaden, lifted. She even felt comforted and warmed. Cold, indifferent and even arrogant as Jim might seem in the affairs of the day there was something in him that understood that sometimes a person likes to be alone . . . whether it was with her troubles or with a brilliant star-ridden sky on a still warm night didn't matter. Perhaps he understood she had not been defecting from her mother's sick-bed on the day she had sat by the billabong when the doctor called.

The funny thing about sitting alone like that was that really you were longing for something, or was it someone? Not anyone, some particular *one* who must be somewhere in the world waiting for that moment in time when Fate would point a finger at you, and at him.

Even in the dark Gerry blushed. She had never really thought as explicitly as this before. Thank goodness it was dark and Jim would never know how her own thoughts had discomfited her.

It was he who broke the silence between them.

"Gerry, you've done a lot of things on a station. You can muster horses and cattle, mend a fence and climb a windmill. You can even cook a good meal in the homestead kitchen. Have you ever run a mustering team as the boss?"

Gerry stiffened. Now it was coming, she thought. The only thing she didn't understand was the quiet note in his voice.

"No," she said. "I haven't. We used to have an overseer."

"And that overseer only kept his authority amongst a group of hard-riding hard-bitten men by iron rule?"

"It never hurt anyone to be kind and sympathetic," Gerry said.

"Exactly." Jim's voice was tighter now. "Have you worked it out how an overseer or muster boss shows his sympathy with his men? He does what they do and he never asks them to do something he can't or won't do himself. He'll always ride down the first and the wildest of the mad bulls. They know he knows what it's like if their timing is out by the fraction of a second."

"Yes, I think you're right," Gerry said.

"And on the other side of the page the story goes on that he gives the men an order, they obey it or they're out."

"You mean my ride this morning? Jim, I knew what you didn't know . . . those cattle had been handled before. They were safe and would not stampede."

"That's got absolutely nothing to do with it. I gave an order to you as a member of my mustering team. You disregarded it."

"If you're lecturing me, Jim, I can see your point. I'm sorry and I won't offend again."

There was a few minutes' silence and when he spoke his voice was quiet again.

"That bunch of stockmen back there are the toughest south of the Gulf country, Gerry. One chink in my armour and I wouldn't hold them."

Gerry laughed softly.

"You're not calling me your chink, are you, Jim?"

She felt him stiffen beside her.

"Letting you get away with that ride would have been a chink," he said coldly. "Quite a different matter."

"Yes, I see that it is," Gerry said soberly.

"Well, that's cleared the air, I think," said Jim, and he stood up.

Gerry remained unmoving. She would have liked to stand up too just to savour that height beside her own. Standing near Jim Conrad gave her a very small feeling but it also gave her a comforting awareness of his strength. It was strange how divided her feelings were about him. One moment she was afraid of him and what he might be doing on Yandoo. The next, willy nilly, she had a wild inclination to lean on his authority, to give him her burden of worry.

But she remained seated.

"By the way," Jim said from a long way up above her, "you will probably be interested to know David Randall rode into the homestead late this afternoon. When I got up with Bill Seddon Lulu was giving him dinner."

Gerry turned her head eagerly. All she could see of Jim was his black shadow against the glow of the camp fire yards away along the bank.

"Did you . . . did you tell him where we were? You will give him a job in the mustering team, Jim?"

"He said he needs a rest-off to-morrow. He's come a long way."

Gerry didn't know whether there was sarcasm in Jim's voice or whether she imagined it. Jim would know she knew that the men already with them had come a long way; had turned into the quarters very late at night but had been up before daybreak to start the first long day on the cattle hunt.

"David's different from these stockmen," Gerry said in excuse for him. "He's only learning how things work on a station for his company in the city. He's not corn hardened to the saddle like . . ."

64

"Of course not. Don't worry, Gerry. We won't kill him even if we do work him hard. Now if you'll excuse me I'm going back to the homestead. Randall did at least bring the mail in with him and Lulu and I'll go through it to-night. I'll see you in the morning."

Without another word he was gone and presently Gerry heard the sound of a horse's rhythmical canter as Jim rode away.

The magic spell of the creek was broken. Simon was winding in his lines and talking to himself; the men round the camp fire were turning in and Gerry could hear the rattle of tin on tin as the camp cook made the last-minute damper to put in the oven under the coals first thing in the morning.

It was time the world went to bed, yet Jim Conrad was riding those five miles back to the homestead to sit poring over an office table with Lulu beside him. Gerry had a mental picture of that intimate scene. Deliberately she switched her thoughts away to David Randall. She didn't want to be grateful to Jim Conrad for taking on Yandoo's jackaroo again, but she was very thankful that he had all the same. David being on Yandoo was like old times. They had had fun together, swimming in the billabong and playing squash on the concrete square outside the garages.

Gerry let Simon boss her just a little bit about the business of putting their fishing gear away, and washing at the creek edge and turning in at the correct distance from the rest of the swags now lying somnolent around the dying fire.

"I guess I'd better sleep between you and the bogies," Simon said but Gerry noticed that he put his sleeping-bag down between her own and the creek. Just what were Simon's ideas of bogies, she wondered. She must remember to ask him in the morning. She couldn't ask him to-night because he was asleep instantly, like the turning out of a light. And she . . . well, she was almost asleep herself.

CHAPTER SIX

FIVE DAYS LATER Gerry returned with the mustering team to the homestead square.

"A day's lay-off," was Jim Conrad's curt instruction. "Thursday morning report at the office door five a.m."

He was speaking to the men but his words included Gerry.

Throughout the five days he had treated her as a team member, the only time he had spoken to her separately was each night before she turned in.

Every night he had gone back to the homestead in Bill Seddon's truck and every night he had come back on his change-horse to see if the camp was settled down. It was on those occasions he would have a little desultory but impersonal conversation with Gerry.

He rarely bothered with the boy Simon except to say, "How are you going, mate?" Simon would answer him with the same laconic reply that the stockmen gave. "Fine, thanks."

Once Jim said to him, "You looking after Gerry all right?"

To which Simon replied, "I got my weather eye on her. She's doing fine . . . for a girl."

Gerry affected indignation.

"The only girl on your horizon, Simon, is trying to teach you to speak the Queen's English and read a book from end to end without getting bored half-way through."

"Aw . . . books!" said Simon.

"What's that?" said Jim. "Don't tell me you're going to school out here at a muster camp."

"Half an hour every raking night," said Simon wearily.

"Leave out the word 'raking,'" said Gerry reprovingly, "and sound your 't' on the end of night."

"See what I mean?" said Simon with the kind of dead pan face with which all the stockmen asked searching questions.

Jim looked at Gerry.

"Quite a job you've taken on, Gerry," he said. "Is that what Bill Seddon brought those books down for?"

"I'm amazed that no one else has thought of taking it on," Gerry said, trying to sound as if she was not lecturing *him*. She was too frightened of Jim's scarifying tongue to book an open fight with him. All the same she was astonished that he would travel round the outback with a nine-year-old boy and not bother about that boy's education. What were Simon's parents thinking of, letting this state of affairs continue?

She knew, of course, that catastrophe in the nature of a cyclone had completely dislocated the boy's home but it was increasingly clear to her, and it must have been to Jim, that Simon's only ambition in life was to emulate the stockmen . . . their skill and intrepid daring on horseback and their speech. Even if Simon was going to spend his life on an outback station he should add something to *that*. He should not be ignorant of other ways of life. It wasn't right but she

66

wouldn't dare say so to Jim Conrad. She just hoped he'd give it thought now that he noticed someone else thought the boy was entitled to an elementary education.

Jim's eyes were searching her face so she turned quickly away.

"Going up to the homestead again to-night?" she asked.

"Yes. Have you got any messages for Lulu?"

There was something sardonic in the question as if he knew she would not have messages for Lulu but would like to send one to David Randall. She would have done so every night only again she had been afraid of that knowing glint in Jim's eyes. She felt instinctively he didn't care much for David Randall.

Well, David Randall was *different*.

Little passages like these had passed between Gerry and Jim on that five-day muster but at the end of it she still knew no more of his intentions.

To begin with, how was he going to pay this mustering team, including herself, since he had put her . . . just plain G. Meredith . . . on the tally sheet, casual rates?

On the last night at the camp before they returned to the homestead she put this problem to Bill Seddon. The camp was well away from the homestead on this night and Bill Seddon had driven Jim down in the truck. Jim was now detailing plans for the morrow to Twisty, the small wiry man who was obviously the leader of the men who formed Jim's muster team.

"I don't know why you don't give up worrying, Gerry," the old stockman said kindly. "Everything's fair and above board, square an' honest as far as I can see. Tell you the truth, there was nothin' fer you to lose on Yandoo, Gerry. It was a fair goner, anyway. With them two hundred steers drafted and branded in the gully, an' a buyer comin' along at the right moment Jim Conrad'll have more'n enough to pay wages an' carry on too."

"But will a buyer come along at the right moment? The water level in the hole is going down rapidly. Why doesn't he drive the cattle into the big paddock?"

"He's fattening 'em up quick in that gully, Gerry. They're easier to get handled there and you know what buyers are like. They don't like wild cattle. They pay better for stuff well handled."

Gerry thought for a long time.

"Bill," she said tentatively, "has it occurred to you that
67

mob of cattle could very easily be eased along that narrow cattle pad at the back end of the gully. And be gone in a night."

"I guess that's what the buyer'll do when he comes along. Don't you worry, Gerry. I never seen a straighter eye than Jim Conrad's got . . . even if it's a cold one when he's in one of his moods."

Gerry lifted her head curiously.

"What moods do you mean, Bill?"

"Those crack-on-the-pace and to-certain-raking-places-with-dawdling moods. Then what with half the night in the office and all daylight with the team I reckon he's pretty tired most of the time. He don't get in a temper when he's tired. That's one good thing about Jim Conrad. He just goes quiet and like a slice of the south pole. He sort of has leave-me-alone signals oozing out the pores of his skin."

"Yes, I've noticed that," Gerry said soberly.

She wished her feelings weren't so divided about Jim Conrad. When she saw the pace at which he worked, the terrific drive with which he egged his men on, the astonishing feats of horsemanship which he performed without apparently knowing he did them, everything in her applauded him as a man of great strength and endurance. Specially if he was doing all this for Yandoo and not himself.

Then cold anxiety would settle on her heart when she thought of Simon's innocent words . . . "My uncle's always got his eye out for a bite into another station. My dad reckons he'll own all the stations in the State one day."

And she could not but feel anxious about the cattle in the gully. They were the pick of the mobs they had mustered. The cows, calves, weaners and rough stuff had all been drafted out. Only the best had been branded . . . if they were clean-skins . . . and mobbed in the gully. And unless a buyer came in the next three or four days the water would have all dried out.

It was in this frame of mind that at the end of the fifth day Gerry returned to the homestead.

There had always been something lovely about returning to the homestead after a muster when she had been a child. The homestead had seemed to be waiting for them. Certainly her mother was waiting with extra fine fare for dinner, baths and a clean change of clothes for Gerry and her father.

Then had come the bad days after her father had gone, and her mother no longer was watching the horsemen coming

home from the rails by the saddling paddock. Those had been
the days when Gerry went inside and retrieved her dinner
from the oven. Aunt Sally Sylvester knew little of station life
and had never understood that special feeling about coming
home after a muster. And Gerry was so grateful to her aunt
for shutting herself away on Yandoo and looking after Mrs.
Meredith that Gerry never told her that for herself the house
no longer welcomed. It no longer had the special look of waiting specially for young Gerry Meredith to come home.

All the same Gerry knew it was going to be different this
time. To begin with, there was a whole muster team to be
camped down at the homestead and that meant there would
be singing and the sound of the mouth organ and concertina
as the men sat outside their sleeping quarters the other side
of the station square. There would be laughter and yarning
and the sound of their voices wafting across the still gum-
scented night air. There would be *life* in and around the place.

Lulu was used to Jim Conrad riding or driving up to the
homestead each night so she would have prepared something
for their evening meal.

And there would be David Randall.

Jim had said there would be a day off for all. That would
include David too, surely. Perhaps they would swim in the
billabong.

The only swims Gerry had taken in the billabong in six
months had been in the nature of quick washes because she
didn't have time to go up to the homestead for one.

Gerry left Mandy in the saddling paddock. Johnny the
faithful native was waiting to unsaddle for her. She joyfully
threw him the reins and ran up towards the garden and the
house.

Goodness, the garden had been cleared up! The engine
house was humming with sound and water was being pumped
from the bore into the sprinklers. Who had been responsible
for all this? And in five days!

It was wonderful. Even the shrubs . . . the oleanders, the
bougainvillæa and the hibiscus . . . seemed to have taken a
new lease of life. Their leaves glistened as if they had been
drinking water long and deep and the old dead flowers had
been cut and cleared away, leaving only a gorgeous array of
pink, red and tangerine flowers.

As Gerry jumped up on to the veranda outside the office
Lulu came out.

Even Lulu had changed. She had always been attractive

but now she was something more. She was like a woman in command of a very pleasing situation. There was an air of composure and satisfaction about her. One glance in the office and Gerry thought she could see why. Even in her father's lifetime it had never been so tidy. And there were *flowers* on the table and filing cabinet. A real welcome for Jim Conrad, anyway.

"Golly," Gerry said. "What have you been doing, Lulu? The place has been spring-cleaned!" Then she added impulsively, "You must have worked hard, Lulu."

"Oh, Jim and I decided that no one can work efficiently in a muddle. We both agreed that some of the furniture could go out and the rest of the stuff be moved around. Of course we burnt barrow-loads of old useless files."

"We? But when was he doing it? I know he put in a few hours each night up here but he slept and worked out at the muster camp."

"Oh, you would be surprised at what can be done in a few hours when two people are of one mind," Lulu said sagely. "As a matter of fact Jim and I are kindred souls when it comes to office work. We both seem to understand what the other is thinking . . . without putting it into words."

Gerry felt she should not be silent, but she was. This was an aspect of Jim Conrad so foreign to her that she could hardly believe Lulu was speaking of *him*.

What was it Simon had said about his uncle not being able to stand women round the place? Of course that had only been a child speaking but Gerry's own contacts with Jim had certainly not been that of a soul-mate.

Still, she must be generous to Lulu for the other's wonderful assistance. She wondered secretly if Lulu too had been added, a mere name, to Jim's wages tally, but she didn't ask Lulu. Obviously her cousin's air of composed dignity was not consistent with being asked if she was a wage slave. And she was wearing the prettiest dress of her whole wardrobe.

Simon had already arrived and had entered the homestead from the other side. He now came through the passage leading out the side door beside the office. He picked his way across the veranda delicately like a ballet dancer. Gerry, smiling, wondered who Simon was emulating now.

"Don't put dust on the passage floor now, Gerry. And wash your hands. Snakes alive, how can a young fella like you get all that plurry dust in five days. You bin rollin' in the dust like that fella dingo."

70

This was a lubra talking.

"Lulu!" cried Gerry. "Don't tell me we've got kitchen help?"

"Old Mary and her daughter Jeannie have come across from Ruloo Station," Lulu said with the faintly bored accents of one who thinks there's nothing odd in this occurrence. "Naturally Jim didn't expect me to be in the kitchen and office at one and the same time. What is more . . ." There was a long dramatic pause intended for effect. "I don't think he expects me to be in the kitchen at all."

Yes, looking at her cousin, Gerry realised she was far too nicely dressed, her hair too well groomed and the nails of her fingers too perfectly painted to have come from a hot stove preparing dinner for the musterers' come home. Even Lulu's eyebrows were pencilled and there was mascara on her lashes, forcing one to concentrate on her eyes when one looked at her. Lulu's eyes were a light blue but the mascara enhanced them. They looked so clear.

"And there's a cook down at the quarters," Lulu added for further effect. "I was just not prepared to put up with a whole gang of men eating in the kitchen."

Gerry passed her dusty hand over her dusty face.

Jim Conrad was the man who hated a dawdler, who made everyone work at top speed from before daylight until after dark. Everyone, that is, except Lulu. Lulu must be given assistance.

But then, why should Lulu work? After all, it wasn't *her* station. That was probably how Jim had reasoned.

"As a matter of fact, Jim and I . . ." Lulu began.

Jim and I! Gerry thought she might cry out if Lulu used that expression *Jim and I* again. Somehow it didn't belong . . . and for some strange reason it hurt.

At that moment Jim came up the path from the saddling yard. He too was covered with dust, and his eyes were almost hollow with tiredness. His face, weather-beaten a new brown, was streaked and the wrinkle lines at the corners of his eyes showed white because the skin there did not burn when he screwed up his eyes out on the run to see into the distances.

Lulu did not finish her sentence. Instead she began another.

"Oh, Jim, would you like to bath up at the homestead to-night? I'm sure the men will have hogged the shower down at the quarters. And I've got a large roast dinner for you." She smiled charmingly.

71

Jim came carefully up the three steps. He stood looming over the two girls.

"Thank you, Lulu," he said. He took his eyes from Lulu's face to Gerry's. "What about you, Gerry . . ." And then he looked up with a jerk of his head.

There were heavy footsteps round the corner of the veranda. Gerry turned to follow Jim's gaze. Round the corner came David Randall.

Gerry took one glance at his fair smiling face with the curious wave of hair that always hung over his forehead in a lock. He was spotlessly clean in fresh khakis, and had brown shoes on instead of elastic-sided boots. He looked so clean and just-bathed that Gerry felt that in looking at him she had drunk a whole demi-john of iced water.

"David!" She gave a joyous cry. She ran down the veranda and for some entirely unpremeditated reason ran straight into his arms.

"Whacko!" said David. "Look who's come home!"

"I'm so glad to see you," cried Gerry.

"What do you think I came back for, young 'un?"

Gerry extricated herself from David's embrace. She took his hand and turned.

"Jim . . ." she said.

But Jim with Lulu had gone into the office. He was, at that moment, quietly closing the door.

CHAPTER SEVEN

LAY-OFF DAY on a station was a day upon which people, willy nilly, were to lie up and rest. It meant recognition of the hard work done and anticipation of hard work to be begun again on the morrow. It was everyone's duty to be ready for that work.

Gerry for the first time since she had come home from school, a year ago, lay in bed the following morning.

She had woken as usual at four-thirty and half asleep had begun to feel for the floor with her reluctant feet. Then she remembered. She was home. Someone was organising the work on Yandoo. It was somebody else's responsibility to know how many bores were in order and working: what the fences were like at the out-stations fifty miles away . . . how the cattle were round the natural water-holes.

She didn't know whether to like that or not, worry about it or not. She didn't have to get up, she could put her head back on the pillow and sleep and sleep and sleep. It was like Sunday mornings in boarding school. One woke at six but remembered with joy and relief that to-day one had an extra half hour. One could close one's eyes and go to sleep again.

To-day, here on Yandoo, she could close her eyes and sleep all day if she wanted.

Gerry withdrew her feet from the floor and stretched them out on the bed. She turned her head into her pillow and was asleep before she had stopped thinking about this strange phenomenon.

Each time Jeannie, the young lubra who had come across from Ruloo Station, put her head in the door Gerry was still asleep, her position exactly as it was the first time.

"Mine tink that one sleepy fella," she said to Jim Conrad as she passed him in the passage with the tray of tea and toast she had prepared for Gerry. "When that gul las' get a goo' night's sleep, huh?"

Jim paused and looked at the slowly cooling tea.

"She's not ill?" he asked.

The lubra shrugged.

"Mine tink she sleep like dead fella."

Jim strode up the passage to Gerry's door. It was ajar and he did not knock. He pushed the door open and walked across to Gerry's bed. He stood looking down at her.

There had only been a few occasions when he had seen Gerry without a layer of dust on her face. Her skin was very clear and her lashes lay long and peacefully on her cheeks. The sprinkling of freckles on the bridge of her nose gave her face a very young look.

Jim Conrad's face was a quiet study. No wonder Simon had taken to Gerry's company. Two young things . . .

She looked so defenceless lying there with her arms outflung on the bed covers where the covers were turned back. He bent down and lifted her wrist to feel her pulse. It was smooth and strong, yet as he held her hand he felt a faint tremor pass through it. He let her hand lie in his for a moment and he stood looking down at it. How soft and delicate it was! He could see the sunburn line where the fingers emerged from the half gloves she wore when riding. They were the long narrow fingers of a young girl's hand.

Gerry stirred and Jim put her hand gently back on the

73

bed. He was still looking down at her when she turned her face a little and opened her eyes. Jim smiled.

"Sleeping the sleep of the just," he said. He turned away towards the door.

Gerry blinked and shook her head trying to shake away the veils of sleep. Was she still dreaming . . . because she *had* been dreaming. She had been dreaming she was calling out to him but that he went on ahead and would not turn back.

He would have gone straight through the door now, without turning his head, except that David had arrived there in search of Gerry.

Jim stood aside as David hesitated in the doorway.

"Your patient . . ." Jim said, waving his hand towards Gerry. There was a cynical edge to his smile as he greeted David. But a minute before his smile had been different, Gerry was sure of it.

David looked into Gerry's room and lifted his hand in greeting.

"You're not ill, or anything like that, are you, Gerry?"

"No. Just overslept myself," she said gaily. She felt happy to see those two men standing there like that. It was nice to be cared about.

"I'll see you later," Jim said to David, and he went rapidly down the passage.

David made a wry face at Gerry.

"That means he'll see me right now at the office door," he said. "Glad to see you're okay, Gerry. I'll be seeing you."

Gerry took a shower and dressed hurriedly. She felt gloriously refreshed from her long sleep, and even the growing heat of the day did not damp her spirits.

The two lubras in the kitchen made it a gay place with the sunshine of their smiles. Gerry loved the black girls. They were the most happy-go-lucky and the sunniest race in the world. Only the fact that Mary was a little more portly than Jeannie portrayed which was mother and which was daughter.

"You bin shut-eye long time," Mary said. "You close-up dead. Proper tired. How 'bout cuppa tea, eh?"

"That's what I've come for," said Gerry. "Golly, it's nice to see you and Jeannie here, Mary. It's like old times. Are you going to stay for good?"

"We bin stay alla-same long time," Mary said. "That boss up at Ruloo he say 'You fella git down there to Yandoo. I bin come for you someday, maybe.'"

They laughed.

"Let's hope his 'someday' will be a long way off," said Gerry.

It was grand about the way the manager had been so neighbourly and co-operative with Jim Conrad. There was no doubt about it, Jim's wish seemed to be taken as a command by everyone from the manager of Ruloo to Bill Seddon on her own station and the two girls now in Yandoo's kitchen.

The three of them laughed and talked while Gerry made some toast and Jeannie made the tea and set out a cup and saucer on a small tray. The two lubras chatted on, telling Gerry all the news of Ruloo.

"Black fella up at Ruloo say this fella Jim Conrad maybe sometime marry Lulu, eh?" laughed Jeannie.

"Oh, Jeannie, don't talk like that!" Gerry said. "Both Jim Conrad and Lulu might be properly mad if they hear you."

"How about you bin properly mad, eh?" laughed Jeannie. "How 'bout you marry this fella Jim Conrad, 'stead of Lulu? Alla-same maybe you marry that fella jackaroo David Randall, eh?"

Gerry buttered the toast lavishly.

"You don't think of anything but somebody marrying somebody else, Jeannie," Gerry said severely. "How 'bout you marry someone yourself one day pretty soon? What about that Charlie horse-breaker up at Ruloo? He's a pretty smart black fellow for you to marry."

This was received with gales of laughter from both lubras. Jeannie threw her apron over her head and ran shrieking with laughter from the kitchen.

At that moment Lulu came in the opposite door.

"Really," she said, "this place might as well be full of cockatoos as two lubras. They're making far too much noise. Why don't you keep them quiet, Gerry?"

Gerry put a finger of hot buttered toast in her mouth. Lulu didn't know much about station life and Gerry was sorry for her on that score.

"I couldn't keep them quiet if I wanted to, Lulu," she said. "But I wouldn't want to, anyway. They're happy. When the natives were here before Father died, you could hear them chattering and laughing all day long down at the camp."

"Plenty alla-same magpie," said Mary, smiling. "Cockatoo him screech."

"Well, what was that I heard when I came in?" asked Lulu.

"That was Jeannie laughing," explained Gerry. "Have a
75

cup of tea, Lulu? First it makes you hot but you feel cool afterwards."

"I think Mr. Conrad is entitled to peace and quiet in order to get on with his work," Lulu said from rather lofty heights.

Gerry took another bite of toast. She pushed the bitten piece into the corner of her mouth.

Who was the "*Mister* Conrad" for? Mary and Jeannie? The black people did not understand courtesy names and surnames. They only understood a name as a name. Well, Gerry would have to explain all this to Lulu somewhere else, not in front of the lubras. So she changed the subject.

"Is Jim working in the office? What is he working at, Lulu?"

Lulu looked disdainful.

"I don't ask you what you do on a horse all day out on the run, Gerry, because I wouldn't understand. So I don't think you would understand what bringing the ledgers and accounts up to date means."

Gerry was determined not to be hurt by Lulu's tone. Moreover, there was some logic in what Lulu said. All the same the reminder of books and ledgers brought back that old feeling of unease. Surely this would be the business of the manager when he came?

Gerry remembered she had been going to write to the manager. Now that she was back in the homestead she must do it.

"I'd like to go and see Jim for a few minutes," she said. She picked up her cup and saucer, balanced another piece of toast on the saucer and went towards the door.

"You'll do nothing of the kind, Gerry. For goodness' sake . . . the man is *busy*. Haven't I just been explaining that."

The two girls were within a few feet of one another now. Gerry looked into Lulu's eyes. There she read something cold and self-certain. It was like a stroke across her own heart. Lulu was standing guard over Jim Conrad, and perhaps over the affairs of Yandoo.

"You mean he has shut the door again?"

"Yes, against *all* interruptions."

Suddenly Gerry knew that Lulu had changed out of all recognition. The graceful bored girl who once had lolled on the veranda chairs of the homestead was gone. This was a young woman of poise. Her bearing was alert and confident. Her prettiness had been groomed to sophistication. Her couldn't-care-less attitude had given place to one of careful purpose.

What or who had done this to Lulu in little over two weeks? Or had she always been like this underneath that veneer of disinterestedness? Maybe, before, she had had no direction in her life. Now she had one. If it was not Yandoo, then it must be Jim Conrad.

"All right, Lulu," she said quietly. "If he's as busy as all that I won't disturb him." She took another step and was in the doorway. She turned her head to look at Lulu again. "Do you know where David Randall is?"

"Yes, off to the Number Two Bore. Something was repaired there the other day and Jim told David to go out and turn on the mill, a few minutes ago."

"Turn on the mill!" That was not work one gave a jackaroo, unless a jackaroo happened to be passing that way. A jackaroo was on a station to learn the business of station management. One did not send him to do an ordinary labourer's work. Jim Conrad would have known that if Lulu didn't. Had he done this deliberately to humiliate David?

Gerry not only bit her toast, she bit her lip.

She took the rest of her tea out on to the veranda and sat looking over the newly tidied garden while she finished it.

As far as she knew there were no new hands on the station other than those in the muster team and Jim's own native who had gone with Bill Seddon and Johnny to mend the pump rod at Number Two. Then who had cleared the débris from the garden? Not Mary and Jeannie and certainly not Lulu. Jim couldn't in all conscience have got David Randall to do it? But that was impossible. David could simply have refused.

Gerry put her cup and saucer on the floor under her chair and left it there. She reached for her felt hat from the side veranda peg where it was always kept, pulled it down on her forehead and went quickly down to the stables.

Mandy was out to rest so Gerry saddled her change-horse, Sultan. A few minutes later she was riding across the saddling paddock. Sultan was a hurdler and with effortless grace Gerry sailed over the fence. From a canter to a gallop she gathered speed as she went down the flat towards the creek.

Past the elbow of the creek she galloped along the old cattle pad leading out on to the plain and the desert lands beyond. Four miles out she came to the Number Two Bore. David Randall was sitting in the shade of a tree smoking a cigarette. Gerry swung herself from the saddle, threw the reins across the cross-bar of the bore trough and came and sat down beside David.

He grinned when he saw her riding up but he did not make a move to greet her. Gerry had always been just a kid to him but he was beginning to think life on Yandoo had an ageing effect. Gerry, even in the same old jeans and same old shirt and same old felt hat, had looked mighty like a young woman when she had come racing along the veranda last night to meet him. Even with those layers of dust it was a rather attractive woman too.

But he wasn't going to let Gerry act too grown up with him . . . yet.

He didn't have to worry. Gerry threw herself on the ground beside him in the shade of the tree. She picked up a dried twig and chewed it.

"David," she said, "where have you been all the morning?"

"You can talk," he said with a derisive smile. "The last time I saw you, round about eleven ack emma, you were just waking up."

"Why shouldn't we sleep till eleven o'clock. It's lay-off today."

"Not for me, I fear. Don't forget I haven't been out on a muster. I've just been round the homestead wielding a rake and a pair of clippers in the garden."

Gerry was shocked.

"Didn't you mind . . . just gardening?" she asked.

David now looked surprised.

"Why should I? Boss's orders for one thing. For another I've heard a thing or two about Jim Conrad on a muster. Riding with Jim Conrad gives a half-baked horseman like me a two to one chance of coming home with a broken neck. I'll take the garden any time."

Gerry considered this. There was something in it. True, David was not born in the saddle like station people and stockmen. He hadn't come into the outback to ride as stockmen ride . . . only to learn *how* they rode and *how* many men it took effectively to muster sizeable mobs of cattle. David probably didn't even know that stockmen regard gardening as an under-privileged job fit for the rouseabout only. For that matter, Gerry supposed as she thought about it, he need never know. Only silly people like herself and Simon cared that the stockmen should think they were as good as themselves. After all, horsemanship wasn't everything in the world, as she had been trying to teach Simon.

"Have you finished down here, David?" Gerry asked

brightly. "Aren't you good and hot? Wouldn't a swim in the billabong be just the very thing?"

"Gerry, you never uttered fairer words."

David unwound himself and stood up. He took Gerry's hand and pulled her up with a jerk. He took her reins from the cross-piece of the trough and threw them to her.

"On your way, mate," he said cheerily.

Gerry smacked Sultan gently and he tossed his head and broke into a run. With deft speed she twisted the left stirrup with her hand as she ran beside him, thrust her foot in and with her back to Sultan's head mounted from in front of the foreleg. Her body described a perfect three-quarter circle in the air. David pushed his hat on the back of his head.

"You ought to be hired out to do that in a circus," he called. "You'd make a fortune."

Gerry laughed back over her shoulder.

"I didn't know I did it that time. I just do it automatically."

She cantered ahead but not so fast that David could not overtake her.

"Doesn't matter how hot we get," she called gaily. "The billabong's at the end of this ride."

They galloped along the flat hard pad of the cattle track.

At the billabong David stripped off his shirt and Gerry went into the water clothes and all, except for her riding boots and socks. This was common usage and neither cared. There were no such things as swim-suits in their saddle bags.

"Race you to the old log," David shouted, shaking the wet hair from his eyes.

"Right. But you'll win because I've got too many clothes on."

"And because I can beat you, anyway. Right? Then *go*!"

David beat her easily and not only because of Gerry's clothes. He had learned his swimming on the beaches of Bondi and Manly while Gerry had been limited by a hundred yards of water in the loop of a creek.

All the same it was a good race and they clung to the log laughing and shaking the wet hair from their eyes.

"David . . . why did you come back to Yandoo?" Gerry asked.

"The best way to learn station business for my kind of a job is to have plenty of change. I know I'd been on Yandoo before but it would be quite a thing down south to say I'd worked with Jim Conrad."

"Everyone seems to have heard of Jim Conrad. I didn't even know who he was when he rode in here. Why is he well known, David?"

"I don't know. Just one of those legendary sort of fellows people make up yarns about. Probably did a few rash and hardy things years back, and he has a reputation for first-class horsemanship. After that, folk-lore does the rest for a chap. Someone to talk about round the camp fire at night and everyone's got to tell a better yarn than the last one. It can give a man quite a build-up."

"Do you . . . will you like working with him?"

"Oh, he's quite a decent chap. Knows a fellow's limitations and doesn't push him too hard."

This sounded out of character to Gerry. Jim was a hard driver out with a muster team.

David ducked his head under the water and blew bubbles. He came up and shook his head so that water drops flew out in a spray all around him.

"I'm no stockman, Gerry," he said with an affable grin. "It's no good my trying to compete with those fellows out on the run. You know that."

"Yes, I suppose I do," Gerry said soberly. Then her face broke into a smile. "I bet you can keep ledgers and make balance sheets, and deal with the customers and take the right man out to dinner to clinch a buying deal though."

"That's just routine, my girl."

"Do you know what, David? I think it's *clever*."

"Thank you. If I wasn't treading water I'd take a bow. Now how about taking ten yards' start and I'll still beat you back to the bank?"

"Right!"

With the splashing of arms and the patter of feet they raced through the water.

David pulled himself up on the bank and leaned down to give Gerry a hand. She could see the play of big muscles on his chest and arms. Gardening wouldn't be so much hardship to him, she supposed. He was very strong. Oh, well, every man to his taste. When David finished with his station experience he would go back to the city company and probably make a fortune compared with what a hard-riding stockman made, working at one of the world's most dangerous occupations.

When they straightened themselves she stood admiring David. His wet tousled hair hung over his forehead in that wayward lock. He was beautifully and evenly sunburned and his white teeth enhanced his attractive smile.

He in his turn looked down at Gerry. She looked quaint in those dripping clothes now definitely sagging round the ankles. But she was a young woman all the same. Where her wet shirt clung to her body he could see her soft rounded shoulders and the clear young throat rising out of a water-flattened collar. He also liked the freckles on her nose. They made her human, whereas Lulu up at the homestead with her carefully cared for skin and lofty manner disturbed him. He had a vague feeling that Lulu might be mostly façade, whereas this kid . . . this young woman Gerry, was sterling through and through.

He put his arm along her shoulder.

"Dry out on horseback?" he said. "But young woman . . . no racing me to the homestead. I don't like being beaten before lunch-time . . . ever."

This time Gerry mounted her stationary horse in a less spectacular manner. She would have hated David to think she was showing off. She turned her head and watched David drag on his shirt and then mount his horse. When she turned round again she saw two horsemen coming steadily through the trees further along the billabong bank. They were riding the track that led round the elbow towards the gully beyond the main creek bed. It was Jim Conrad and Yandoo's own stockman, Bill Seddon.

Jim's eyes flicked from Gerry to David. It would be quite clear to him what the pair had been doing. Water was still streaming from David's pants and Gerry's jeans, and both had got their riding boots cradled up on the saddle in front of them. Bared feet clung to the stirrup irons. Wet hair clung to their temples. It was also quite clear to Gerry that Jim was not pleased with what he saw. His mouth tightened and his eyes remained cold.

It was Bill Seddon who gave them a broad grin of welcome. It made the old stockman happy to see Gerry playing for once. She was too young, he reckoned, to work a ninety-hour week and have no fun. It was a good job that David Randall had come back.

"Gerry girl," he said, "did you see if the billabong level is up?"

"It wouldn't be up much, Bill, if at all. It's due to go down, isn't it, with this dry weather?"

"There's been a big cloudburst up the country," he said.

"That means the rivers and creeks up there'll fill up, maybe run a banker. With luck we'll get the overflow."

"Oh!"

Gerry wheeled her horse and walked it back to the bank. She threw one leg over the pommel and slid off her horse and knelt down by the bank.

"Yes," she said. "I believe it is. It wouldn't be more than an inch . . . but it could be rising." She lifted up her face sunny with joy. "That means the water down in the gully will rise. The cattle will be all right."

Her eyes moved from Bill's good-natured face to Jim Conrad. He was leaning forward on his saddle, resting his hands, one on the other on the pommel. There was a sardonic gleam in his eye but he said nothing. His expression said everything for him.

Water rising in the billabong, creek and gully meant life . . . and fortune. Gerry, whose whole concern it should have been, hadn't even noticed. She had been frivolling in the water with David Randall, who probably should have been about more important business while a verdict of life was being pronounced on two hundred head of cattle in the gully. Just as she had been sitting dreaming by that billabong while a verdict of life had been passed on her mother.

She knew what that twisted expression on Jim Conrad's mouth meant. Call herself a station owner's daughter? Think she could run a station single-handed with only Bill Seddon and one native in train? When the lifegiving water was rising in the billabong she didn't even notice!

Gerry flushed. The freckles on her nose faded under that tell-tale colour.

"Well, it's good luck," she said. "It's wonderful good luck."

She got up and mounted her horse again.

"Not good luck, good judgment on Jim's part, Gerry," Bill Seddon said. "I was mighty uneasy about the cattle in the gully meself."

For the first time Jim spoke.

"Neither good luck nor good judgment," he said dryly. "Listening in to the weather bulletins covering the north of Australia will tell a man working farther south what to expect. I recommend it as a worthwhile evening pastime, Gerry." Then he wheeled his horse. "Right, Bill," he said. "Let's get along and see what we can find grazing down at the Number Ten."

Bill saluted with his stockwhip and turned to follow Jim.

"Very high and mighty, this morning," David said of Jim affably as he and Gerry rode towards the homestead. "You know, Gerry, even the greatest of us has his human weaknesses. Jim Conrad was fairly certain that water would rise when he put the cattle in the gully. He just likes being right."

When they got up to the saddling paddock David lifted his saddle to carry it into the harness room.

"I'll see you later, Gerry," he said. "I've got to go through the stock in the storeroom and get one of the natives to cleaning it up ready for the next load of stores." He looked over his shoulder at Gerry with an amused grin. "Considering the low condition of that stock, old thing, I shouldn't be long," he added. "Be seeing you."

"Be seeing you!" Gerry answered as she slung her own saddle over the rail and prepared to loose Sultan out into the grass paddock.

Jim had given David three jobs to do to-day. Turn on the mill at the Two Mile, and check the stock, which was so low it almost wasn't there at all, and set someone else to clean out the store.

There wasn't a quarter day's work in that. Gerry felt uneasy. Why was Jim, the slave driver, using David so lightly? And no wonder David thought Jim an easy-going boss. David just didn't know the other side of Jim's character.

She wondered if Lulu had something to do with this but if so Gerry couldn't imagine what. Lulu had no interest in David whatsoever. She had ignored him as small fry because he was not a station owner nor did he own his own business in the city.

There were too many puzzles on Yandoo these days, Gerry decided. And once again she thought she must write that letter to the manager. She owed it to everyone, including Jim Conrad, that the manager should know just how things were going on the station. And she would do Jim Conrad justice. She would tell the manager how ably Jim had got things working again. Maybe the manager would give Jim the job of overseer . . . if Jim stayed on.

CHAPTER EIGHT

GERRY WENT UP to the homestead. Lunch was over and it was the siesta hour. She went into the kitchen and opened the refrigerator. A piece of lettuce, a tomato and a slice of cold meat in her hand was enough for Gerry. She was a little hungry but decided that at her age self-denial was good for the figure. It would be nice to have a good figure like Lulu.

Gerry went to the shower room, shed her half-dried shirt and jeans and took a shower.

Well, she hadn't any fat on her yet. And that reminded her . . . where was Simon? She put on a shirt and shorts and went round the verandas looking for him. He was fast asleep stretched out on his iron bedstead.

She smiled as she looked down at him. If he was dreaming, what great character in Australian outback life did he dream he was now? What legendary bush-ranger or stockman was he seeing dressed in Simon's shirt and shorts?

She went back to her own room and stretched out on her bed, but she had slept too well and too late into the morning to be able to doze off now.

All she could do was lie and think; and thinking made her heart contract because she remembered waking this morning to see Jim Conrad standing beside her bed.

Presently she got up and went to the office. How cool and tidy and efficient it looked! Never in all Gerry's life had it looked like this. And those bougainvillæa flowers made a splash of colour on the mantelshelf and the table. Also the floor had a carpet on it. Where, Gerry wondered, had Lulu got that carpet? Then she remembered her father's room which was now used as a box-room. Lulu had taken the carpet from there.

Well, the carpet looked very nice and the office didn't look like an office any more. It looked like a study in some professor's house. Oh, well, Gerry supposed Jim Conrad liked it that way.

She took writing paper from a box on top of the filing cabinet and sat down at the desk and began to write. She didn't know the manager's name but she would send the letter to the "Manager of Yandoo," care of the bank.

She began:

"Dear Manager . . ."

How did that look? Gerry put her head on one side and the tip of her tongue showed at the corner of her mouth. She frowned thoughtfully. Oh well, she couldn't help how it looked! The thing to do was write that letter.

She began by saying things were looking up here on Yandoo. He'd be surprised when he got here because doubtless the bank inspector's report had been unfavourable. Her mother had temporarily entrusted the care of the station to a man called Jim Conrad. This man, Jim Conrad, was well known for his efficiency and skill.

Gerry frowned and thought a minute. Yes, she had to be careful to be very just about Jim Conrad. She had to put down faithfully all that he had achieved in so short a time and just how able he was in handling the men and getting things done.

Gerry began to write again. She wrote and wrote, covering first one page and then another. She was amazed at how easy it was to write about the happenings on Yandoo. She certainly hadn't been able to write essays at school as easily as this. Every time she wrote that Jim Conrad did this and Jim Conrad did that she told herself she was being very scrupulous about giving Jim his due. She must let the manager know all about him and all that was being done . . . but never would she be guilty of sticking a knife in a man's back.

"Jim Conrad is the finest horseman that's ever been on Yandoo," she wrote. Then she went on to describe Jim as being tall and good-looking and stern and of iron will. If what Simon had said about Jim wanting to get a "bite" into every station he cleaned up had been just childish prattle the manager would know that Jim would be a very good man to act as overseer. If not—well the manager would know what to do about it.

Gerry ceased writing and bit the end of her pen. If Jim wasn't trying to take the station from them she wanted him to stay on.

Suddenly there were tears in Gerry's eyes.

She wanted to like Jim . . . if only he would let her.

She wanted to let him shoulder all the worries. If only he didn't treat her as if she were some sixth-form schoolgirl who should keep her young and irresponsible head out of the management of her own station.

Did Lulu's superior years make her so much more useful

to Jim? Or was it her office training? Or was it that Lulu was tall and her skin was smooth and clear and beautifully kept? And her dresses and shoes and hands were immaculate?

Gerry filled the fountain pen again. She wrote on:

"My cousin Lulu is of great assistance to Jim Conrad. They get on very well together. I wish I could be as helpful but I guess I only know about horses and cattle and whether the sand dunes are blowing too near the boundary fences and likely to smother them up."

Then she added:

"Oh, by the way, Jim Conrad has his nephew Simon, aged nine, with him. You'll like Simon. I do."

She thought a long time about how to end the letter. Then quickly she added:

"You'll like Jim Conrad too. I do, only I'll never let him know it. He thinks he's the Prime Minister anyway."

She added "Yours sincerely, Geraldine Meredith of Yandoo Station," blotted, folded and sealed the letter in an envelope without reading it. If she re-read it she might have to re-write it . . . and she would never do that. For some reason or other writing that letter had opened the floodgates. She felt better.

She addressed the envelope to the Manager of Yandoo Station, care of the Northern Bank Ltd., Sydney, and printed across the bottom of the envelope "Please Forward at Once."

She put the letter in the mail bag which already had a number of letters in it. The store and mail waggon was coming in to-morrow. Soon that mail bag would be on its way to Sydney.

Gerry went outside and closed the office door behind her. It was sundown now and the station was stirring again. Through the shrubs in the garden Gerry could see the pink splash of Lulu's dress. She was walking with someone.

When the two figures came into view from behind a clump of oleander trees Gerry could see it was Jim Conrad walking and talking with Lulu.

Well . . . it was his lay-off too. Why shouldn't he walk about a garden and talk to a pretty woman? Any man is entitled to relaxation.

Gerry went inside, had another shower, and changed into a dress. She brushed and brushed her hair until it too shone. She put on a lovely pair of white whittle-heeled shoes her Aunt Sally had sent up from Sydney. Aunt Sally, when she had written to say how well Mrs. Meredith was doing, had sent shoes and hair shampoos and face cream for Gerry.

"Darling . . ." she had written. "It is time you stopped looking like a female edition of a stockman . . ."

Gerry looked at herself in the mirror. Golly, she did look different!

Out on the veranda once again the first person she met was Simon.

"You went swimming in the billabong without telling me," he began accusingly.

"I know, darling. But you see, David and I . . ."

She got no further.

Jim and Lulu were both coming up the path to the foot of the veranda steps. Jim was looking at Gerry closely but Lulu had raised eyebrows. Then she laughed. There was a delicious tinkle of bells in her voice.

"Yes, Simon," Lulu said, but looking at Gerry and not Simon, "David has certainly had a revolutionary effect on Gerry. Swimming in the billabong, and now looking as pretty as a picture!"

She turned to Jim Conrad for confirmation. What Jim thought not even Lulu would have known because he had just thrown down his cigarette and had bent his head as he stamped it out with the toe of his shoe.

Jim didn't appear to notice she was in a dress and not in shirt and jeans. And that her hair had been brushed till it shone. Or if he did, it was immaterial to him.

Lay-off day, like all holidays, had to end on a special note. Lulu had inherited from her mother a taste for good well-cooked food and though she did not cook the evening meal herself she gave Mary and Jeannie the kind of instructions they couldn't confuse. David Randall, who had been given a small room that used to house the over-flow from the store in the days of abundance, came up to dinner at the homestead as did Jim Conrad.

The best cut of beef had been sent to the kitchen and Mary, chief cook, had done it justice. For dessert they had home-grown melon that had been well iced, with ice-cream . . . and for Simon, the raspberry sponge cake.

Not only had the outside run of the station sprung to life

but so had the old dining-room. The mahogany chairs and sideboard brought from England by the first generation of Merediths shone with polishing, and an old Irish lace cloth covered the table.

Gerry felt reborn herself. Gone, it seemed, were the days when she had to come in, still unchanged and unbathed, and get her left-over dinner from the oven.

Only Simon objected to the glamour.

"Golly," he said. "A man gets hungry waiting in between courses."

Jeannie the lubra brought the raspberry sponge cake from the sideboard and set it in front of him.

"Gerry say this fatten you 'm up, young fella," she said. "You eat 'um up quick."

Simon looked at Gerry from under considering brows. He wanted the raspberry sponge cake but he didn't want to concede he needed fattening up. His glance went round the table from one face to another. Lulu was not looking at him. She was looking at her own reflection in the mirror of the sideboard that was on the opposite side of the room from her seat.

"Maybe if you're fat enough and strong enough next week, Simon," Jim said, "I'll let you throw a bullock."

Simon said nothing but instantly he put out his hand and took an enormous slice of cake. Gerry's eyes flew to Jim's face.

"You wouldn't . . ." she began.

Jim nodded his head in the direction of the boy.

"He believes me," he said. "Look at the amount of cake he's getting through." He meant what he said.

Gerry bit her lip. She could not talk to Jim about this in front of Simon, and neither David Randall nor Lulu knew anything about the skill required and the danger involved in throwing a bullock.

What was the man made of? First of all, he had been indifferent to the boy's scantily covered bones. Now he was bribing him to eat by offering him something the boy's heart would crave after but which only the most skilful and daring of stockmen could do effectively.

Gerry ate her melon in silence.

When they went out on to the veranda for coffee David Randall went into the office to listen in to the open session on the air. Ruloo Station was talking to another station farther outback and David was garnering the news. Lulu went to have a few last words with the lubras in the kitchen.

Funny, Gerry thought, but it's more Lulu's homestead now than mine. But that is because I'm always out on the run.

Jim Conrad sat in a low-slung cane chair and meticulously rolled a cigarette. When he had got the paper folded tightly round the tobacco he held it out to Gerry.

"Yours," he said. "It will keep the mosquitoes away."

Gerry took the cigarette from him and thanked him. He held a match for her to light it. She looked up beyond the cigarette into his eyes but his own were on the flaming match. He flicked it out and put it in the ash tray.

"Jim . . ." Gerry said nervously. "You wouldn't let a little boy like Simon try to throw a bullock . . ."

Jim finished making his own cigarette and then he lit it. Only then did he look at her.

"Those men out there," he said, nodding his head in the direction of the quarters, "learned when they were Simon's age. Only the young have got nerve enough to try it the first time."

"But . . ."

"There are no buts. Simon learns now, or never. My decision is for now."

Lulu came round the corner of the veranda. Jim stood up and poured her cup of coffee for her.

"Would you mind bringing that into the office?" he asked. "I'm sorry to trouble you, Lulu, but I need your help for about half an hour."

He stood aside so that Lulu could precede him in through the door. He turned to Gerry.

"I'll send David out to keep you company," he said.

Gerry hardly heard him.

He was going to teach Simon to throw a bullock! A little boy like that! There was no mercy in the man.

CHAPTER NINE

LAY-OFF DAY had been on a Thursday so that Friday and Saturday were devoted to rounding up strays in the open paddocks and beginning the laborious task of drafting.

At the office door on Sunday morning Jim Conrad gave the team their instructions for Monday. Sunday was the only day on which men could go over their harness and gear ready for the following week's work.

It was, however, an easy day because the men sat under the bush shade outside their quarters while they rubbed up and mended leather horse-gear, twisted long leather thongs for their stockwhips and even got to work with hammer, sprigs and last to mend their footwear.

A good deal of shirt washing went on down at the creek and all the time there was the sound of men's voices and men's laughter.

On Monday the team was to be broken up. Bill Seddon with the native Johnny and two of the new men were to ride the far boundaries on an out-station that had not been visited since the first of Yandoo's own stockmen had defected.

Gerry wished Bill Seddon and Johnny weren't both going to the out-station.

She could not help feeling that their entire fortune was wrapped up in that mob in the gully. Fattened and sold it would pay the running costs of the present and the next few weeks. Her imagination boggled at the thought of the disaster if the new manager or a bank inspector arrived to find a mustering team clamouring for wages, and a storeroom newly stocked with provisions not yet paid for. Without Bill at hand she did not know to whom to turn for advice.

Lulu, with all her office work for Jim, probably knew a lot more about how the finances stood than Gerry but when Gerry had diffidently approached her on the subject Lulu had been at her most lofty.

"This station is in a most frightful mess, Gerry," she said. "For goodness' sake give Jim and me a chance to straighten it out."

"Well . . . I *am* my mother's daughter," Gerry began.

"You could have been that a bit more effectively a year ago and got these books straightened out."

This was unjust. No one human being could work the run and do the management side of a station. To the young girl coming home from school the most important thing had seemed to be to save the cattle. And in Lulu's own words, Gerry had not understood books. She was an intelligent girl and could have learned to understand them if she hadn't come in weary at nine o'clock each night from a long hard day's work on the run.

Gerry might have retaliated that Lulu, with her training, might have done something about the books herself in those long months when she had done nothing but loll about the

90

homestead, bored, and with eyes turned always towards Sydney and the highlights.

Gerry turned away. It wasn't any good quarrelling with Lulu. She had no right to expect anything of Lulu at all. She had, instead, to be grateful for Lulu's staying on now and being so great a help to Jim Conrad.

The mail had come and gone. It brought further good news of Mrs. Meredith. She was beginning to take an interest in affairs again. Mrs. Sylvester would shortly take her to the Blue Mountains for a real holiday.

Gerry's letter to the manager was winging on its way. She liked to think of it passing from station to station, from mail plane to mailman and from mailman to stockman travelling the cattle route. Or maybe the manager in his long trek had reached the sheep country between the rivers and the coast.

As Gerry changed into a cotton dress and her whittle-heeled shoes for Sunday high tea on the veranda she could see her letter pursuing the man who was coming to manage Yandoo across mountain, river and plain.

How far would he have come now? That cloudburst up the country that had filled the creeks and billabong of Yandoo would have caused the rivers and creeks up north to run a banker. He could be held up on the far side of any one of them. Or at least his horse plant and gear could be held up.

Gerry finished dressing and went out to join the others on the veranda. Jim Conrad and David were sitting on either side of the doorstep, a long cold drink in their hands. Lulu was lying back in an easy-chair. Her hands were clasped behind her head and this attitude enhanced and displayed her figure. She wore her prettiest dress and she too had on the whittle-heeled shoes that were all the fashion. The Sydney store the family dealt with had their fractional shoe fittings and Mrs. Sylvester had been able to send both girls these shoes.

Jim and David were talking about the weather conditions. They were certain that the Dry had set in and Yandoo would see no more rains for seven months. The last of the rains in the far north were keeping the creeks flowing and Jim told David now was the time to clean out as much of the cattle from the scrub and the outback waterholes as possible.

Simon and Lulu noticed Gerry's soft coloured dress and her pretty shoes and that her hair was freshly shampooed and brushed hard, so that one saw golden lights in it instead of red dust.

91

Lulu smiled. Gerry was sorry that Lulu, these days, affected a more sophisticated manner than she had had before. After all, Gerry too had had many years in Sydney at a well-known girls' school. She too had been taken on well-conducted tours by the mistresses to music clubs, the theatre and opera; elegant little dances conducted conjointly with boys' schools.

Maybe she didn't know about night-clubs but then she didn't think Lulu knew that much either. Aunt Sally Sylvester had a nice little home on the fringe of one of the best suburbs but she didn't have great wealth. She had just enough on which to live comfortably. Hence Lulu's training in a secretarial course.

Privately Gerry would have thought Lulu didn't have enough energy to take up any work enthusiastically.

As she noticed Lulu's condescending smile she wondered what really had brought about this swift change in Lulu? It couldn't possibly be a real interest in Yandoo. It must be Jim Conrad. Was it that he had the capacity to inspire service in anyone or did he have something special for Lulu that awakened both energy and enterprise in her?

Lulu's eyes, with that odd smile in them, moved from Gerry to David and back again. There was something knowing in them. Yes, David was immaculate in clean well-pressed tropical clothes. There was something a little extra about the way that lock of hair was licked down into order.

Gerry's heart beat faster. Could it be David was doing it specially for her? That was unmistakably the message in Lulu's eyes. Also Lulu's eyes were saying that Gerry was "dressed up" for David.

Gerry's heart lifted a little. It was very nice that someone in the world thought of her as an attractive young woman . . . as different from just Gerry Meredith sunburnt and sand-dusted racing over the plains of a big station.

Had she been thinking of this herself when she had shampooed and re-shampooed her hair and put on this dress and felt a special lilting delight in the pretty delicate shoes Aunt Sally had sent up?

It was an effort for Gerry to drag her eyes away from David to Jim.

At last she stole a surreptitious glance in his direction. It was to find Jim, at that moment, glancing at her. She thought there was something puzzled in his glance but all the same it was not unfriendly.

Jeannie came round the veranda corner and spoke to Lulu.

92

"Well, I suppose you men want your tea," Lulu said lightly. "I'll just check on the cook."

Both men stood up as Lulu got up from her chair. Their conversation broke off and they watched her walking gracefully away with Jeannie. Then they sat down again.

Simon was cleaning the inside of a snake skin preparatory to making another snake belt.

"Do you think you'd better wash your hands, Simon?" Gerry asked.

He closed his clasp knife and hung it on to the belt he was wearing at the moment.

"Golly," he said, "women are fuss-pots."

"I'm sure your Uncle Jim tells you to wash your hands before a meal when you're travelling with him," Gerry said with gentle mockery.

"He does not," said Simon flatly.

"Then when do you wash your hands?"

"When Uncle Jim washes his. I do what he does. That's good enough for me."

Jim heard Simon's words.

"I'm not going to get up and wash mine again, young fella. Spring to it . . . and see you're back here in five minutes. If you're late for tea you go without."

"Okay, okay, okay!" said Simon patiently. But Gerry noticed he was very quick about hanging the snake skin on the veranda rail and disappearing in the direction of the washroom.

The boy certainly took notice of his uncle; his uncle's way of speaking to him was like a field-marshal giving orders to a private. Gerry wondered if there were ever any occasions when Jim addressed the boy as a very young human being, which was what Simon was.

David took out a packet of cigarettes and shook the last one out. He screwed up the empty packet.

"Can't offer you fellas one," he said, including Gerry. "It's my last. I guess I've got another five minutes to get down to my room and get another packet."

He stood up, stretched himself a little which was a gesture that increased his height and showed his considerable expanse of powerful chest and shoulders.

"See you in a minute," he said. He took a step and turned and smiled at Gerry. "Tell Lulu not to miss a beat of the stroke if I'm three and a half seconds late, will you?"

Gerry laughed. There was something winsome about David's

smile and he had rather neatly summed up Lulu's present way of running the homestead. Everything had to be done to the minute and when anything was delayed it seemed to put her out of routine and irritated her. Sunday night tea was a casual affair. David's few minutes wouldn't matter. They would eat buffet style from traymobiles on the veranda and the only hot thing was the coffee that followed.

The departure of Lulu, Simon, and now David left Jim and Gerry sitting alone.

Jim carefully rolled and made a cigarette. Gerry deliberately let her gaze wander far out, beyond the garden fence to the stubble paddock that lay beyond. She could not bring herself to break the silence. It seemed full of unspoken words and thoughts.

Suddenly Jim stood up and came across to her chair. He held the cigarette he had made towards her.

"Yours," he said.

Gerry couldn't decline it. When Jim made her a cigarette and handed it to her he left no opening for a refusal.

"Thank you," she said.

He struck a match for her to light it. She was a little clumsy about it, maybe because her nerves seemed tensed up, almost as if something cataclysmic was going to happen. There was nothing that could happen except that Jim would flick out his match and go back to his seat on the veranda step.

Gerry concentrated on the match and the end of her cigarette. When it caught she had perforce to lift her eyes. Jim was looking at her with grave concentration.

"Thank you," she said.

"It's a pleasure," he said. But he didn't smile. Exactly what did he mean by that, she wondered.

He went into the office and brought out a tray with sherry in small glasses. At that moment Lulu came back and David appeared on the garden path. A half sigh escaped Gerry's lips. Was she relieved the others had come back? Or had they broken a spell? It had seemed as if Jim had been about to speak to her about something, and now had changed his mind.

"Sit down, Lulu," Jim said. "You're the one who is going to be waited on this time. We can't have you doing all the work."

Lulu smiled and sat down in a deep chair.

"Thank you, Jim. I think that's very nice of you."

He carried her a sherry.

"Mildara Dry is yours, I think," he said.

Then, when Lulu had taken her drink, he put down the tray on the table beside her. He walked over to David and held out his hand for the new packet of cigarettes from which David had just taken the Cellophane outer paper.

"Thanks, old man," Jim said. "I'll borrow one of these for Lulu." He held the cigarettes towards her and when she took one he struck a match and lit it for her.

"Coming, David," he said. He sent the packet spinning back through the air. David caught it deftly with his left hand.

"How about yourself, Jim?" he asked.

"I stick to the aristocrats," Jim said. "I like to roll 'em."

He was stooping over Lulu to light her cigarette. Gerry could see his long lean back as he bent to the low chair but Lulu's face was in full view. Lulu drew on her cigarette and then looked up at Jim. There was something intimate and almost conspiratorial in the smile of thanks she gave him. For a frozen moment the pair of them were isolated alone there. Could it have been something about Lulu Jim had been going to tell her? Was his attention to Lulu now his way of telling her?

David came across to Gerry. He picked up a sherry from the tray and brought it with him.

"This must be yours," he said, giving it to Gerry. "I only drink beer."

It was Gerry's turn to look up at David and thank him. Actually she felt momentarily grateful because he had casually and easily broken what was an awkward moment. Gerry's blue eyes smiled her thanks.

Jim Conrad turned round.

"There's a bottle of beer in the fridge, David," he said. "I'll join you in it."

Simon came back flipping his half-dried hands in the air. Just ahead of him Jeannie was wheeling the traymobile loaded with delicious salads and cold meats.

"Did you make any raspberry sponge cake, Lulu?" Simon asked.

"To tell you the truth, Simon," Lulu said distantly, "I didn't consider your tastes when I was arranging a menu. However . . ." Lulu was sounding didactic and not for the first time Gerry thought she didn't have much patience with small boys. "You must have got somebody's ear in the kitchen because I saw a raspberry sponge cake, with far too much cream for good digestion, on the side table."

The lubra beamed on Simon.

"You get plenty fat on that one, young fella," she said.

"Jeannie," said Simon disdainfully, "you're talking like Gerry."

"Well, she arright, that one," said Jeannie with emphasis. "She tell me make raspberry sponge every time I see that young fella Simon. Maybe she bin think you get properly thin in your country. You bin come down here close up Yandoo and get fat quick fella."

Simon looked imploringly at his Uncle Jim.

"See what I mean?" he said.

Jim was wearing one of his rare smiles.

"I think there's a conspiracy between Gerry and the kitchen staff," he said. "But out of it you seem to get a spate of raspberry sponges. Any complaints?"

Simon grinned. He brought a plate over to Gerry and as Jeannie held the dishes to Gerry for the latter to serve herself Simon reduced his voice to a whisper.

"I reckon Lulu thinks about Uncle Jim, and no one else," he said.

Gerry put her fingers to her lips to enjoin silence or at least discretion.

"Without Lulu we'd hardly eat at all," she whispered. "She's the homestead manager now. So be grateful."

"So you say," said Simon. But he didn't sound as pleased as he might.

Gerry looked down at her pretty cotton dress and at the elegant little shoes. She thought about her shining hair. Why did she think it was all in vain even though David had noticed? She felt that in dressing thus she had been importunate and had failed to touch the hearts of those who had not chosen her with *their* hearts.

Deliberately she had deceived herself, for she was afraid to admit that it had not been *their* hearts being touched that had mattered, but *his* heart. Just one person sitting there in the magic aura of the softly lit veranda with its decorations of hanging ferns and richly scented pot-plants had a heart that really mattered.

Later, when David put some records on the radiogram Simon went away to bed. Presently Gerry went around the veranda to his special place to wish him "good night."

Simon leaned over the side of his bed and examined her feet.

"Those aren't proper shoes for Sunday tea, Gerry," he said

reprovingly. "They're made for dancing, aren't they? You ought to wear them for a ball."

For a minute Gerry felt dashed. Even Simon's censure hurt. Then she tossed her head gaily.

"One can dance even in a homestead," she said. "Listen! David must have heard you for that's a waltz he's playing on the radiogram now."

It was one of Strauss's Viennese waltzes. Gerry twirled round on her toes to the rhythm of the music. A few practice steps were enough. Like the morning of the muster when one stretch of gallop round a real professional muster had been enough to let something loose in her blood so that she had galloped on, round and round, so now she twirled in waltz-time round and round.

She was a young girl, and she wanted to dance. Simon had said her shoes were for dancing.

Round and round, her skirt swirling out like a ballerina's, her head thrown back and her eyes closed, a smile almost of ecstasy on her lips, Gerry danced to the tune of Simon's shouted laughter and the radiogram's hi-fi rendering of a Strauss waltz.

Nothing mattered very much in the world except the tingling in her blood and the twirling of her neat feet in their pretty dancing shoes.

She knew that David had come round the corner of the veranda for she heard his footsteps, and some extra sense told her exactly where he stood without her having to open her eyes.

The music began to die away and with one extra twirl Gerry brought herself to a standstill in front of David. She dropped to a curtsy at his feet, her head bowed well down in mock humility. She stretched up her hand for him to take it.

"What will you of your handmaiden, Sir David," she cried, imitating the pathos of a medieval slave. "Speak and your word shall be law."

She opened her eyes. Whose shoes were those she was looking at? Not David's!

With a swift panicky movement she lifted up her head. It was Jim Conrad who had taken her hand. It was his eyes that were looking down into hers.

"Wrong man, I'm afraid, Gerry," he said.

She sprang up, and he dropped her hand.

CHAPTER TEN

THE ROSTER as arranged on Saturday had suddenly and dramatically to be changed early on Monday morning.

On Sunday night when Jim Conrad had gone into the office to listen to the weather bulletin for the far north and pick up the local news from other stations on the air he had heard from Ruloo Station that a buyer was on his way to Yandoo to look over the mob Jim Conrad had mustered. This was the mob in the gully.

In a characteristic fashion Jim Conrad did not discuss his changed plans with anyone. He merely announced his arrangements for the following day.

"The team going to the out-station goes as detailed," he said at the office door in the morning.

That, as Gerry knew, included Bill Seddon and Johnny the Yandoo native.

"Ben and Twisty, get out to the gully and comb the sides and scrub and see that the mob is together. Sam Small, you'll have to go alone to the Number Two Bore and check there. The other two can round up the horses and get riding gear ready."

He turned to Gerry.

"You'd better stay with the horses, Gerry. You and David can meet the buyer with me and come along with us."

Jim never gave instructions to Simon, Simon just went along with Twisty if he thought that whatever job Jim was on was not interesting or exciting enough. With Twisty some rough riding was always guaranteed.

It was barely five-thirty.

"I'd better wake Lulu," Gerry said. "We'll need to entertain the buyer. Who is he, Jim? Someone from Young, Brown and Company?"

Jim answered her shortly.

"No. This man operates his own agency. He's building it up and I'll get the best prices from him. He's John Slater and he buys for the overseas market."

"Has he got contacts amongst the drovers? There are no drovers about . . ."

"He'll bring his own drovers. They take the cattle to the

yards this side of the airport. The beef is freighted out in the same planes that bring in the bagged petrol and oil."

Gerry's eyes betrayed her astonishment.

"Petrol in bags?" she said.

Jim's smile was sardonic.

"You don't keep up with the times for a station-owner's daughter, Miss Meredith. The Vacuum Oil Company air-freights out the oil to stations in anything up to 1,200-gallon rubber bags. At the station they fold up the bags and air-freight beef back. Simple?"

Gerry felt snubbed. When Jim was being superior he called her "Miss Meredith."

Perhaps one of the reasons why Yandoo had fallen back so badly was it hadn't kept up with the times. It hadn't even an airstrip of its own and was dependent on all deliveries coming through Ruloo Station.

"I'd . . . I'd better wake Lulu," she said lamely.

Jim's voice was a staccato command.

"Leave Lulu where she is," he said. "There's nothing to take up Lulu's time till sundown to-night. There is no reason why she should be disturbed."

He was quite angry and he showed it. Gerry was surprised at his expression.

"We'll give Slater some tea down at the quarters. We'll want to get over to the gully as soon as he arrives," Jim added.

Speed and efficiency again. Gone were the days when the buyer was entertained to ceremonious tea on the homestead veranda, pleasantries exchanged and messages of goodwill delivered. Jim Conrad's way was to get on with the business and be done with it. No time for the leisured elegancies of her father's day.

Well, thought Gerry stubbornly, something worthwhile was lost and one day she would tell Mr. Conrad so. She called him "Mr. Conrad" when she was hurt or angry with him, as he called her "Miss Meredith" when he meant to deflate her.

It was mid-morning when the buyer John Slater and his offsider arrived on the outskirts of the Yandoo bullock paddock. A mob of horses had been rounded up and without any ado the buyer and his man got out of the utility truck that brought them and mounted horses.

The greeting between Jim Conrad and this man was short and Gerry noticed there were not exactly any pleasantries passed between them. Yet they seemed to understand one another. Mr. Slater took it for granted that saddled horses would be waiting for him.

Gerry wondered how often these two had met like this before. It was clear the buyer was another man of Jim Conrad's kind. Few words and to business and work at once was the order of the day. There were no delays. They didn't have to explain this to one another. Each knew it.

Gerry longed for comfortable Bill Seddon's company. He would have been able to explain this strange phenomenon to her.

In her experience buyers had come to the homestead and it had been two or three hours, after much conversation and tea drinking, before they left with an elaborate bunch of stockmen as escort to see the cattle.

This little group of men met on the paddock boundary. Mr. Slater and his man got out of the truck and on to the horses with barely a word exchanged.

Gerry was holding the spare change-horses in the background. She debated in her mind whether she should ride up and introduce herself as Geraldine Meredith of Yandoo.

But was she? Wasn't she just G. Meredith, a name on the wages sheet—casual rates? Oh, why had her mother just handed over the station to Jim Conrad like that!

Then Gerry felt a flicker of remorse.

"Poor mother," she thought. "She was so ill. And it was our fault. Aunt Sally's and mine. We should have made her see a doctor."

Gerry's remorse battled with her will to push forward and tell this buyer who she was. In the end it was Jim Conrad's implacable back that defeated her. He was simply riding forward with Mr. Slater and paying no attention to Gerry.

Gerry fell behind with the change-horses as this was the job given to her. If she broke the rules and had an idea of her own Jim might speak to her the way he had spoken to her when she'd ridden out of place on the first day of the muster. That she would not like in front of the stranger. When they got to the gully she would tell Mr. Slater who she was.

However, when she got to the gully Mr. Slater and Jim were already riding round and round the mob that Ben and Twisty were holding together. Every now and again Mr. Slater would point out an unwanted bullock and either Ben or Twisty would cut it out from the mob and send it racing out of the gully to join the others on the plain.

There were very few rejects and Gerry knew this was a tribute to Jim's judgment in good cattle. More than ninety per cent. of what he'd got there in the gully was good stuff and having been kept there, with himself or Twisty riding among them every day, they were docile. This was something highly prized by a buyer. Touchy or undisciplined cattle took too much flesh off themselves playing up on the stock route on their way to the yards.

It was early afternoon before they called a halt to eat and by that time Ben and Twisty had taken over change-horses from Gerry and she had led the others off to return them to the grass paddock. She ate her lunch with Simon on the bank at the creek elbow. She still hadn't met or had a word with Mr. Slater.

It was late afternoon and the buying over before Gerry finally came anywhere near the buyer. Her chore still being the horses, and not the cattle, she had had to ride back to the homestead with the last mounts changed. It was close on sundown then so she went up to the homestead, had a bath and changed her clothes.

Lulu already looked as if she had stepped first out of a bath and afterwards out of the covers of a magazine.

"Everything's well organised in the kitchen," she said. "Thank goodness someone up at Ruloo taught Mary to cook a good roast dinner. I expect these men will be staying."

"I was sorry not to let you know about them before we went out," Gerry said.

"Oh, it's all right," Lulu said casually. "Jim sent one of the men up with a message after lunch. He's quite considerate about things like that."

"Yes, I think he is," Gerry said soberly. "He didn't want you disturbed early this morning."

There was a strange smile on Lulu's lips.

"Well, we did have a late session last night," she said cryptically.

Jim and Lulu had been in the office when Gerry had gone to bed the night before. She wondered how late a late session was . . . and if it involved work all the time. Lulu's smile seemed to imply something different.

Gerry put the sherry and glasses on a tray ready to take on to the veranda. "I think we'd better leave the beer in the fridge till the last minute," she said. "It will stay cold that way."

David appeared in the dining-room doorway at that moment.

"Leave the beer to me, Gerry," he said. "I'll act barman."

Gerry smiled.

"Thank you very much. That's a big weight off my mind."

"Meaning there'll be too many bottles for you to carry? Well, what's the good of top prices and a good sale if we don't celebrate?"

Gerry looked at him curiously.

"Did we get top prices?"

"You bet. Things are looking up on Yandoo, young Gerry. I'm glad I put my money on Jim Conrad and came back here."

Gerry said nothing. She was too hurt to let anyone see that David Randall knew of the success of the sale, and she, the owner's daughter, did not. She carried the tray with the sherry glasses on to the veranda. The office door was wide open and Jim and the buyer were inside talking business. Gerry could hear their voices. They were talking about the drovers who were camping up the creek and who would come in to move the cattle for Mr. Slater.

Then suddenly the conversation took another direction.

"I'll give you my cheque now, Jim," Mr. Slater said. "Do you want it made out to Yandoo Pastoral Company or to you?"

"Make it out to me, John, I've got plenty to do with it now."

"Right!"

There was a silence that meant the buyer had taken out his cheque book and was filling in the form. After a minute or two there was a sound as he handed the cheque over to Jim.

"That's all clear, I think," Mr. Slater's voice came again. "I've made it out to you and left it an open cheque. Don't leave it around, it's money."

Both men laughed.

"Up to the same old racket, I can see," Mr. Slater added. "Oh, well, good luck to you. You certainly know how to make a go out of these stations that are slipping."

Gerry went and sat on the veranda steps. She felt as if cold water was dripping down her spine. What did the buyer mean . . . "Up to the same old racket"? And why was the cheque for Yandoo's cattle made out to Jim Conrad? Everything that came into Yandoo, and was on Yandoo, belonged to her mother except the one-third that had to go to the outside shareholders. And since the bank had taken over the finances of Yandoo everything that came and went on the station should be through the bank.

All the old worries seemed to slide back on to Gerry's shoulders. The old doubt nagged at her. Who was Jim Conrad? Where had he come from? Aunt Sally said her mother was better and beginning to take an interest in things again now. Would it be fair if she, Gerry, wrote now to her mother and asked for the full story of how Mrs. Meredith, or Gerry's father, had known Jim Conrad well enough to hand the full control of the station over to him in the interim period.

Gerry couldn't bear to worry her mother unnecessarily . . . and besides, when she thought of the trust the men had in Jim and of the straight look in his eye she was ashamed of her own worries. Too ashamed to put them into writing. Yet they would not leave her. They were like some unwanted minute demons that sometimes slept and sometimes pecked at her thoughts to take all rest from her.

If only Bill Seddon had not been sent to the out-station! Bill was a shoulder to lean on, his commonsense so often allayed her anxieties.

And why should both Bill and Johnny the Yandoo native have been sent to the out-station at the time the cattle were due to be sold?

There were heavy footsteps coming out of the office door on to the veranda. Jim Conrad was saying something to the buyer about having another mob ready in three to five weeks' time when he saw Gerry sitting alone on the step. He stopped short. At that moment David Randall came out of the passage door.

"You'll have a drink, Slater?" David said. "Just relieve me of one of these bottles, will you?" He too saw Gerry. "Will I pour a sherry for you, Gerry?" he said. "By the way, you have met Mr. Slater, of course?"

Gerry stood up and came towards the chairs by the table. She nodded and forced a smile.

"Oh, yes, we've been meeting all day," she said. "In fact we've been working on the same job."

Mr. Slater lifted his head and looked at Gerry with puzzlement. His swift glance took in her gaily coloured cotton dress and even the pretty white whittle-heeled shoes. At close quarters Gerry saw he had the same cold businesslike blue eyes that Jim Conrad had.

"Have we?" he said. "I'd begun to think Yandoo was a bachelor establishment."

"I had the horses," Gerry said.

"You mean you were ringing the changes with the horses?" Mr. Slater looked surprised. His eyes lost some of the coldness. "But that was a young stripling of a fellow . . ." He looked at Jim Conrad for confirmation.

"I'm afraid your young stripling of a fellow was Miss Meredith," Jim said.

"Well, well!" said Mr. Slater. "You did a good day's work, young lady. I'm sorry I hadn't realised . . ."

"It's all right," Gerry said. "Mr. Conrad did not introduce us."

Jim pulled in the corners of his mouth. He knew that when Gerry referred to him as "Mr. Conrad" she was angry. She was being Miss Geraldine Meredith of Yandoo now.

"*Gerry,*" he said, underlining the word, "knows the rules of the run when we're out on a muster. There are no 'misters' or 'misses.' Just hands with a day's work in front of them."

David had poured out some sherry for Gerry and he handed it to her. There was something rallying in his smile.

"Tough going," he whispered in an aside. "These two bush-whackers don't intend to give ground to the homestead fry, do they?"

It was the time-worn joke. The man out on the run always knew better than the people who lived in the homestead. So often the joke had the bitter barb of truth in it but it was unfair in Gerry's case. For one whole year she had known and run that run. Jim Conrad knew that, so she could not guess what his motives were in keeping the business of Yandoo from her. Unless . . . ?

Ah, that dreadful, worrying *unless.*

For three days Gerry worked out on the run on routine drafting of cattle through gates, from one paddock to another. Some cutting out was being done but mostly the cattle were getting used to being handled. On this point she knew Jim was right but all the time her heart hankered after the stray stuff in the scrub. Cattle refuging in the scrub were generally fat though wild. Captured, handled, branded and mastered, they meant the kind of big money the cattle in the gully had evidently brought.

Jim Conrad said nothing to her of this money until knock-off on Friday. He told all the men to be at the office door at sundown.

Gerry, when she left the saddling yard, went straight to her room, picked up her towel and toilet things and made for the shower-room. When she had bathed and dressed for dinner she went out to the veranda. The last of the men was leaving the office door. Gerry knew quite well what he was carrying in his hand. She had seen this happen before. The men were being paid off and they carried their cheques. They would be cheques on Jim Conrad's account, not Yandoo's account. This, of course, was why he had the cheque for the cattle made over to him but wages would only be a small bite of the total amount.

Jim came out of the office door with the staff sheet on its board in his hand. He looked at Gerry with a hint of a smile.

"Apart from three men at the out-station who won't be in for a week, G. Meredith is the only one who didn't turn up for the pay-off," he said.

Gerry took up her favourite position on the veranda step. Her back was to Jim.

"What do you take me for, Mr. Conrad?" she said. "I do not . . ."

"Accept wages for a good season's work? Or is it you just don't like being classed as a hand . . . G. Meredith, casual rates?" His voice was mocking.

Gerry did not turn round. She rested her elbow on her knee and her chin on her hand.

"In due course," she said very quietly, "my mother will get her share and she will give me whatever allowance she can afford."

There was the sound of Jim putting the tally board on the table. He came across the veranda and sat down on the step beside Gerry. She did not move.

Jim put his hand in his shirt pocket and brought out his tin of tobacco and began to roll a cigarette. Gerry knew that he would take his time, but that in a minute he might explain a few things. That is . . . if Lulu didn't come and spoil it all.

Jim finished making the cigarette and handed it to Gerry. "Yours," he said.

Gerry took it. He rolled another for himself and when it

was made put it between his lips and took out his matches. He lit first Gerry's cigarette, then his own. For a moment their heads were very close together. She could see the tan overtones of his skin, the wrinkles at the corners of his eyes. She could see that his eyes were flecked with little spots that gave them both depth and darkness.

She was so close to him it unnerved her.

His gesture in making the cigarette and lighting it for her had been so open, so regardless . . . regardless of his earlier mockery of her status, and of the embarrassment of being so close their shoulders touched . . . that her heart contracted.

Was that sudden change a mark of contempt for her adult status, or was he playing games with her? Winning her as he must have won Lulu and Aunt Sally Sylvester and even kind, trusting Bill Seddon? Was it nothing more than a change of tactics?

"You see, Gerry," he said as if he was just going on from a sentence he had begun earlier, "you wouldn't get anything at all if I didn't do it this way. Wages have to be paid before the books are balanced. Then if they don't balance, the owner and other creditors, go without. But not the wages man paid on casual rates. He works for cash, and gets it."

"Is that why those men . . . Ben and Twisty and the others . . . will always work for you?" She forced herself to sound natural.

"Yes. They work hard and they get paid well. Casual rates are higher rates than permanent wages."

"So I get more by being a casual hand?"

"You do, Gerry. You had to have something to carry on with, you know."

"I never need money. I never have money."

"No. You have accounts. Well, I guess you're grown up enough to know those accounts are closed."

Gerry felt this like a blow between the eyes. She didn't ask Jim another question. She knew what he meant. The bank had closed down all credit with Yandoo's usual agents, dealers and stores.

The world slid a little sideways and then steadied.

"I can't pay money to a Meredith as such, at the moment," Jim Conrad went on. "Any moment now that bank inspector will take it into his head to call again. The books have got to be square and above board. There is no Miss Geraldine Meredith of Yandoo . . ."

"I know," said Gerry. "Only G. *Meredith, casual rates*, doing the same work as any other stockman on the place."

"Exactly."

"And when that bank man does come . . . and he is *not* an inspector; he is to be the manager, you know . . . when he does come, how will you account for everything then?"

She looked at him with serious eyes. He was very close to her. The little muscle in his cheek was working and for an instant there had been a look of incredulous surprise in his eyes. Then quickly they were hooded as if he was looking into the sun. But there was no sun. Maybe he was just looking into his own thoughts.

"Oh, yes . . . the *manager*," Jim said at length. There was a sharp satire in his voice. "I'd forgotten about him. Wasn't he a friend of the family? A very reliable fellow, or something. A first-class cattleman too, I believe?"

He was using her own words.

Fortunately the dusk hid Gerry's blush. She remembered telling Jim Conrad that the first day he came to Yandoo. That had been to keep him in order because, before he had ever seen Yandoo, he had sounded too independent for safety's sake.

The silence was so long that Jim Conrad turned his head and looked at Gerry."

"Wasn't it that?" he insisted. "Wasn't he a very paragon of all the virtues?"

His tone steadied Gerry's unreliable heart beats. He was being sarcastic again.

"You will see that for yourself when he comes," she managed to say. "In the meantime I cannot accept wages, if there are other creditors."

"I'm sure *you* cannot accept wages, Gerry," he said with irony. "But I think G. Meredith, casual rates, would be advised to do so. The other stockmen would blackball her, otherwise, and down tools. All the unions in the industry would blackball everything coming off Yandoo. Too much free labour in the country would do every stockman on the routes out of a job."

Gerry knew what he was telling her. When she had left her name on that wages sheet in the first instance she had automatically joined a union. She had to abide by the rules.

"I suppose I can always give it away, after I have received it," she said a little bitterly.

"You can toss it in the creek, if you like," said Jim coldly.

"But don't forget to cash the cheque first because drowning the cheque will leave the money in my account. I'm sure you don't want me to be any better off . . ." There was bitterness as well as anger in Jim's voice too.

Gerry heard sounds of heavy footsteps coming down the passage.

"Jim . . ." she said. She wanted to ask him so much so quickly. But David Randall came out on to the veranda.

"Hey, what goes on?" he said. His voice was jocular yet there was a note of irritation in it. "That's my girl, you know," he said as Jim stood up. "You have to get my permission to sit as close to Gerry as that."

"My dear David," Jim said. His voice was so loaded with sarcasm that even David could not miss it. "I don't ask anybody's permission to do anything. However, if you like Miss Meredith's company in particular . . . the top step is yours."

He moved over to the table, picked up the tally board and went through the office door. He closed the door behind him.

"An edgy brute," David said as he sat down by Gerry. "Can't take a joke."

Gerry did not answer. Instead she watched the stars come out, little points of light on a great velvet cloth. She had known all along that someone would come: that the explanations would cease—and that Jim Conrad would not begin them again. And that she had angered him deeply.

This time David's presence did not bring back her happiness so easily.

CHAPTER ELEVEN

THE MUSTERING TEAM had gone for a four-day break to the township on the upper reaches of Yeebong Creek. They would cash their cheques, have a wonderful talking spree with the oldtimers sitting under the pepper trees on the main street and return to be re-entered on the wages sheet on Tuesday.

On the station there was only Jim Conrad and his native Dinny, David Randall, Simon and the two girls.

On Saturday Simon and Gerry helped Jim muster up horses that had been out to grass so long Simon said they would have to be broken all over again. There were new foals, a delight and joy to both Simon and Gerry.

David Randall's job was to take stock of all station equipment, beginning with the tool house and the machine shed.

Bringing in the horses was wonderful fun. They were fleet but so was Mandy, Gerry's horse, and the two mounts Jim and Simon rode. Even Gerry knew the three of them made a good team. There was nothing Jim Conrad could tell Gerry about bringing in horses and there was nothing Simon *would* be told. He learned his business the best way of all, by example. He watched with his bright eager eyes everything his uncle did and promptly did likewise.

Gerry hoped for Simon's sake that Jim would never do anything on the wrong side of the slate and she wondered if he was aware of the tremendous influence he would have on the boy's whole outlook on life. On the surface he appeared to take little notice of his nephew and when he spoke to him it was only in monosyllables.

On the Saturday evening when they returned to the saddling paddock Jim was first on the ground and his saddle off. Gerry, her head bent, was unbuckling Mandy's girth. Jim threw his saddle over the top rail and came over to her.

"I'll lift your saddle for you, Gerry," he said.

She looked up to meet his eyes across Mandy's back. Gerry smiled.

"I've lifted my saddle all my life," she said.

"Well, supposing we begin to-day by having someone lift it for you."

Before Gerry could answer he swung her saddle in the air and hung it across the top-rail. Gerry was embarrassed. She didn't quite know how to take this sudden chivalry. Her father, in her childhood, had taught her to handle her own horse gear on the principle that independence was a girl's greatest safeguard if ever she was caught out alone at far distances from the homestead. Fearlessness of the bush was any person's defence on a property that stretched for hundreds of thousands of acres and which covered everything from verdant gully, menacing scrub, creeklands, to plain and thirsty desert.

She ran her hands down the sides of her jeans.

"Well . . . thank you, Jim," she said.

"Simon," Jim commanded, "take Mandy's bridle and the rest of the gear and put them in the harness room. Hang them in the right place."

"Okay, boss," Simon said nonchalantly.

Gerry felt at a loss. She stood and wrinkled her fore-head, then blinked.

"You'd better not get me into bad habits, Jim," she said.

But she felt pleased all the same. Jim had formerly treated her either as another hand on the place or as a juvenile member of the Meredith family who needed suppressing. Since the night when she had asked him how he would account for everything when the manager came he had treated her with a coolness that appeared to hide a kind of anger. Gerry wished she had never asked that question.

As they turned through the gate to go up to the home-stead she ventured a smile in Jim's direction.

"Thank you very much," she said again.

"It's good for Simon," Jim said. "He has to learn that it behoves a man to help a woman."

Gerry felt dashed. He'd only done it as an example to Simon! All the same it did show he was aware of some responsibility towards the boy's proper education.

She pressed her lips together.

When they reached the homestead veranda Lulu was coming out of the door.

"You're early," she said. "I'll put the ferns on the table and pull the chairs round."

"Here, let me . . ."

Jim lifted the pot plant from its hanging basket and put it on the table. He then dragged round two of the easy-chairs that had been used farther down the veranda during the day.

"Oh, thank you, Jim," Lulu said casually. Her manner implied she'd been having similar services all her life.

Gerry whacked her riding boots with her stockwhip and tried not to watch the little ceremony.

David Randall came along the path from the engine room. "That billabong's wet, Gerry," he said. "And it's been a mighty hot day."

Gerry's face broke into a relieved smile. She wanted a swim but she also wanted to get away from Jim and Lulu.

"Right," she said. "I'll meet you under the red gum in five minutes. Lulu, will you tell Simon?"

David took two of the three steps on to the veranda in one stride. He folded his arms and leaned against the railing.

"Dear Gerry," he said. "Do you think we could take Simon some other time? I have things to say . . ."

"Don't you want someone to witness you beating me by

yards? Besides, David, I couldn't leave Simon out. He'd be disappointed."

Jim had been rolling himself a cigarette.

"Never mind Simon," he said. "I'll take care of him."

"But he likes a swim . . ."

"He can like a shower to-night by way of a change."

Gerry pressed her lips together again. Sometimes she just hated Jim Conrad. There was something hard and cruel about him. He didn't care how Simon would feel about being left out. As if anything David had to say could matter that much!

But she couldn't have an argument there in front of David and Lulu, especially one in which she would end up by being bested.

"See you later," she said to David and turned on her heel and went down the passage to her own room.

Half an hour later David had suitably beaten Gerry in a free style race the length of the billabong and they were sitting up on the bank, their knees hunched up and their arms wrapped round their knees.

"Tell me, Gerry," said David. "Have you noticed our Lulu is a different person lately?"

He was chewing a gum twig and looking at the water reflectively.

"Yes, I have. I expect it is having interesting work . . . and responsibility. Probably Lulu needed that all the time."

She hoped she didn't sound like being laboriously loyal. In her own heart she thought it was Jim Conrad who had worked the oracle.

"You know what . . ." David continued in the same thoughtful tone. "Lulu was born to stand at the head of a staircase. You know what I mean? Receiving the guests dressed in shimmering cloth of gold. Is there such a thing as cloth of gold?"

Gerry shrugged her shoulders.

"I suppose so," she said. Then after a minute's silence, "What made you think of Lulu and staircases and cloth of gold?"

"*She* makes me think of them. She ought to marry one of these big business magnates, or a Prime Minister, or something." His voice waxed enthusiastic. "You know, Gerry, she's really beautiful and she knows how to put it over. I don't just mean her good looks, I mean that disdainful head-of-the-staircase look. If I was a big business magnate and looking for the right wife to carry off the job I'd look for someone like Lulu."

Gerry looked at David in surprise. She had no idea he thought about these things at all.

"Don't men marry for love? Wouldn't you marry for love . . . irrespective of the staircase and all that?" she asked.

David laughed and threw his twig into the water. He broke another from the fallen branch beside them.

"I guess everything depends on the man. There must be some who just get 'hit' and then get married. I think I'm the kind that would find the right girl for the job. Mind you, Gerry, I wouldn't marry any girl if I didn't love her. I'd just take care to love the right girl."

Gerry frowned.

"I'm not sure that doesn't sound a bit calculating," she said reprovingly.

"I don't know whether it is or not," David admitted. "But it's a sound investment for the future. For instance, if I was going to live a life on a cattle station I'd marry a girl like you. If I was going to try for the top class in business, I'd marry a girl like Lulu."

"But you'd have to *love* the girl?"

"You bet." He flicked Gerry's arm with the tip of his finger. "Don't worry, old thing. I believe in love with a capital 'L.' "

"I think this is a silly conversation," she said. "Why did you start it?"

"Because I can't work out what Jim Conrad is up to. If ever there was a man with his head on his shoulders it's Jim Conrad. But he seems to be making a line for a girl who'd never, never be the right girl for a man who leads a life in the saddle moving from one station to another; and half his life on the stock route."

Gerry was silent for a few minutes.

"I think he's something more than that," she said slowly. "I think he has shares in a number of stations. Perhaps he means to be one of those men who own or control big properties." She looked at David soberly. "In the end it might mean one of those harbour-side mansions with . . . well, with a staircase . . ."

David bit on his twig.

"Could be," he said reflectively. "Could be." He picked up a gumnut and threw it in the water. "If what you say is true

I'm all the more glad I threw in my hand with him. Those big owners mean big business to a pastoral agency like ours."

Gerry was very silent. After a while David noticed it. He turned to look at her. Her head was sunk a little on her chest and she was watching the tiny water midgets in the pool between the roots of the big tree where they were sitting. David leaned forward and lifted her chin with his thumb and forefinger.

"Maybe I'll come back as manager of Yandoo one day, and marry the squatter's daughter, hey?" he said with a laugh.

"Don't forget to make sure you love her," said Gerry. "You might find she's gone and married someone else meantime."

"That 'ud just be my bad luck. It wouldn't be hard to love you, Gerry. In fact, just too darn easy."

"Thanks a lot, mate," said Gerry, imitating Simon's style with the stockmen. "And now for washing the mud off our legs. How much start do I get this time?"

"Twelve yards. Are you ready?"

They both stood poised on the bank.

"*Right!*"

The two figures shot into the water. The birds with a whirr fluttered and rose from the surface as Gerry and David raced to the other side.

Simon, at the dinner table, was too polished about the face and hair, and complacent in his manner, to make Gerry's heart feel easy. He ought to have been reproaching her for swimming in the billabong without him. There was something unnaturally angelic about his manners as he passed things to other people.

When the meal was over and Jim and David had gone across the homestead gravel to their own rooms adjoining the store Gerry walked around the side veranda where Simon kept his possessions . . . no more than a change of clothes and his riding gear . . . in a box under his bed. He was sitting on his bed pulling off his boots.

"So early to bed, Simon?" she asked. "It's Saturday night."

"Yep, but I'm getting all the sleep in I can in the next thirty-six hours. I've got a big day on Monday."

"Oh, have you?" Gerry said with raised eyebrows. "And what have you got on Monday that the rest of us haven't got?"

"I'm going to throw a bullock on Monday." He said it casually as if this was something he might get around to doing

113

in the course of events if he felt inclined that way. But Gerry knew that to Simon the summit of all achievement was to throw a bullock. At the same time she felt shocked. She had hoped Jim had forgotten or thought better of that promise. The sale of the cattle had taken all their minds off hunting wild cattle.

"Look, Simon . . ." she began.

"Aw, you girls worry too much," said Simon at his most bored. "You get scared and het up about nothing at all. It's just nothing to throw a bullock, Gerry. I've seen my uncle do it a hundred times."

Gerry bit her lips.

"All right, Simon," she said at length. "I suppose you men know best about these things. Good night now . . . and don't throw anything about in your sleep, will you?"

"Good night, Gerry."

Lulu was altering a dress in the sewing-room so Gerry sat alone in the office and listened-in to the open session of the air. She could hear Ruloo Station talking to a station in the dead centre. They were passing on the message that Slater, the buyer, was on his way. They gave the news of the district. "Jim Conrad was doing fine down there at Yandoo and the latest about Mrs. Meredith was that she was on the mend. Due out of hospital any time, so they said." The "they" being, as Gerry listening-in well knew, the other gossips of the stock route and the air.

Gerry took some paper from the box on the filing cabinet and wrote to her mother.

"Jim Conrad was doing fine." That was what Ruloo Station was telling the world when it was talking on the open session like that. Well, so he was. Cattle had been sold and they had got good prices. That was good news that would cheer her mother. Was it safe to put that? Would her mother want to know for how much and where the money was?

Gerry could not bring herself to risk worrying her mother in any way. Perhaps it was still too early to ask for all those details about Jim Conrad's background.

Gerry tore up the letter and started again. She wrote of all the daily doings on the station. "Jim Conrad is doing fine" is all she wrote about him.

When she went to bed she thought quite a lot more than she would ever have written to anyone. Was it irresponsible to let a child like Simon learn to throw a bullock? Gerry supposed Jim had been right when he had said that it was in youth one learned to do things that older people would not dare. One had to learn to dive in deep water when one was very young because one didn't understand of what one had to be afraid.

All right! Perhaps Jim was right but please God keep a weather eye on Simon.

Perhaps *David* was right too when he said a man should marry the right girl, even if it did sound calculating. Unfortunately girls didn't have the same choice. What happens to a girl if the "right" man passes her by, or falls in love with another, or doesn't come her way at all? What does she do then? Go without, or are there always several Mr. Rights in the world for any one girl?

Gerry knew that if Jim Conrad was going finally to set himself up as a master pastoralist, a major station-owner, he would be Mr. Right for Lulu. And she supposed Lulu would be the right girl for him. As David had said, Lulu could stand at the head of a staircase. As for herself . . .

She thought of David telling her it would be easy to fall in love with her. That was nice of David, but quite meaningless. To begin with, he wanted to be a big business magnate, to be at the head of a big pastoral agency in Sydney, and Lulu, in that case, would be the one to stand at the head of *his* staircase.

"So what!" thought Gerry, punching her pillows irritably. "Lulu can't marry them both."

As she fell asleep she had a vision of Lulu in wedding dress and orange blossom standing beside a shadowy man. Then inexplicably, as is the way with half dreams, it wasn't Lulu at all in that lace and misty veil. It was herself. And the man wasn't shadowy any more. It was Jim Conrad.

Gerry shook herself awake.

"No, never!" she said. "Oh, how could I have dreamed such a thing!"

The next day was Sunday. The girls did not see Jim or David all day though Simon said he saw them riding out towards the scrub down in the west paddock.

"They should take it easy to-day," Gerry said.

"Oh, they will," Simon advised. "They're only gone to look for cattle tracks in the scrub. That way Uncle Jim's got a good idea where we can hunt them to-morrow. We got to be down

115

there before dawn, Gerry . . . that's when the cattle come out to feed. Soon as the sun's well up they hide in the scrub again."

"Yes, I know," Gerry said soberly.

"You coming, Gerry?"

"I don't know, Simon. I just . . . just can't make up my mind."

Simon looked at Gerry with a solemn face.

"I'd like you to come, Gerry," he said. "I'd like you to see me throw my first mickey."

Gerry looked searchingly in Simon's eyes. She dared not tell him how afraid she was herself. If Simon was to do this thing then he must go into it with his nerve unshaken. She must not under any circumstances communicate her own fears to him.

"All right, Simon," she said at length. "I'll come."

Monday was a free day as the routine work did not begin until the muster team signed on again on Tuesday morning. But Gerry did not ride with Simon on his first bull hunt.

She was up early and down to the saddling paddock at the same time as Simon. Jim Conrad was already there.

"I'm sorry, Gerry," he said. "You're not coming."

"Of course I am," said Gerry. "I promised Simon. Besides, when there is anything on . . . I go."

"Not this time."

"I . . . What do you mean, Jim?"

"This is something between Simon and me. You're not coming, Gerry."

"But supposing something happens?"

"I'll take care of it."

The only light was from the hurricane lamp hanging on a nail in the post. Gerry could see, however, that Jim's jaw was set in that forward thrust that meant he would brook no opposition. His eyes were just pools in dark hollows. Gerry knew that Jim wouldn't take her. It was no good fighting him.

CHAPTER TWELVE

SIMON WAS THE first in that evening. Jim Conrad was still down at the saddling paddock. Evidently he did not intend coming up to the office, as was his usual routine, before dinner.

Gerry had busied herself all day round the homestead. Never since she had left school had she had the opportunity to do things about her own home that so badly needed doing. The beautiful but old mahogany furniture needed polishing. Curtains needed to be taken down and in some instances actually scrapped. Others should be mended.

Lulu was doing an expert job with the office work and with the direction of Mary and Jeannie in the kitchen. Like her mother, Lulu liked good food daintily, even extravagantly, prepared. But she had no zest for curtains and shabby chintz covers and leaky cushions.

Gerry, in a cotton house dress instead of her usual uniform . . . shirt and jeans . . . worked hard all day trying to keep her mind from Jim and Simon out there chasing wild cattle on the fringe of the scrub.

Aunt Sally, in Sydney, had delighted in the success of the whittle-heeled shoes with Gerry and Lulu. Aunt Sally had a "thing" about shoes. Gerry had never seen so many shoes, out of a shop, as Aunt Sally had. And all beautiful and expensive.

"Doesn't matter what else you've got on," Aunt Sally used to say, "if your shoes are good and well kept, the day is saved."

Pleased with the girls'- delight in the whittle-heeled shoes, Aunt Sally now sent each girl a pair of pointed-toed flatties with buckles across the front. They had come three days before.

Lulu had been a trifle disdainful because she said she never wore flatties. The buckle and the Italian pointed toes, however, intrigued her. The shoes were a perfect fit but she had put them aside. "I'll see . . ." she said non-committally.

Gerry for her part was thrilled. She thought the toes were the silliest things imaginable; like little flowery hats, silly but endearing. As for the gilt buckles with their Florentine designs. . . .

Gerry had put her shoes on, found them a perfect fit, and now longed for the day when she could wear them. But no more dancing at Jim Conrad's feet.

In the afternoon when she had showered, and shampooed her hair to take out the household dust, she put on a square-necked fresh cotton dress, and the new shoes with the gilt buckles. She brushed her hair till it shone, telling herself household dust was infinitely worse than red earth dust. The latter was at least healthy.

Lulu had been resting most of the afternoon. When she

hadn't been dozing she had been reading. She emerged for the sundown drinks looking as svelte and rested as ever, but she wasn't at all sure about Gerry's shoes.

"Don't you think those buckles are just a little elaborate for the homestead?" she said.

"Well, the shoes are flatties," said Gerry excusingly. "And when would I wear them? I mean they're sort of comfortable house shoes, and this *is* afternoon. Besides, the men will probably come up for drinks before dinner."

"Oh!" said Lulu. "They're for the benefit of the men, are they?"

Gerry would have liked to ask Lulu why she took such elaborate pains with her own toilette but she knew it would sound petty. Besides, it probably was a little petty, for Lulu had always spent a lot of time arranging her hair, her finger-nails and the small details of her dress.

"Oh, well," Gerry said lamely, "it's company, having the men come up for dinner."

"Fair enough," Lulu replied, conceding Gerry's point. "You don't mind my saying, Gerry, but David's reappearance has made quite a change in you. You appear more often in a dress. And your hair! Well, to tell you the truth I had forgotten your hair was the colour it is. Mostly it has been well toned down with the desert red."

Lulu was speaking humorously.

"I don't suppose David's had any effect on you, Lulu," Gerry said kindly, "but he thinks you're immensely attractive. He told me so."

Lulu's eyes widened.

"That's very kind of him," she said. She looked at Gerry sideways. "And didn't you mind, just the littlest bit, that he was praising another woman?"

Gerry, who was now sitting in one of the veranda chairs, bent over and flicked a speck of dust that had dared settle on the gilt buckles.

"Oh, no," she said. "He likes me for one thing and you for another. Men are like that, you know."

"Oh, not all," said Lulu. "Take Jim Conrad for instance. Neatness, efficiency . . . the flawless jewel . . . that is Jim's standard."

It was Gerry's turn to look at her cousin in surprise. Were those the sort of things Jim Conrad talked about to Lulu when they had their late sessions?

She tried to imagine Jim's mouth expressing words like *flawless jewel*. Who knows what a man is like when he is not his working self?

Well, she, Gerry, would never measure up to that standard. There was the dusting of freckles on the bridge of her nose to begin with. And no matter how hard she brushed her hair it never attained that polished look that Lulu's seemed to have all the time. Lulu's skin *was* flawless. And her nose and mouth *were* perfectly shaped.

David had wondered what Jim was up to. Well, here was the explanation. It wasn't the head of the staircase business at all. It was the flawless jewel.

From round the corner of the homestead the girls could see David coming up the track in the utility. He had been to the out-station with provisions for Bill Seddon and the group out there.

Gerry heard the utility go into the garage. Lulu decided she would make a sortie into the kitchen and make sure Mary was adding the proper sauces and in their right proportion to the evening meal.

Gerry was alone on the veranda when David, covered in dust, came through the garden. He was swinging the heavy jute-fibred mail bag. He threw it up on the veranda near Gerry's feet, and he saw the buckles and the little pointed toes.

"Wow!" he said. "Who is all the shine for, Gerry?"

"For myself, of course. Tell me all about Bill and Johnny. What are they doing out there and are they all right?"

"Happy as a bunch of sandboys. No women around to see they have a bath and a shave. And they're mending fences. They've fixed a stretch of about forty miles now. There's been fire out there and a lot of the straining posts were burnt through."

Gerry bent and drew the mail bag towards her chair.

"How'd you get this?" she asked.

"The Ruloo boundary rider took it across to Bill Seddon at midday. Jim evidently told Ruloo on the air last night, I'd be going out there to-day. Jim and Simon in yet?"

Gerry shook her head.

"Not yet."

David grinned.

"Want me to send an ambulance out for them?"

Gerry was not amused.

"If they don't come in by sundown I'll go with you, David . . . to look for them."

David turned round, pushed his hat down over his brow to keep the light of the sinking sun out of his eyes.

"One dust cloud about half a mile down the straight," he said. "They're coming."

Gerry got up and stood beside David and watched the dust cloud grow larger and larger.

"There's two of them. They're alive, old thing," David said and patted Gerry's shoulder. "You must be the only person in the world who worries that Jim Conrad won't come home safe and sound in wind and limb."

"I was not thinking of Jim," Gerry said. "I was thinking of Simon."

"That kid's all right. He can do more than I'd be game to do, you know."

"You're not a stockman, David. There are things you can do Jim and Simon and the rest of us can't do."

"Like beat you in a hundred-yards race down the billabong?"

"No. Run a business . . ."

David patted Gerry's shoulders again.

"One day we'll show 'em, hey?" he said. "Me and you? What do you say to that?"

"Don't be silly, David. Go and have a shower and change before dinner. Lulu will expect you to come up for drinks."

"You never said fairer words. Excuse me . . . I'm off."

As David went off through the garden Gerry opened the mail bag. There were three letters for herself. One, a thin one with frail handwriting on the envelope, was from her mother. One was from Aunt Sally and the third one bore the imprint of the Northern Bank Ltd., Sydney, in the corner.

Gerry opened her mother's letter quickly. It was only a few lines, but they were the first Mrs. Meredith had been able to write. There was a note of optimism and happiness in them.

". . . I'll soon be well, dear, and I'm looking forward to coming home. How I wish we could afford to have the homestead done up. But never mind . . . we'll do our best together as soon as I'm strong enough."

Gerry thought of all the rubbish she had unearthed that day; of the dusty and shabby curtains, the faded chintz. Before her mother came home she must do something about all that.

Aunt Sally's letter could wait until after dinner and Gerry was in the privacy of her room. Aunt Sally would be full of wisdom about how to dress and behave and speak and look in order to be a becoming young woman. Advice, Gerry thought, can always wait. The letter from the bank came first in importance. What could they be writing to her about?

Eagerly she tore the flap of the envelope and drew out the single sheet of beautiful linen finish paper. The letter was typed. Puzzled, Gerry began to read.

"Dear Miss Meredith,

"We are instructed by the Manager of Yandoo to inform you he has received your letter of the 18th inst. He appreciates very much your full account of affairs on the station and wishes us to thank you for the interesting statement. He will reply to you in person when he has the opportunity.

"He further requests us to add a personal note on his behalf. It is to the effect he would like you to know he respects very much the considerable contribution you have personally made towards the rehabilitation of Yandoo Pastoral Company. He is very impressed by your loyal service to the property."

Then followed the signature: B. M. Everard, Pastoral Inspector.

Gerry's heart for some unaccountable reason was beating faster. At first the cold official atmosphere of the letter chilled her. But she re-read it three times and as she did so her spirits rose.

He'd got her letter. He didn't mind her writing to him. What she had written had been interesting . . . he had said so.

And he knew about her, Gerry. Unlike Jim Conrad, he knew she was not just G. Meredith, hired hand on casual rates. He knew she was someone who cared and loved Yandoo and would have given her life to help save it.

He knew. She didn't know how he knew . . . but he knew. It was all there camouflaged under the austere official jargon of a bank executive.

Oh, Gerry was going to love this man when he came! She didn't care whether he was bow-legged and had cross eyes. She was going to love him. He *understood*.

"We'll see about being G. Meredith, casual rates, when the manager comes," Gerry said, tossing her head a little.

Then suddenly she remembered that though Jim and

121

Simon were on their way home, and so were alive, she didn't yet know how much alive they were.

She went to the edge of the veranda again. She could see the two horses carrying Jim and Simon entering the lower end of the saddling paddock. The two dogs were running madly ahead.

Gerry gave a sigh of relief. She went back to the mail and sorted out the letters. There were two for Lulu and several for David. There were three for Jim Conrad. Gerry could not help looking at the imprint on the official looking envelopes. Two were from the Northern Bank. So they knew all about Jim Conrad! That was a relief. She wondered if he'd written in and told them about the sale of the cattle. The third one bore the imprint of Centro-Northern Airways Ltd. Perhaps Jim was buying himself an air ticket somewhere. He'd probably go away about the time that manager came. Gerry couldn't see Jim Conrad knuckling down to any manager.

And to-night, after dinner, when everyone else was in bed she would write to him, the manager, again. She would tell him all the lovely things about Yandoo. How the grass sparkled in the crystal clear mornings . . . if one was up early enough. How the birds came home to the creek pools at night and you could always tell the time by them. How Bill Seddon and Johnny were putting all the boundary fences in order. That four bores were now in working order and the bullock paddock was stocking up with cattle drafted and branded. How bit by bit the scrub was being combed for strays. The engine room was working . . .

As Gerry thought of it all she knew again that all this had come about because Jim Conrad had ridden into Yandoo not so very many weeks ago.

She would have to do justice to Jim. Yes, she would tell the manager all about Jim. That was only fair.

As she put the rest of the mail on the office table Gerry wondered why the manager had not written to her himself. Well, perhaps he wasn't a writing man. More likely he was camped down on some river bank with his horses tinkling their night bells all around and only stubby pencils and an old notebook with which to make his communications. The bank, being a pastoral bank, was used to that kind of letter writing from its outside men. But it wouldn't be quite correct to write like that to a young lady who was a station-owner's daughter.

122

"G. Meredith, casual rates!" Gerry said to herself again, pressing in her lips severely.

Well, it was a good job *Mister* Conrad was bringing in Simon safe and sound, otherwise both G. Meredith and Miss Geraldine Meredith would have had something very important to say to him.

Gerry took Lulu's two letters to her in the kitchen annex where she was putting sprigs of mint, some sliced orange and small tinned cherries in a fruit drink Jeannie had made. Then Gerry went back to the front veranda. Simon came up the steps.

"Oh, Simon!" Gerry cried. "Your face!"

"I hope it looks as bad as it feels," said Simon with an air of satisfaction. "It feels like a balloon. I came a beaut whopper with my first one, Gerry. I got the second and sat on his haunches all right but he was a bit big and kindà threw me off. But the third one I got and I got the nick in his ear too so he's not only got Yandoo mark on him. He's got *mine*."

"Three bullocks, Simon! You didn't throw three, did you?"

"Well, the first was a bit of a muff. But Uncle Jim says you've got to do everything three times. Then you know you're good. You don't worry any more once you *know* you're good."

Gerry felt a shiver down her spine. What did that man have in place of a heart that he could coldly and with calculation make that boy repeat his feats after muffing the first and doing all that damage to his face? Simon had a cut lip, a long cut on his forehead. One eye was nearly bunged up and the whole face was bruised.

"Come on inside, Simon, and let me do things to your face."

"No fussing now, Gerry," said Simon. "That face of mine is kinda sore. I don't want you rubbing round the sore spots."

"I'll be careful."

She took Simon into the bathroom, added some antiseptic and boracic acid powder to warm water in the bowl and took some fresh cotton wool from a packet.

"And just how many bullocks did your uncle throw?" she asked, more to take Simon's mind off what she was doing, as, carefully and gently, she began to sponge away the dust and grime from the cuts.

"Crikey, Gerry! He threw the biggest mickey you ever saw in your life. He had horns a yard wide and you know what? He was that mad at Uncle Jim when he got up he charged him . . ."

"Keep still, Simon, like a good boy."

"Yeah, but look, Gerry! That bull was the fastest brute this side of the Gulf country. Uncle Jim . . ."

The boy pulled his head away from Gerry's ministering hands and looked at her with eyes almost feverish in their awe and admiration for both that bull and his uncle.

"You just ought to have seen Uncle Jim . . ."

"Has he got a bruised face?"

"Aw, gee no. He knows how to throw a bull properly. But he cut his hand."

"The marks of trade, or the marks of heroism?" Gerry thought. "I don't know which . . . but all good stockmen are the same."

Jim Conrad did not come up for drinks that night. It was dinner-time before he put in an appearance. They were all just going into the dining-room as he came along the passage from the veranda. As he held open the door for Gerry he glanced down and saw her shoes.

He smiled and then he glanced up and caught her eyes. One eyebrow flickered and the smile spread to his eyes. Gerry pretended she didn't notice he had noticed her shoes but she could not help a little tell-tale blush mounting her cheeks.

"Have you had a good day?" she asked.

"Simon had," he replied. "Just look at him."

"I have, and I've been repairing his wounds. You didn't do much for him when he came in."

"No." Jim spoke so softly only Gerry could hear him. "I knew you would do it, Gerry."

Gerry looked at him quickly. Was he laughing at her? But no, he was quite serious, except for that smile about her shoes that still lingered in his eyes.

They took their places at the table and when Jim put his hands up to take his knife and fork Gerry could see the wide band of plaster across the back of his right hand. All around the region of the plaster was bruised and a little swollen. She noticed he had difficulty with his knife. She would have liked to offer to help him but somehow she had not quite the courage to face Lulu's raised eyebrows or David's grin.

In the end it was Lulu who came to Jim's aid.

"I don't know what you've done to your hand, but you can't cut your food that way, Jim," Lulu said.

Without ado she got up, walked round the table and took

124

Jim's knife and fork from him. She leaned over his shoulder and cut up the larger pieces for him.

Gerry kept her eyes on her plate. Lulu's head was very near Jim's. Her hair must be brushing his cheek. He would feel it . . .

When Lulu went back to her place only Simon made a comment.

"Gee, Gerry," he said, "you'll have to help a man out. I have to use a *kid's* fork."

"Pass me your plate, Simon," Gerry said.

When he had done so she carefully cut his food into small pieces.

"What a day you two fellows had," David said. "You have to come home to a couple of nursemaids."

Jim ignored this.

"How are they doing at the out-station?" he asked.

David told him.

"Jeffers, the bloke out there with Bill Seddon, wants to know if you want him in here with the muster team when they sign up to-morrow? I'm taking some sharpened tools down again in the morning and I can let him know."

"I'll leave him there a few more days," Jim said. He turned his eyes to Gerry. "You can take it easy in the morning, Gerry. I won't be needing you at the office door at five o'clock. I'm taking only a small team out."

Gerry's heart stood still. To-morrow was signing up day. If she didn't sign up to-morrow when would she do it? There was something behind Jim's words.

"You mean you don't want me out on the run?" she asked.

"Not just yet awhile, Gerry."

Gerry concentrated on her plate. This, she would have to have out with Jim in privacy.

After dinner Jim went straight down to the office to look at the mail and Gerry followed him. As she went inside she closed the door behind her. This time she was not going to have David or Lulu come before she had finished her conversation with Jim.

"What you said about not signing up to-morrow, Jim. . . . You mean I'm out?"

He was standing up behind the table, his hand with the plaster band on the letters on the desk. His face was quite serious.

"Yes, that's what I mean, Gerry!"

"Why? Because I wanted to turn in the wages?"

"Partly. I've got to keep my team together and thinking the same way. But there is another reason. I can take you out on the run to do a stockman's job, Gerry, but I can't send a stockman in here to jack up the homestead. Lulu's got her hands full, and . . ." He half turned away to slit open one of the letters with a paper-knife. "Yandoo's not her interest really. It's yours."

He flicked open the sheet of notepaper but still made no attempt to read it. He turned back to Gerry.

"You see, Gerry, I think you could do it. And I think you will."

"And how do I read on the wages sheet? G. Meredith, *domestic* rates?"

"No, you don't read on the wages sheet at all. I'm afraid you revert to being Miss Geraldine Meredith. You know, like you were when I met you out at the boundary fence."

Now he was being sarcastic, though there was no sign of it in his face.

"I see," said Gerry.

She turned away to the door. She didn't know what to think. She knew from her activities to-day how much needed doing in the homestead. But how did Jim know? And even if he knew why should he care? Maybe he was just making it easy for her to take her dismissal.

But could he dismiss her from her own run?

"There's no reason why you and David shouldn't potter round the paddocks if you want to," Jim said rather cruelly. "But I can't take you in that muster team again. I'm sorry."

Gerry looked at him out of big serious eyes.

"I don't understand what pottering round a paddock means, Mr. Conrad. All my life I've ridden a horse with the men."

"I know," Jim replied. "I was thinking of David. And you're rather partial to his company."

"You give David only the light jobs to do. I sometimes think that is almost a gesture of contempt on your part. If you feel that way about him, why did you take him on?"

Jim looked across the table directly into Gerry's eyes.

"Because Lulu asked me to take him on."

Gerry felt as if a beam from the roof had fallen and hit her between the eyes.

Jim, the tough and unbreakable cement-hearted attorney and director—*pro tem*—of Yandoo Pastoral Company, had actually taken on a man with no particular capabilities because Lulu had asked him to do so!

And why should Lulu ask for David?

Quite dazed, Gerry felt for the door handle. Jim came round the table and opened it for her.

"Gerry," he said quietly. "Thank you for being kind to Simon."

Gerry stared at him uncomprehendingly and then went quickly through the door.

She went up to her own room and sat on her bed for a long time. Nothing added up. Jim Conrad was the most unpredictable man imaginable.

When she wrote to the manager now she would have to tell him she was out of the muster team . . . confined to barracks, as it were. He wouldn't be able to send a message back this time appreciating all she, Gerry, was doing for the rehabilitation of Yandoo. Doing things to the homestead probably wouldn't mean anything to him.

And Lulu had asked for David.

David had said Lulu was beautiful and was born to stand at the head of a staircase. But Lulu wanted Jim Conrad . . . that was as clear as her own hand was clear before her. Perhaps it was one of those peculiar games one read about in books about playing one man off against the other!

Gerry gave it up.

Anyhow, the homestead did need jacking up. It needed it badly and it must be done before her mother came home. Her mother had to come home to everything sparkling and attractive. She had a new life before her.

As usual Jim Conrad was right but it didn't make it any easier for Gerry to get the sack. Because that was what it was.

Gerry got up from her bed and combed her hair. She looked in the mirror and saw that her face did not show how disappointed she was, then she went out through her veranda door, around the side of it to Simon's bed.

Simon was sitting on the side, carefully rolling his snake belt.

"It's a bit dried out," he explained. "If I roll it up it won't crack."

Gerry sat down on the bed beside him. She put her arm along his shoulder.

"Simon," she said, "does your face hurt? Would you like an aspirin?"

He was about to say something but the words remained unuttered. Simon with mouth open, was looking down at Gerry's feet.

"Golly," he said. "Where'd you get *those* shoes?"

Gerry thrust her feet out for Simon to see them better. Her own head was a little on the side as they examined them.

"Do you like them, Simon? Aunt Sally sent them to me."

"They're beaut. Can I look at them?"

"Well, you are looking at them, aren't you?"

"I mean take one off. Can't you take one off, Gerry? What's the matter? You got a hole in your sock?"

Gerry laughed.

"You think the worst, you little wretch," she said as she slipped one shoe off and gave it to Simon.

Never before had Gerry seen Simon handle anything gently. Not even his snakeskin belt had felt such tender fingers. He stroked the pointed suède toes and delicately touched the gilt buckle.

"Gee . . . it's lovely, Gerry," he said wistfully. "Here, put it back and let me see them both on again."

Gerry did as Simon asked. He looked at them admiringly.

"You know what, Gerry," he said. "Lulu's feet aren't as nice as yours. I wish my Uncle Jim had you for his girl instead of Lulu. I guess I'll tell him . . ."

"Don't you dare!"

"Why? Do you want to be David's girl?"

"I don't want to be anybody's girl. I want to belong to myself."

CHAPTER THIRTEEN

GERRY WAS AWAKE in the morning when the men came up to the office door for instructions. She heard their heavy boots on the gravel and the sound of their voices as Jim Conrad told each man what to do. She lay there listening and feeling wretched. The men would notice she wasn't with them. They would know Jim had put her out of the team.

Sacked on her own station! That was a funny one!

She would jack up the homestead and fix up new or clean curtains, polish the furniture and even transplant some of the ferns that were overcrowding the pots around the veranda but she wouldn't be doing it for Jim Conrad's sake. Or because he told her to do it. She would do it for her mother's sake and because her mother should have a bright homecoming.

Gerry waited until she was sure the last of the men had gone before getting up. As soon as she was dressed she went round the veranda corner to see if Simon was still asleep. His bed was empty.

Simon, with that bruised and cut face, had gone out with the men. Jim Conrad must be mad. Here was an absolutely experienced and useful hand in Gerry Meredith and he leaves her behind and takes out a nine-year-old boy who ought to see a doctor about his face.

Had he been as angry as all that because she had threatened to pass in her wages or could it possibly have been that Lulu didn't like curtains and mending and had suggested it to Jim? It had been Lulu who had asked him to take on David Randall.

That could be the explanation, but was it?

Beginning with her mother's room, Gerry worked at taking down curtains and turning out cupboards with a kind of silent patience. She wondered if she was to be out of that team for good and all? Or just until the homestead was up to scratch.

After a brief lunch Gerry sat down and wrote her three letters. One to her mother full of good cheer, one to Aunt Sally all about the success of the shoes, and one to the manager. To him, unconsciously she poured out a little of her heart.

She described the day by day rebirth of Yandoo. She told how the water in the creeks had brought all the bird life back and brought life to the grasses all along their banks. The wildflowers were like a carpet along the western boundary. He would love Yandoo because it was so beautiful and he must come before the Dry had turned it all to brown paper. The cattle were doing fine. Jim Conrad was doing fine.

If Gerry spoke of Jim Conrad in every third sentence it was because she had to be fair to him. Besides, it was Jim Conrad who was responsible for everything. He left no task undone. Even the homestead was going to get a face lift. Jim Conrad had seen to that. Well, she, Gerry, couldn't be in two places at once, of course. Jim Conrad was quite right. Somebody had to jack up the homestead.

Gerry blotted, signed and sealed her letter. Together with the other two letters she put it in the mail bag.

She considered she had taken up her siesta hour and so she went back to the work of taking off the cushion covers.

She felt a lot better now. Funny how writing a letter like that seemed to take a load off one's chest! Maybe she was just imagining it but somehow she felt she had a friend in that manager. He was getting to mean more to her than even David Randall. David, after all, was a bird of passage. Besides, he made a joke of everything, even work. At times Gerry thought he might try to be just a little more daring. He could actually ride quite well. He just didn't want to *try* to compete with the stockmen.

At four o'clock Gerry made herself a cup of tea. Lulu was not yet stirring in her room.

Gerry had been all day in the homestead and she could not believe the run was still safe and sound in her absence. She must have one short ride over it before nightfall. She got into her riding clothes and went down to the saddling yard. One clear whistle brought Mandy to the outside rail.

In five minutes Gerry had saddled up and was astride. Mandy too thought something was wrong that she had been yarded all day and had no work to do. She galloped smartly down the rise towards the elbow of the creek.

"We'll go and see how the cattle are," Gerry told her. "Those drovers are due here any day now."

Gerry galloped a good mile along the creek flats. Then she slowed down to a walk as she turned to see if there was any sign of the mustering team in the bullock paddock. There was no sign of human life anywhere.

Presently she broke into a canter and then a gallop again. At the elbow she forded the creek by an old stock route. There was a short cut up the steep hill that formed the northern flank of the gully where the cattle were grassing. She let Mandy quietly pick her way up the steep pad. At the top was a lookout from which she would be able to see over the gully.

A quarter of an hour later the horse and rider came out between the tall trees that crowned the top of the hill. Gerry looked down into the gully. The cattle were gone.

Gerry shook her head, blinked her eyes and looked again. The cattle were gone, the gully was empty.

Why hadn't Jim Conrad told her?

Usually when drovers came in they had to be fed at the quarters. There was a sort of formal meeting between them and the stockmen handing the mob over. There was a ceremony in the business of handing over. The stockmen always rode out so many miles with the drovers to see them on their way.

How could the cattle go without Gerry knowing?

And Bill Seddon and Johnny were at the out-station miles and miles away across the sandplain!

Oddly enough, Jim did not come up to the homestead for dinner that night. He sent a message up to say he was in too late and too dusty. He would have dinner with the men down at the quarters.

"Where did you go to-day, Simon?" Gerry asked curiously.

"Out to the waterhole at the Twenty Mile," he said. "We were mustering and branding cleanskins all day."

Gerry could not bring herself to ask him any more questions. Simon would answer her clearly and freely if she asked him for information. She knew that. But she could not ask him to report on his uncle.

The meal was a sombre affair. Clearly both Lulu and Simon did not find the hour so interesting when Jim absented himself.

David had had a boring day at the out-station. He found nothing fascinating about the business of boundary riding and fence mending, and he said so.

After dinner he listened in to the open session for a while and then said he'd see if he could get a game of cards with some of the men down at the quarters. Old Jim was probably on to a good game of poker. It wasn't often Jim didn't come up to the office to see if anything had come through.

Simon and Lulu both retired early and Gerry did likewise. First, however, she went down to the home paddock. She knew she could catch Mandy without any trouble early in the morning but to-night she had to find Sultan. She knew what she was going to do now. In the morning she was going to ride out to Bill Seddon at the out-station. Bill would tell her what to think and, above all, what to do.

Gerry was a born bushman. She knew what to do about preparing for a long ride through bush in the heat. She rode Mandy and led Sultan, and it was Sultan who carried the two canvas water-bags, the saddle pouches of food . . . flour, sugar and tea . . . and the billycan.

Riding one horse and leading another meant she greatly lengthened time in getting to the out-station but her father's greatest legacy to Gerry had been the strict injunction that when you took risks in the bush, you took calculated risks. That is, you knew what you were facing and you took the required precautions.

All being well, Gerry could have ridden Mandy with one water bag on the saddle and reached the out-station by late

131

afternoon without misadventure. But her training bade her do otherwise. Bill Seddon out at the boundary did not know she was coming nor did anyone in the homestead know she was going. So she took the usual precautions against mishap.

No one in the homestead would wonder about her absence, she felt. All the year she had been rising before sun-up and riding out on the run. Jim Conrad and his men would be out and away before they knew she too was abroad.

She didn't tell anyone she was going, because she didn't want to be stopped and she knew Jim Conrad was too strong for her if he opposed her. At the best he would have insisted on someone going with her. This Gerry did not want. There were things she wanted to say alone to Bill Seddon.

It was well after sundown when Gerry got to the out-station to find it deserted.

She took some tinned foodstuffs from the men's stores, built a camp fire and made herself some supper. She hobbled both Mandy and Sultan and turned them out to feed. As she leaned back against one of the saddles preparing to sleep, she could hear the nearby tinkle of their bells.

She was up before daybreak. Even hobbled Sultan took some catching. He was a good horse, very amenable to discipline, but he loved to make a game of being caught. The easiest way would have been to catch him on Mandy but Gerry had much to do in a short time and she didn't want to go to the extra trouble of handling two horses. So she walked after Sultan to find him hiding, in dead silence in spite of the bells, in a clump of trees on the other side of the waterhole.

Gerry made her breakfast and by that time the sun was up and she started to hunt for the most recent tracks which would tell her whether Bill had gone north or south along the boundary fence. Fortunately all three men had gone in the same direction and she knew they were working together. Ten minutes later, water bags filled and hung to her saddle, she set out.

The going was good now. There was a well-defined track along the boundary fence which meant Sultan could go at a good pace.

At mid-morning she had not yet found the men. They must have worked a long way from the camp.

Gerry sat down under a tree, drank some of her water and nibbled biscuits from her saddle bag. Sultan had to have a rest. She watched him cropping grass and promised him a

132

drink of water at midday. Even if she hadn't found Bill Seddon by then she knew she would have reached a water soak that had never been known to go dry yet.

As she sat under the tree, wondering at just what hour she would strike the men, she heard the sound of a motor vehicle passing somewhere near at hand.

There were no vehicle tracks along the boundary fence so it meant the car or truck . . . whichever it was . . . would be having a bumpy going over the tufty grass and grey anthills that covered the ground everywhere.

The sound came nearer and Gerry knew it was coming along the boundary from the direction in which she herself had come. She also was certain she knew who and what it was.

Jim Conrad had sent David in the utility after her.

She felt encircled and imprisoned by the authority of Jim Conrad.

"Heavens!" she said to herself in exasperation. "Before that man came I could ride over every inch of Yandoo and nobody know or care. Now I'm not allowed out with a muster team and if I dare disappear from within view of the homestead he sends a policeman out for me. Yet he lets a little boy like Simon go out and get himself a cut face throwing bullocks."

She remained sitting with her back to the tree, watching the long snake of wire fence which presently would become enveloped in the dust cloud bringing the utility.

"As for David acting policeman . . ." She felt exasperated.

However, when the utility arrived it was not David alone. Jim Conrad was there too, plus his dog Ratty.

"Quite a posse," Gerry said, trying to make it sound light. "Don't you think I'm safe on my own station, Jim?"

He stood, his hands in his leather belt, and looked down at her. His hat was well down on his brow and his eyes were thundery.

"If we'd known where you'd gone, and why . . ."

"I've never had to explain my actions before," Gerry said, determined to sound polite.

She looked from Jim's face to David's. David had an amused grin which showed his even white teeth and made his eyes seem both light and bright. He wagged a finger backwards and forwards at Gerry.

"No can do nowadays," he said. "Two defenceless women left on a station is the grave responsibility of one Jim Conrad plus one distinction-class jackaroo named Randall."

133

"Don't be silly, David," Gerry said. "What do you think Bill Seddon and I have been doing for months?"

She had not got up from her sitting position against the tree trunk. She was not going to spring to attention because the police had come for her. Did they think she was a runaway child, or something?

"You mightn't have known it, Gerry," Jim said icily, "but there was never a minute of the day when Bill Seddon didn't know exactly where you were. He had a sense of responsibility you did not appreciate."

Gerry flushed.

"Yes, and I knew where he was. That's just commonsense."

"Does it occur to you that no one knew where you were during the last thirty hours? Seven hundred and fifty thousand acres is a wide stretch of country, specially when most of it is waterless."

Gerry felt defeated. He would argue her into being wrong whatever she said or did.

"Well, now you've come," she said, "what do you do now? Take me home, a prisoner?"

She wondered if she sounded like a sulky child. As a matter of fact that was what she felt like.

David squatted down on his heels beside her.

"Bet you we've got something nicer to eat in that ute than you've got in that saddle bag."

"David, you are trying to placate me," Gerry said, looking at him sombrely.

Looking right into her eyes, David saw that Gerry was distressed but also that her eyes, when one looked into their depths, were truly beautiful. There was a soft liquid quality about them that betrayed a sensitive nature.

"Come on, Jim," he said. "Let's get the party out. We'll cheer Gerry up with fruit salad and lemon squash straight out of the Eske freezer."

Jim had lifted a wide-mouthed water bag off the back bumper of the utility and was giving Sultan a drink.

"Let's wait till we catch up with Bill and the men," Gerry said. "They'd think fruit salad was manna from heaven."

"*If* we caught up with them this side of to-morrow," Jim said coldly. "They've gone through to Ruloo. If you had announced where you were going you would have been told that."

Gerry felt a shock like a charge of electricity go through her.

She was rebuffed by the quality of Jim's voice and at the same time she understood why the two men had come after her.

When she had been missed from the homestead they had picked up her tracks and known where she had gone. They had also known what she had not, that the team at the out-station had gone much farther afield than she would have anticipated.

Gerry was standing up now. She looked at the ground and bit her lips. Then she looked up at Jim. She felt very small between the two men and was conscious of her old felt hat and the freckles on her nose.

"Why don't you tell me what you are doing when you organise things, Jim?" she asked. "Why shouldn't I know where Bill Seddon has gone? And . . ." She caught her breath and went doggedly on. "And where the cattle have gone? And when they went?"

Surprise chased cold anger from Jim's face.

"If you had asked you would have been told," he said. "I happen to be a very busy man, Gerry. I haven't got time to go round explaining myself to all the members of the family. Moreover, I've learned, through many years of experience, that the least said to members with a vested interest in a property, the less argument and frustration I'm likely to en-counter."

He was speaking rapidly for Jim, and there was a punch in every word.

"I took over this place to make it run," he said tersely. "The less time I waste in argument and explaining the why and the wherefore the sooner I'll get it running. Now if you'll sit in the utility David can give you something worthwhile to eat."

Gerry felt as she had felt whenever Jim closed the office door. There was a "Keep Out" sign in the anger in his face.

Gerry walked over to the utility and got in. David had opened the Eske and he handed her a little plastic tray with the sliced fruit and wafer biscuits on it. He poured some lemon squash into another plastic tumbler and gave her that.

Although the fruit and the cold drink were delicious Gerry hardly was aware that she took them. Jim Conrad had absolutely flattened her as far as her curiosity about the affairs of Yandoo were concerned.

"Cheer up, old thing," David said quietly. "His bark is worse than his bite."

"Yes, but I still don't know why Bill Seddon's gone to Ruloo," Gerry said.

David shrugged.

"Ours is not to reason why," he said. "Leave the bear be. He always seems to turn out right in the end."

Gerry looked into David's face. She hoped he was right. But how did he know?

Jim had removed Sultan's saddle and was now tying the horse to the rear of the utility.

"Move over," he said to David. "I'll drive as far as the out-station. You can take over then."

At the camp Jim caught Mandy, and took off her hobbles.

"They'll both go home, I suppose?" he said. "I'll turn them loose."

Gerry nodded.

"Sultan will have a holiday and take his time but Mandy will go straight home," she replied.

He fed and watered both horses and turned them loose in the bush.

"How's the Eske?" he asked David.

"Empty," he said. "We ate the lot and lemon squash doesn't keep in this heat."

"You checked the water in the utility?"

David nodded.

"I've just refilled the drinking tank," he added.

David emptied Gerry's water bags and threw them in the back of the utility.

"We don't want them," he said. "We've got four gallons in the water tank."

Gerry said nothing because she knew that in addition to the tank three canvas water bags were always carried on the crossbar under the canvas cover of the truck part of the utility. They could almost swim in the amount of water they were carrying. Ratty, the dog, sprang into the back and they were ready to depart for the homestead.

"All right, David," Jim said. "You take the wheel now. I'm going to sleep. It'll be moonlight mustering to-night to finish yarding that mob we brought in from the Twenty Mile."

This, Gerry supposed, was Jim's method of recrimination. Her "rescue," if that was how he looked on it, had taken him off the run and away from the muster team at a crucial moment.

She and David had some desultory conversation for the first few miles but they did not talk about Gerry's misdemeanours. They talked about the absence of track and the degree of heat that was beating down on them. Jim folded his arms and leaned back in the corner. Gerry supposed he was asleep but she would not look at him to see.

Presently the heat, the rhythm of the engine and the gentle rocking of the car on its springs over the disused track caused Gerry to grow drowsy too. She struggled against it for a while, well knowing that over a rough outback road two people should always remain awake, but her sparse sleep against the saddle last night and her long ride the day before took their toll. Gerry too fell asleep.

CHAPTER FOURTEEN

THE UTILITY hitting its sump box against an anthill, hovering balanced for a fateful moment on two wheels, then crashing over on its side, woke her.

The driver's door, now on the upper side, was flung open and David crawled out. Gerry followed and Jim came last.

They all stood, a little dazed. Dulled from sleep, it took Gerry a few minutes to realise what had happened, and the same must have been the case with Jim.

They looked at one another with astonishment. They were all uninjured.

"Thank God they make those raking cars steel strong these days. Bodywork can stand anything."

"What happened?" Jim said.

"Sump box hit something."

David turned round to see what the car had ridden over that had upset it. It was then they saw the water tank had been stove in. Its sides had burst and the water and the petrol from the petrol tank were all over the ground.

"Didn't you see it?" said Jim, exasperated. "You can't drive a car with a fourteen-inch clearance over an eighteen-inch anthill."

David did not answer. He was looking aghast at the water and petrol rapidly sinking into the ground.

"A tin . . . a can . . . get something quick!" he shouted. He stooped down, trying to scoop up the water in his hands. But the earth was bone dry. Even as he tried, it trickled away and sank into the sand.

Jim's voice was ominous.

"Those water bags are hanging in the back?" he asked. At the same time he started to pull away canvas to get to the rear of the damaged truck.

"It's no good, Jim," David said, his own voice quiet and defeated. "I didn't fill 'em up. I reckoned the tank had enough for a regiment to cross the whole station."

Jim looked at Gerry.

"Your bags?"

She shook her head. She did not say David had emptied them and thrown them on the floor of the truck.

"They're empty," David said with a flat note in his voice.

Jim stopped trying to force an entry into the rear end of the truck. Ratty, the dog, was sniffing, his ears pricked, at the damp earth that had swallowed the last of the tank water.

Jim's voice was steady.

"What was left in the Eske?" he asked.

Again David shook his head.

"I'm sorry," he said. "It's empty."

Jim pushed his hand through his hair. Then he walked across the ground, picked up his hat and put it on. Gerry's hat, oddly enough, was still on her head. When they hit she must have unconsciously pushed it further on. David's hat was somewhere in the cab of the truck.

"Get your hat, David," Jim said. "We've got a long dry walk."

David reached into the car, found his hat, and put it on.

"Say, listen," he said. "That's too far to walk in this heat. It would be near on forty miles just by how the speedometer reads. The heat would kill us inside ten. If we rest up here someone will come for us."

"When you went up to the homestead did you tell anyone where we were going?"

"Lulu wasn't about, and you don't tell those two silly lubras anything."

"Well, sit down there in the shade, both of you," said Jim. "I'm going to tell you what we're going to do and then we're going to do it . . . and no talking. Talking takes up energy and dries out the membranes of the mouth and throat. You'll need every drop of moisture you've got in your bodies."

David and Gerry sat down under a bush by the damaged car. Jim was rather wonderful, Gerry thought, that he reproached no one for what had happened As for David having no alternative supply of water . . . well, Jim was almost entitled to shoot him for that.

138

First rule of the bush . . . carry alternatives.

"Now listen," Jim said. "I'm not going to repeat myself because I've a feeling for saving my own energy and body moisture. The homestead doesn't know in which direction we've gone. The muster team won't get in till after dark and unless Lulu raises an alarm they won't know we're missing till morning. If they know before that they can't pick up our tracks till it's daylight and can see them. Dinny's the only tracker amongst the lot and he was to stay out at the Twenty Mile. Half a day would be gone before they'd find him and bring him in to find our tracks. At the best we'll be found mid-day to-morrow. At the worst sometime to-morrow night. At the best we've twenty-two hours without water. At the worst . . . well, work it out for yourselves."

Jim was silent for a minute. He bent down and took Ratty's collar off his neck. Every ounce of weight mattered even to a dog in temperatures that were over a hundred and eight in the shade.

Jim looked up and spoke to Gerry.

"We stay here in this heat, and wait . . . maybe until to-morrow night. Or we walk. Can you walk forty miles, Gerry?"

She nodded.

"Yes."

"Good. All right! No talking. We'll keep an even pace—not too slow and not too fast. We'll cover more ground if we stick to a rhythm. I'll go first."

They fell into single file, Gerry between the two men. It was true that not a single minute or word was to be wasted. All energy was to be carefully conserved and meted out to get them to the nearest water, three miles this side of the homestead, in the shortest possible time.

Gerry knew they had a hard and exhausting time in front of them but she was not unduly worried. Thirty hours without water would not kill them if they kept their senses. The intervening night would help. The worst would be the mid-morning heat to-morrow, when they were perhaps at their lowest ebb. By that time help would probably be at hand. If it wasn't, then to-morrow afternoon. Well, a good bushman would let to-morrow afternoon worry about itself so long as he conserved himself this afternoon. To keep control of one's thoughts was the thing. Thinking badly would consume more energy than physical movement. Tensing up the nervous system would make the mouth drier. Every school-girl going up to get a prize knew that.

Gerry had drunk a lot of lemon squash at the boundary fence where Jim and David had found her. She remembered Jim drinking some too. She'd had another drink of water at the camp. She couldn't remember David drinking at either place. If he hadn't he would be more dehydrated already than either herself or Jim.

She turned her head to see how David was getting on. His hat was pulled well down on his brow and he did not look up to meet her inquiring gaze.

"He's worrying," she thought. "Maybe he hasn't had a long drink since morning."

The heat blazed down on them from the sky and hit back at them from the earth. It had the wrath of God in it.

Jim, in front, turned his head to see how she was getting on. She smiled at him cheerfully. Her mouth was already like leather. Thinking made it that way.

They tramped on another few miles. She heard David appear to stumble behind her and she turned her head. He was walking all right now but his head was well down. Ratty, the dog, had his tongue lolling and several times he sat down as if to indicate to his master it was time they rested or drank. Jim flicked his fingers at the dog and commanded it on.

Gerry heard David stumble again.

"Jim!" she called.

He turned his head. Gerry nodded back over her shoulder. They stopped. David propped himself against a tree and looked at them both out of dazed eyes.

"Keep going, man," Jim ordered. "If we break off for rest it's harder to start again." His voice croaked a little bit and Gerry knew he was feeling thirst but there was no real danger in being thirsty—not for the next few hours anyway. As David had not had a drink, it was different with him.

David did not move. Jim met Gerry's eyes and a message passed between them.

Jim pulled David upright from the tree and pushed him out into the open again. He nodded to Gerry to indicate that she was to walk behind David and keep her eye on him.

They went on for something like another four or five miles. David kept stumbling but each time he righted himself. The sun was westing but the heat, though the blaze had gone out of it, was sticky and humid. Two hours before nightfall, four before it was really cool.

140

David wrenched his hat off his head and threw it to the side of the track.

Gerry had to call to Jim again. Her own voice cracked a little. She knew she couldn't be as dehydrated as all that. It was the knowledge that there was no water that made one so thirsty.

They stopped and Jim and Gerry looked at David's hat lying in the dust. They knew what it meant. The first really bad sign was when a person began discarding his clothes. Next the shirt would go . . . then the boots.

David sank down on his heels and Ratty lay down panting beside him. Jim picked up the hat and rammed it tight on David's head. He jerked him upright.

"Get going, and keep going," he said.

Gerry flinched but she knew Jim had to do it. He had to make David walk and he had to keep him from throwing his clothes away. He nodded to Gerry and this time she went in front and Jim walked behind with David.

Gerry began to tire and she knew her feet were lagging. The thing was to think of something else. Think about what? Think about new curtains for her mother's room . . . about another letter she would write to the manager. . . . Another mile or two passed under their feet.

There was a scuffle behind her and she stopped and turned round. It would be so much easier to stop anyway. In a kind of divorced way she watched Jim struggling with David to make the latter keep his shirt on. The hat was on the ground again. In the end Jim hit him. It was a whacking punch and Gerry closed her eyes.

They walked on again for another mile and then David fell down. This time he wouldn't get up.

Jim dragged him under the shade of a tree and they all sat down in silence.

At last Jim cleared his throat.

"There are two alternatives, Gerry," he said, sparing each word as if it were a precious jewel. As a matter of fact each word was a drop of life's blood. "We all stay . . . and wait. Or one goes on."

Gerry nodded.

"You go on, Jim."

"I can't leave you here. He will probably go berserk. You couldn't handle him."

Gerry waited a few minutes to be sure she could spare the energy and the words.

"You can't do anything else, Jim . . , if we want to save him."

"You're a young girl . . ."

"I'm a stockman. You said so. G. Meredith, casual rates."

A tired grin fleeted across Jim's face. He thought for a long time.

"We have to do it, Jim," Gerry said at length. "It's the rule of the bush you know. Two stay and one goes on. It will be night soon."

He looked searchingly in her eyes. Gerry did not flinch.

"I won't go without him," she said. He knew she meant it.

Jim got up slowly. Gerry could see it was not so much that he was tired as that he was conserving everything. He unstrapped David's belt, pushed David's arms behind him and strapped his wrists to the butt end of a fallen tree. He strapped them very tight because he knew he had to keep him there a prisoner. It would hurt and if many hours passed the pain would be excruciating. But he had to make him a prisoner to save him from something much worse. If he wandered away Gerry would never hold him. She was small and David was thick-set and powerful.

Gerry leaned against the tree trunk beside David. She smiled at Jim.

"Be seeing you!" she said. It sounded like Simon and she would have liked to add a message for the boy but she couldn't spare the words.

Jim stood above them both, looking down at Gerry.

"Be seeing you."

He nodded his head, flicked his finger for Ratty to stay with Gerry and began to walk away. Ratty went after him. Already the dog was limping, and swaying from one side of the track to the other. But he would not leave his master.

Jim unbuckled his own belt, made a sling round his shoulder and picked up the dog. He went off, Ratty's head lolling over his shoulder, the sling of the belt taking his weight on Jim's chest.

Gerry watched the little dust cloud that was the two of them disappearing over the anthill plain. Their eyes had met in the kind of farewell the two of them had meant. She was satisfied.

David stirred once and began to struggle violently but the belt held. Gerry stroked his forehead with her hand.

"Steady, David, steady," she said. "Help's coming."

He calmed down and seemed to go to sleep, his head hanging

forward on his chest, his manacled hands keeping him slouched upright against the tree branch.

The pain in Gerry's throat and chest kept her awake. Funny how she had come out here looking for Bill Seddon because she didn't know whether she trusted Jim Conrad or not. Yet now, in a moment of crisis, she had felt the ultimate in companionship. He had not uttered one word of recrimination. All he had said was "Be seeing you," yet he had just done the hardest thing it was possible for a man to do. He had left a girl alone in the bush with a thirst-crazed man, because he knew it was the only possible way of saving that man. He didn't think she, Gerry, was such a helpless schoolgirl, after all. He had paid her the highest compliment imaginable. He had known she would not leave the sick man and he had known she would not be afraid to stay. He'd given her equal status with Twisty and Big Ben. How green with envy would young Simon be!

The sun was well down now and the bush in front of Gerry was full of shadows. Her eyelids drooped over her eyes. When she opened them she thought a shadow moved. But shadows don't move at sundown. They only fade. She blinked her eyes. It was true there was a mist in front of her eyes and that was because she was both thirsty and exhausted. But that shadow moved again.

Then she saw it quite clearly. It wasn't a shadow, it was a bush native coming towards her. He had nothing round his waist but his dilly bag and nothing in his hand but his spear; but this man came from God's right hand as far as Gerry was concerned.

She pointed to her mouth and after that she didn't have to worry any more. She roused herself enough to point up the track where Jim had gone and see the native crouch down and search for and count the tracks of three people and a dog. Then she knew he knew that Jim had to be found too.

After that she went to sleep.

It was dark when she felt water trickling in her mouth. There was a small fire just bursting into flames a few feet away and there was another black shadow crouching over it. Another one was trickling water in her mouth out of a coulabash . . . a dish made of bark.

David was still strapped to the tree but the native poured water in his mouth and then splashed it over his face. Some time later he untied David. David slumped down on the ground, his face in his hands. Presently the native gave him a little more water.

Then Gerry saw they were cooking a small kangaroo in the coals of the fire.

She felt as if she had never looked at two human beings in all her life with so much love and gratitude.

She pointed up the track where Jim had gone and the native nodded. He made his fingers walk along the ground, telling her in sign language that Jim was coming back.

The kangaroo was just about cooked when Jim came back with the third native. He looked at Gerry but they said nothing to one another. There was nothing to say. They both knew everything.

When the kangaroo was eaten the natives faded away into the background. Gerry and Jim stretched David out comfortably. They could see he was just sleeping now. When he woke up he would be all right. Jim massaged David's wrists where he had strapped them and kicked a hole with the heel of his boot in the ground for Gerry, and she lay down in it to sleep. He stretched out on his back a yard away. He put out his hand, and across the distance Gerry put her hand in his. It was a truce.

In the morning Twisty came down from the homestead in the big truck. The natives had sent a message into the homestead by Jeannie and Mary. They would not go into the homestead environs themselves, and when the truck came through the bush they packed up their bark vessels, their spears and their woomeras and disappeared back into the bush.

David was a little shamefaced and Jim had to help him into the truck.

"That's okay," Jim said when David attempted to say something. "Gerry and I had about twice as much water in us when we started out. If you're feeling weak put your head on her shoulder. She saved you."

"We weren't in any danger. It was just dreadfully unpleasant," Gerry said but when David leaned his weight against her she let him slump forward in the seat and do just what Jim had counselled . . . put his head on her shoulder.

Gerry's arm stole round David's shoulder and she moved a little to let his head rest more comfortably in the hollow of her neck.

Twisty in the driver's seat moved further over. Jim, on the

other side of David, remained looking straight ahead. Gerry stole a glance at his profile. Once again it was cold and austere. Once again he was back to being the man who ran a station and brooked neither explanation nor interference.

Yet last night, he had put out his hand. Gerry could feel its strength and its warm assurance as he had closed his fingers over hers.

A little colour stole into her cheeks and she closed her eyes. Then tears smarted behind them.

He had only been kind . . . and perhaps just a little grateful. While she. . . . It wasn't any good being hurt by him, or distrusting him, or wondering where he came from and why he was on Yandoo. Because she was a little in love with him.

But it would be Lulu, up there at the station, on whom he would smile.

CHAPTER FIFTEEN

A FORTNIGHT passed and in the conversations exchanged between David and Jim at the dinner table at night Gerry got a clear picture of what was going on out on the run. Waterhole by waterhole, bore by bore, it was being mustered. The long task was in handling the cattle that were mustered and drafted. By the end of the Dry there would be a big difference in the condition of Yandoo.

In the meantime another small mob was being grassed and fattened for the buyer.

Gerry could see now how Jim Conrad worked. He mustered as he went, all the time picking out a bullock here and there to form the small prime mob he could quickly fatten and sell for money with which to carry on.

How much the bank knew of the nature of these activities Gerry did not know but whether it was right or wrong by the book she could see it working wonders on Yandoo.

Gerry did not, in the long run, have the kind of talk she had intended with Bill Seddon.

When the stockman had finally returned to the homestead he told Gerry they had worked their way along the fence to Ruloo and then went on into that station to talk over the type of plain country near Yandoo with the airways surveyor who was then lengthening the strip on Ruloo. The surveyor was then to come on to Yandoo and do the preliminary survey for an airstrip on that station.

When Bill Seddon had told her this she knew it was time she gave up worrying about Jim Conrad's movements and motives. It was all too big for her. Airstrips and future aeroplanes landing on Yandoo shook her imagination. She had thought they were all but bankrupt.

It was all beyond her. How was this to be paid for?

One evening at sundown Gerry had gone with Simon for a swim in the billabong where David later joined them.

They had their usual race, with Simon keeping up in second place with Gerry. David's prowess in the water certainly impressed the small boy and while David and Gerry sat on the bank and talked Simon did his best to improve his stroke by emulating David's overarm swing.

"Let's hope that boy never falls in with a gang of safe-breakers," David said. "He'd copy their habits inside five minutes and would be gaoled for breaking and entering within the year."

Gerry thought about this. Simon was a very straightforward boy and if he was the shadow of his associates at least their influence on that side of his character was good. Sometimes she wondered if she had misjudged Jim Conrad about his lack of interest in Simon's education.

Gerry had gone out of her way to be extra nice to David since their escapade on the way back from the out-station. She felt luck had been against David, and she herself should not have let him empty her own water bags. It was a sheer matter of bad luck that, not being the thirsty kind in the ordinary day's march, he had not taken a deep drink since he had left the homestead in pursuit of herself. Everything had worked against him. The only redeeming feature, as far as David was concerned, was the fact that Jim had said not one word to rub salt in the wounds. He well might have done so for David's had been the responsibility of checking the double water supplies.

She sat with David now on the creek bank and admired the powerful ripple of his shoulder muscles as he leaned forward to watch what Simon was doing.

"Use a six-beat patter with your feet," David shouted across the water to the boy. "Forget about your arms."

Having disposed of Simon for the next few minutes, he turned his head and looked at Gerry.

"We ought to bring Lulu down here," he said. "She doesn't know what she's missing."

Gerry shook her head.

"The sun scorches her skin and makes her ill," she said.

"Well, I guess that skin is worth preserving," said David judicially. "I haven't seen anything better east of the rabbit-proof fence." He smiled at Gerry and flipped her chin with his forefinger. "And no freckles," he added with a grin.

"Are my freckles as noticeable as all that?" Gerry asked.

"About as noticeable as beauty spots . . . and about as attractive."

He smiled into her eyes. Gerry smiled back.

"You say the nicest things in the oddest way," she said.

David made a play of counting the freckles on the bridge of her nose.

"Eight," he said, shaking his head sadly. "With all the sun you enjoy, Gerry, you ought to be able to do better than that."

"Not much sun these days, David. I'm so busy in the homestead I'm lucky if I get one good gallop in twenty-four hours."

Simon was scrambling up on the bank now.

"What were you doing to Gerry's face?" he asked. "You were doing things to her nose."

"Counting freckles, old man," David said. "Now don't interrupt while your elders conduct an important conversation." He turned to Gerry again. "What's the big idea . . . sticking around the homestead? When you first came home from school nothing could keep you off a horse."

"Ask Simon," Gerry said. "He told me Jim's reason for confining me inside the garden gates."

"A woman's place is in the home," Simon said coldly.

They both knew, without any shadow of doubt, that Jim had said that just that way.

Gerry smiled ruefully at David.

"Now you know," she said.

"And I guess that's why he likes Lulu," Simon added. "Always round the place when a man comes in tired and wanting his dinner."

Again Gerry smiled at David.

"You see?"

"I see," said David, and Gerry thought he sounded very thoughtful.

Gerry herself thought they weren't being very fair to

147

Simon. His words had a far deeper meaning for her than the young boy would know. She decided to vary the subject.

"You men are all so keen about having the little woman doing things around the place neither of you have even noticed the new curtains in the dining-room or that all the ferns have been repotted."

"No, but Uncle Jim has," put in Simon at once. "First of all he said to me, 'A woman's place is in the home,' then he pointed to the curtains and said 'See what I mean?' So I saw what he meant and the dining-room looks beaut now, Gerry. It's all light and polished looking."

"Thank you, Simon. Do I get up and curtsy?"

"We've got to hand it to Jim," said David. "He's certainly wrought wonderful changes around the place. You know, I think one of the reasons why Lulu has changed is because he's given her interest and a purpose. Why didn't we think of that ourselves, Gerry?"

"Because neither of us is Jim Conrad," Gerry said. "Let's have one more swim and go up. It must be getting on for dinner-time."

Simon sprang into the water but David put his hand on Gerry's arm.

"You don't like him, do you, Gerry?" She knew he meant Jim Conrad.

"Yes, I do," she said slowly. "I like him as much as one can *like* a person who . . ." She broke off, at a loss for words. There was no way of putting those deep tangled feelings into words.

"Who cuts you out of your own muster team?"

Gerry hadn't meant that at all but because she was silent David took her silence as assent and went on.

"Well, he won't be here that long, old thing, and think of what a comeback you can make then. I'm pretty mixed in my own feelings towards him but I'm grateful to him for two things. One, he takes me at my own valuation and doesn't try to make me throw bullocks, and two . . . I'm glad he's done so much for Lulu. He's made that girl happy. I didn't think she had it in her. Well, here's to wetting my head . . ." And David dived into the water.

Gerry hadn't thought that David was so concerned for Lulu's welfare. He too was showing new aspects of his personality. How everyone was changing! Even herself. She was beginning to take a pride in the new look the homestead was getting. She was even wondering how a bracket of indoor growing plants would look in the dining-room, and she was quite certain she didn't want to be invited back into the muster team before she had put all her plans for the home into operation. She wanted it to look really sparkling by the time her mother came home.

That night she wrote her third letter to the manager of Yandoo Station. She had noticed the water level in the creek was lowering. That would be partly due to evaporation but partly to the fact the rivers farther north were no longer running bankers. With the drying out of the land his coming would be quicker because it would be easier.

Gerry studied the pastoral map from time to time and counted the rivers and creeks a man would have to cross coming down from Arnhem Land. He must be far enough south that a river crossing wouldn't be much to him. He must be well forward on the main stock route with its permanent crossings.

He hadn't replied to her second letter, but then perhaps he had not yet received it. But his first message, when she had thought well about it, had warmed her heart. She read into it something inherently friendly.

It wasn't just the "manager" who would come down there on the track from the north, it was a friend.

Already in Gerry's heart, he was *her* friend.

Her third letter was about the changes in the homestead. He would find it clean and sparkling. It would be a homecoming for him as well as for her mother.

She knew her letters bubbled with hope and aspiration but she wanted it to be that way. It relieved her feelings to write and it would make Yandoo seem a desirable place for a weary traveller to come to rest. She was very careful to give all the credit to Jim Conrad. She had never told Jim she had written to the manager and so she had to be doubly careful to be utterly loyal to him and play fair about everything she said of him.

As with the former letters she sealed it and addressed it and put it in the mail bag without reading it over. She didn't want to change her mind about what she wrote. She just wanted it to go the way she felt things at the time of writing.

Each time the mail came in she waited for another letter from the bank for herself but the only letters were the now regular ones from her mother, and her aunt and one or two from school friends.

The only person the bank wrote to on Yandoo was Jim Conrad. Well, at least they knew of his existence and doubtless knew what he was doing. That was a security in itself.

When Jim announced one evening that the Airways surveyor would be down shortly Gerry took her courage in her hands and asked him how he thought Yandoo would ever pay for an airstrip. Also, wasn't it true a station had to pay twenty pounds over and above freight charges for every landing made by an Airways aircraft?

Jim looked at her across the dinner table.

"You have to put money into a place, Gerry, to get money out," he said patiently. "Yandoo, if it is ever going to do any good, will have to move with the times. That means the prime beef will have to go by air. Even road trains will get out of date in the next few years and Yandoo hasn't caught up with road trains yet."

Everything Jim said these days was a shock to Gerry. She hadn't dreamed of a road train, let alone that it could be outdated. She had read in the papers of sheep and cattle being moved over vast distances by huge trucks drawn by a diesel motor engine. These, she had thought, related to other places. Definitely not Yandoo. Drovers and the stock route was the only way of doing things that Gerry knew of.

Jim mistook the expression on her face.

"Aeroplanes don't take all the fun out of station life," he said. "Only first-class stockmen on first-rate horses can muster stock out of bush and gullies. The stockwhip and 'man's friend' the horse will be with the cattlemen always."

She shook her head.

"I wasn't thinking of that."

She was wondering who was going to pay for all this and what further questions she dared to ask. It was an effort to meet his eyes because she knew how forthright his snub could be.

"Jim . . . will the bank extend our overdraft for all this before the new manager and the pastoral inspector come?"

"Forget your manager, Gerry. We'll deal with him when he comes. And forget the bank. You've one-third shares out on the public. They can do a bit of putting money back into Yandoo. They've too much to lose if they don't. Now if you'll excuse me I've some office work to do. Lulu, I wonder if you will give me an hour or two of your time to-night? There's a lot to be got through and I want to leave the office table clear by the week-end."

When he said this he turned to Lulu and smiled at her. Lulu was the only person Jim really smiled at. It brought a twinge to Gerry's heart. She knew now that she wished it was herself who could win that kind of look from him, and that it was herself who would be sought to help him out when he was in a rush of office business.

Lulu stood up, her eyes sparkling.

It was true, Lulu was a different person. She held herself straight and her head up. She smiled glowingly at Jim Conrad. She was eager to go with him into the office and work with him there for hours . . . behind closed doors.

"I'm coming, Jim," she said. "Gerry will see the girls clear away properly."

They left the room and the three pairs of eyes, Gerry's, David's and Simon's, followed them. Then they met one another's.

Simon shrugged.

"Guess I'll get on with that leather belt of mine," he said, "Am I excused, Gerry?"

She nodded.

David and Gerry were left alone at the table.

David took out a packet of cigarettes thoughtfully. He slowly tore away the Cellophane covering but he said nothing.

"He's thinking what I'm thinking," Gerry thought sadly. "There's something between Lulu and Jim."

David lifted his head suddenly. He smiled at Gerry as he offered her a cigarette.

"That little performance makes us look like a couple of also-rans, doesn't it, Gerry? Well, let's make some fun, shall we? How about the radiogram? Even the Spartans made music before they died."

Gerry declined a cigarette with a shake of her head.

"I don't feel like being about to die," she said. "Do you?"

"No. But as far as Jim Conrad is concerned we could drop dead. I'm almost surprised he didn't say so when you started asking questions about that manager and the pastoral inspector. You ought to know by this time, Gerry, that Jim would have to be arrested and gaoled before he took any notice of *them*. Even then I imagine he would take his own route to the police barracks. And choose his own warders."

"I wish . . ."

"Don't wish, worry or wonder, Gerry. You're a minor. They can't gaol you for the theft of Yandoo, that's certain. Come on . . . let's haul Jeannie in to clear away and we'll get the radiogram going."

By the time they had made a selection of records and carried them out to the partly enclosed corner of the veranda where the radiogram stood they were both pretending to be in good spirits.

Gerry went on farther round the veranda to Simon's habitat.

"We've brought your favourites, Simon dear. Come and listen."

Simon was sitting on a box by his bed and his possessions. He was working on his belt. He shook his head and did not look up.

"Don't want to," he said.

Gerry sat on the edge of the bed.

"Simon," she said softly, "what is the matter?"

He darted her an upward glance then went on working the skin with his fingers.

"You know," he said. His words were almost muttered.

"But I don't, dear. We want you to come. That's why we picked your records."

"You might, but David doesn't. Anyway, Uncle Jim doesn't."

"Look, Simon . . . you know your Uncle Jim has to work. You don't mind being with Twisty and Big Ben out on the muster team when Jim is somewhere else on the run. You don't always want to be by his side."

"No, but I don't want Lulu always by his side either."

Gerry gave the kind of laugh that was proper to a small boy making improper statements.

"Lulu's very nice to you. And she always sees there's raspberry sponge cake for you. What's more, you can't direct your uncle's choice of working mates, you know. Nobody can ever tell him what to do, or with whom. You know that, Simon."

"Oh, I told him all right," said Simon airily. "I told him to tell Lulu to fix the curtains and change round all those carpets and things and let you come on the muster team with us, and do you know what he said?"

Simon shook back his hair as he looked up.

Gerry felt her heart twist again. She didn't really want Simon to tell her. She was certain it would be something that would hurt her because she cared very much what Jim Conrad said and yet hated herself for caring.

"Well . . . perhaps . . ."

"He said 'Gerry can take care of herself. Lulu can't.' What do you reckon he meant by that?"

"Just that, I suppose," Gerry said, standing up.

Yes, it had hurt. Somehow or other she should have silenced Simon. He was an unconscious mimic and so she knew just the tone in which Jim had uttered those words. When he had spoken of herself he had used the tone of dismissal. When he had said "Lulu can't" he had been thoughtful and just a little gentle. For once she felt inclined to tell Simon not to repeat conversations he had with his uncle but the boy's down-drooping head showed that he too was hurt on her behalf.

As she stood beside him she ran her fingers through the top of his hair.

"He's quite right, you know, Simon. I've got you and David and Bill Seddon to take care of me. What more could I want? Now come and take care of the records for me, then I'll feel truly loved."

Simon sneaked another upward glance and seeing Gerry's smiling face he smiled himself.

"Okay, mate," he said. "Anyhow, I like you best."

"Simon, will you stop saying things like that! Like us all the best. You'll be happy and we'll be happy that way."

"All right, I like you all best," said Simon as he followed her round the corner of the veranda. "But I still wish you'd like Uncle Jim best. Then maybe you could . . ."

"Could do what I liked on Yandoo Station? Well, that's not a bad idea, Simon. I'll give it some thought."

CHAPTER SIXTEEN

GERRY SAT on the veranda long after David had gone down to his room off the store, and Simon had gone to bed.

The light was still on in the office. Jim had opened the door on to the veranda to get a cooling current of air and the light from it lay across the other end of the veranda like a pale yellow rectangle. Occasionally she could hear the murmur of voices but mostly the only sounds were first the transmitter during the air session and later Lulu's typewriter.

All the time she and David and Simon had listened to the records Gerry had been thinking. She knew she had something she had to tell Jim Conrad. She would have to tell him to-night. His curt dismissal of the subject of Yandoo's manager appointed by the bank, and the bank's pastoral inspector, had turned the knife that was in her conscience. She had been writing to the manager, and the pastoral inspector knew of it. The only important person who didn't know of it was Jim Conrad.

Gerry knew from that one letter she had had that the bank and the manager operated on the conviction that the manager would take over Yandoo. Jim Conrad's manner had implied he didn't care a fig about either and that he, Jim Conrad, was running Yandoo.

Gerry fully expected another snub and that Jim's indifference to her would turn to absolute dislike. Yet she had to tell him. So she sat on the veranda and quietly waited until Jim would have finished his work in the office.

She heard Lulu go out of the office and down the long passage. She could hear her quick light steps going, and some time later, her steps, more careful, coming back. She guessed she was carrying a tray. They would have supper together.

Gerry could have gone along the veranda and joined them but she doubted if she would be really welcome. She had done that once before and though Jim had stood up with a quick short smile and Lulu had said, "Get yourself a cup and saucer, Gerry," by way of welcome, she had felt constraint in the atmosphere. It could have been that they wanted to drink tea and get on with their work at the same time. But it could have been the old story that two's company and three is not.

Gerry lay back in her deep-seated veranda chair and looked out across the shadowed garden to the ghostly silver of the plain. Above, the sky was a velvet dome and the stars a patterning of diamonds.

Then Jim Conrad came striding along the veranda. There was nothing of the weary man in that walk. He was going to bed as purposefully as he went about roping in a horse for the day's muster.

He was past Gerry's chair and almost at the steps before he realised she was sitting there. She had turned the light out long since.

He stopped abruptly, and then turned, bending his head a little to identify her in the blue light of the sky and the stars.

154

"Not gone to bed yet, Gerry?" he asked.

"No."

She wished her heart wouldn't pound so painfully and she hoped her voice didn't sound as wavering as she feared it did. Why was she nervous of him? What had she done of which she need be ashamed? Nothing, really. She was her own mistress and the affairs of Yandoo were deeply hers because of her mother's absence. Yet somehow she was a little afraid of Jim. She had been that way ever since those first few days when he had ruthlessly over-ridden everyone and everything on Yandoo and taken over. And particularly since he had so cuttingly dressed her down for over-riding the team on that first day's muster. She quite expected another dressing down now but somehow she was not going to mind that very much. It wouldn't kill her and she would have done the right thing by telling Jim. It was of *him* she was afraid, not the things he would say, or even do.

Jim Conrad took a few steps towards her and unexpectedly sat down in the chair next to her. It was the one David had been sitting in earlier. On the little table in front of both chairs was the open bowl of the ash tray full of the butts of David's tailor-made cigarettes. The empty packet of the brand he usually smoked lay screwed beside it.

"Do you often sit by yourself like this, Gerry?" Jim asked.

She could see the white flash of his hands as he rolled a cigarette. He was looking at it, not at her.

"Yes, now that I have time. When I went out on the run I was in too late and . . ."

"Were too tired?"

She glanced at his shadowed face.

"You don't seem very tired yourself, Jim."

"I haven't got time to be tired."

He finished rolling the cigarette. For the first time he looked in her direction.

"Would you like a cigarette, Gerry?" The white hand made a gesture towards the table. "Or has David kept you well supplied?"

"Actually I like a home-made cigarette when I do smoke one," Gerry replied. "It's not often, you know."

He gave her the cigarette and struck a match for her. As she leaned forward she was conscious of his voice speaking very near her ear.

"I'm surprised David hasn't woken up to that predilection of yours by this time."

155

What surprised Gerry about this remark was the teasing quality in Jim's voice.

"I've never mentioned it," she said.

"He should have noticed it," Jim added. This time there was no teasing note in his voice.

He rolled a cigarette for himself and Gerry was conscious of the silence between them and of the memory of that night when he had come back with the native to where she and David were being cared for by the other natives. What she thought of was that moment when he had stretched out on the ground and with an unconscious yet supremely comradely gesture stretched out his hand as if he knew Gerry would put her hand in it and as if he knew they shared something in that momentary contact.

Gerry shook her head and shook the memory away. It was no good feeling like that to-night. To-night she was about to earn his everlasting dislike. Better get on with it.

"Jim," she said a little hurriedly, "you rather brushed off the conversation about the station manager to-night when I mentioned it . . ."

She saw the quick impatient movement of his feet and the forward thrust of his big powerful body as he leaned to the table to shake off his cigarette ash. She closed her eyes tight and went on speaking.

"I want you to know I've been writing to him. Just personal, friendly letters . . ." She tailed off. She waited for a cloud to burst or an atom bomb to fall; but nothing but silence happened.

Her voice was a little steadier now.

"I wanted him to feel welcome, and to know that things are looking up on Yandoo."

She stole a glance at him but he sat well back in the shadow. Only his hands were very still. The cigarette in his right hand was burning to ash. She knew her words had some very profound effect on him.

"I . . . I just wanted you to know."

Very slowly he lifted his right hand and drew on his cigarette. But still he said nothing. His silence was more discomfiting than an explosion would have been. Gerry had to keep on talking to prevent the silence oppressing her into rising from her chair and saying "good night." She didn't want to go just yet. She wanted Jim to ask her questions so that she could answer them and in that way make him understand the terrible responsibility for Yandoo that she had felt

156

and the absolute agony of her divided loyalties to the manager on one hand and to Jim on the other, since he was in fact directing the station, and so ably.

"I would like you to know, Jim . . ." Her voice wavered again and she swallowed hard. "To know that I have not been critical. I mean I have . . . well, I've just been friendly, that's all."

Still he was silent but now she gained more courage.

"He will be here soon, you know. And that pastoral inspector too. They can't be ignored. They do exist."

Jim broke his silence at last. His voice was a little deeper than usual and because she could not see the expression of his face she did not know whether this new note was from sheer anger or not.

"My advice to you, Gerry, is the same as earlier. That is . . . forget them. They're my problem."

"Not altogether, Jim." Gerry was speaking almost sadly. "You see . . . just through writing to him I feel that manager is my friend. There is a sort of bond between us. I can't let him down now. He matters to me . . . tremendously."

She was conscious of him turning his head as if to try and catch some glimpse of her face. Then he stood up. This time there was no trouble about identifying the expression in his voice.

"A person you don't know well can't matter to you, Gerry," he said tersely. "Forget him."

Gerry stood up too.

"Jim, I can't. You can't forget him. He will come."

He seemed to look down at her from his great height but it was too dark to read his face.

"I'll deal with him when he comes. My advice to you is to keep out. And I think . . ." He stopped as if he was indeed thinking and when he spoke that deeper almost rough note was in his voice again. "You'd better stop writing to him. No good can come out of *that*."

He turned and without a word of "good night" went down the three steps of the veranda and out through the garden towards his own quarters.

Gerry went inside. She took the supper things from the study to the kitchen and washed them up and put them away. Lulu generally left them for Jeannie but since Gerry had been around the homestead she had taken to doing all the little things that kept the house tidy, almost as if ready at any moment for her mother's homecoming.

157

A dreadful thought assailed her. Was it really just her mother's homecoming? Wasn't she also thinking that any day and any moment now that man would come out of the north? And hadn't she been wanting the homestead to sparkle for him too? Wasn't that perhaps the secret of the pleasure she had been taking in homestead affairs?

How dreadfully bewildered she was! Was she trying to escape from letting herself fall under Jim's magnetic spell by weaving another one for herself which included this unknown man who must ultimately have the destiny of Yandoo in his keeping? Was it because she felt rejected by Jim that she sought to be accepted by someone else?

Suddenly and inexplicably she longed for the old hard-working days of a stricken Yandoo with the dusty but paternal companionship of Bill Seddon. Bill had let her feel she was desperately needed by the station. With him she had not felt rejected.

Jim Conrad had not exploded because Gerry had been corresponding with the future manager of Yandoo. Gerry was baffled at the manner in which he had taken this information because for the next few days nothing happened to show that Jim's attitude towards her was any different from what it had ever been. The only noticeable difference about the following days was that Jim came in later than usual from the run and there was not time for the short before-dinner meeting on the veranda for a drink and a cigarette before Jeannie came out to say dinner was ready. It was as if he was avoiding anything more than essential contact.

On the night immediately after her talk with him on the veranda he worked for an hour after hearing the open session news and without Lulu's aid. He had told Lulu to take an evening off as he wished to get on with some private correspondence.

The following evening he left the homestead immediately after listening in to the weather bulletin and the open session. Gerry heard his voice talking over the air to Ruloo and another station. Then he shut down the transceiver set, walked out on to the veranda and towards the steps.

"You knocking off early, Jim?" David asked, looking up in surprise.

"Yes. I want to be up again to-night."

Lulu stood up quickly.

"Let me make you some tea before you go down, Jim," she began.

"No, thank you. Not to-night."

He stood at the edge of the steps and looked out over the garden. When he turned it seemed to Gerry as if he saw her alone and that she was pressed down into her chair by the intense surveillance of his eyes. She felt it as pointed as an accusation. Then in another instant he had turned his head.

"Good night," he said to nobody in particular, but to all in general. Then he was gone.

Had he really looked at her like that or had she imagined it?

Neither Lulu nor David was inclined to sit late on the veranda that night and Simon, who had been up at four-thirty that morning, had gone straight to bed after dinner.

Once again Gerry sat alone on the veranda. She could see Jim's light on down at the store-house. Presently David's light went out but Jim's remained on. What was he doing, Gerry wondered, in the loneliness of that monastic room? She pictured him there . . . sitting in the hard upright chair by the small table, or perhaps in bed. She had only seen that room once since Jim Conrad had come and she knew it was bare of comfort. There would be no welcoming atmosphere as a man returned to that room each night.

She ought to have thought about doing something to add to his comfort before. Perhaps to-morrow, while the men were away . . .

Then she remembered the vase of flowers on the desk in the office, and the changed carpet. The pick of the fern pots which stood each day on the shelf over the book stack. It had all made Lulu's attitude so clear, almost like shouting a message. No, she couldn't possibly go down there and violate the privacy of Jim's room. She would have to give Dinny ideas. It was Dinny, Jim's man, who looked after him down there at the store.

All the homestead was in darkness now. The only light anywhere was that glow from the window of Jim's room. When Lulu had gone inside Gerry had asked her to turn off the veranda light. She liked sitting there in the half dark of the brilliant night. She could smell the scented earth and the perfume of the dried grasses out there on the plain.

Presently the door of the store house opened and a shaft of yellow light stabbed across the gravel square like a truncated searchlight. Jim's dark shadow broke the shape as he came out of the door and closed it behind him. Only the light from his bedroom window showed now.

Presently she could hear the sound of his footsteps as he approached the garden. There was a faint squeak as he opened the wicket gate. He went round the side of the homestead and Gerry heard him turn on the engine. A little later he came back and picked up a garden hose. The water was flowing freely from it. He began to water the shrubs along the outer fence.

Goodness! Gerry thought. As if she, or David, or one of the lubras couldn't do that. Jim worked an eighteen-hour day nearly every day in the week.

She got up from her chair and went down the veranda steps. He heard her approaching and turned his head.

"Why aren't you in bed, Gerry?" he said. There was no note of pleasure in his voice, only surprise.

"I could ask you the same question with another added to it, Jim. Why do you think you should water the garden?"

"I don't think it. I'm doing it for pleasure. I like to see things growing. I don't happen to feel like sleep to-night . . . but that's quite a different matter."

"Perhaps you should have had that cup of tea Lulu offered. Could I get one for you now?"

Jim shook his head. Then unexpectedly his manner defrosted. He dropped the hose and went over to the tap and turned it off.

"I think a good walk might be the remedy. How are you at walking in the dark, Gerry?"

Gerry felt her heart quicken.

"Pretty good," she said. "Only it's not really dark, is it? I mean there's plenty of stars and the moon will be up soon. There's a silver edge to the skyline now."

"All right, you name the direction."

"The belt of timber on the brow of the hill behind us," Gerry said promptly. "And there's a nice clean log . . ."

She broke off, embarrassed. Jim had asked her to go for a walk and not to go sitting on a log in the tree shadows. Wishful thinking must have governed her words before her brain had had time to think them out.

"It's a good limit mark, don't you think?" she went on hurriedly. "I mean it's always nice to have some special place to get to . . ."

160

They were walking side by side across the grass outside the garden.

"But you said it was a clean log," Jim said.

There was quite definitely a teasing note in his voice now. Gerry's heart beat more quickly. She would have to be careful what she said and how she said it. She must enjoy this stolen moment of comradeship, like that moment on the night when they had been stranded with David out on the track and he, Jim, had put out his hand and Gerry had put hers in it. She must be careful not to spoil it. The wrong word . . . and he might recede back into his shell and be lost for ever.

"Yes, it is a clean log," Gerry said. "The natives chipped all the bark off it for a fire when they were camping up there before going walkabout. We used to sit on it."

"We?"

"Yes. David and I."

That was safe, she thought. He wouldn't think now that she was an over-eager female who had never been for an evening walk with a man before. It would put things in perspective for him.

He made no reply to this and they walked on side by side in silence for a little while.

"We're walking straight at the Southern Cross," Gerry said after a while.

"Yes, and that tree dead centre looks like the spire of a cathedral all set about with stars."

"I didn't know you thought about cathedrals and spires," Gerry said. "I thought you lived only for the bush and the outback, Jim."

"There are more cathedrals and spires in England than there are varieties of trees in Australia," Jim said.

"Have you been in England?" Gerry asked, surprised.

"Twice. I was there last year making contacts for my beef market."

"*Your* beef market?" Gerry bit her lip. Her surprise must be only too evident. *His* beef market. But he was a wandering stockman who took jobs pulling together rundown stations.

Again she remembered Simon's words. "My Uncle Jim gets a bite into every station he cleans up. Dad says he'll own half the stations in the State before he finishes."

His beef market! Where did he keep his cattle, if it wasn't on other people's stations? And was this the kind of tie-up he had with that man Slater, the buyer who had come and whisked the cattle away before anyone on Yandoo Station had known they were gone. But that wasn't Jim's beef . . . it was Yandoo's beef!

Jim had said nothing to her last remark. She had to turn a little to avoid a particularly large and prickly clump of spinifex and Jim took her arm.

"This way," he said. "Look, there's a little path made for us."

Gerry felt his hand cupping her elbow. It was as strong as steel. She was very conscious of his closeness and the magnetic attraction that lay in his strength. Yet fear brushed her like the wings of the nightbird that had been only a silent shadow flitting through the garden.

Yandoo had been Meredith property since the foundation of the cattle industry in Australia. It was all that her mother had. There was no one but herself to safeguard her mother.

This man, Jim Conrad, was the world's wonder at rushing a station together into first-class working order. But what was his price? Ah, if only she knew that!

Jim's hand was still cupping her elbow but she drew delicately away from it as soon as they were on to a more open track.

"Do you always see shapes and fantasies in the trees against the skyline?" she asked lightly. Anything to get her thoughts off cattle and where it was sold and for whom.

"Yes. And monuments in the cloud shadows on the plain," he said. There was something in his voice that suggested he was laughing at himself for this foible.

They came to the log gleaming white against the dark background of the timber. The moon was coming up over the plain like a misshapen apricot over a sea. It was quite light and Gerry could see Jim's profile. He leaned forward as he looked out beyond the trees.

"Do you see the rabbit in the moon?" he asked.

"Is it a rabbit, or a man . . . or just mountains?"

"It's whatever you make it . . . like tree tops and cloud shadows."

"I never thought of making shapes of the shadows on the ground," Gerry said. "But I've often lain on my back and made palaces and castles of the clouds in the sky."

"Have you ever flown over them? Then you see a snowland with the palaces under your feet."

"Once I was flying home from school to Ruloo," Gerry said, "and the plane flew through the clouds when the sun was setting. Oh, it was wonderful. All the colours . . . and the sort of frail beauty of the shadows in the clouds."

Jim had turned and was looking at her. This time Gerry was not looking at Jim but out, wistfully, over the moon-washed grass.

"I think we must be kindred souls after all," Jim said quietly.

Gerry came back to earth with a jolt. What had he said? Kindred souls?

She was very close to him, sitting on the log. Their shoulders touched. Gerry felt a quiver go right through her. She also felt that her fears and doubts and anxieties were falling away from her. They didn't matter any more. Nothing mattered in the face of this overwhelming feeling she had for Jim Conrad. My love . . . right or wrong; good or bad; in sickness or in health . . .

If they lost Yandoo, the world was well lost for love.

She had forgotten about the manager and the pastoral inspector and Lulu. She lived in this one moment in time and nothing else and no one else mattered. It did not even matter that he did not, *could* not, feel this way too. It was enough to preserve the moment in a world frozen by the still trees and silent moon into immobility for ever.

Gerry saw her heart as it really was.

Jim put out his hand and touched her lightly.

"Gerry," he said, "you are very quiet."

"Yes," she said. "I was thinking."

"Of your mother? Of Yandoo? You know I wanted to get away from the homestead and all its interruptions so that we could talk."

Gerry felt herself slowly coming back to earth. The moment was thawing back into moving life. Nothing, after all, stood still.

"Yes?" she said as if her head was not quite out of the cloud castles yet.

He stood up and taking her hand drew her up beside him. He was a long way up there but he still held her hand. That kept her bound to him.

He put his right hand under her chin and looked down into her eyes.

"You're a very brave and a very loyal little person," he said gently. "I wanted you to know I know that."

There was nothing Gerry could say. She could not read the expression in his eyes because though the white light shed by the moon touched the edge of his brow and chin it did not penetrate the dark cavities of his eyes. Her own face was full in the moonlight and he could see every shadowed expression fleeting over it.

He was speaking very slowly now.

"I think Yandoo can manage all right without you for a short while. I think you need your mother, and your mother possibly needs you." He paused.

Gerry's heart did a land-slide back to the earth.

"Lulu thinks so too," he went on. "Though what Simon will do without you I can't imagine."

Her feet had not stopped at the earth; they went on sliding into the pit of disappointment. They were not kindred spirits. He had not come out here to walk with her in the moonlight. He had come to give her marching orders.

With extreme delicacy Gerry released her hand from his and stepped back so that he dropped his hand from under her chin. She turned away and they began walking quietly back in the direction of the homestead.

"I do not know that my mother needs me," she said when she had found her voice. "She is happier with Aunt Sally than with anyone else in the world. They were always very close. But perhaps I need her. I've been making the homestead ready for her. I would like her to come home as soon as possible."

Jim's hands were in his pockets. They picked their way carefully between the clumps of spinifex.

"From the accounts I've had Mrs. Meredith is doing very well indeed," Jim said. "At the same time she should make a complete cure of it by taking a long holiday." His voice brightened as if he was about to make the world's most wonderful suggestion. "You know there's nothing like a trip to round of a long illness and convalescence. New Zealand? How does that strike you, Gerry? Or would you like warmer climates? There's the Barrier Reef or even Singapore, Hong Kong?"

"What would I like?" asked Gerry. "You mean would I like to go for a trip with my mother?"

"Of course. She couldn't go alone and it would be the important break you need."

"If Mother went for a trip she would like Aunt Sally with her. I know that. But Jim, you forget that trips take money and if the stores we've dealt with all our lives have closed our accounts I can't see the bank allowing sufficient money for tripping round the southern hemisphere."

"Have you ever worked it out it is cheaper to live on a ship than at home? Fare money doesn't only get you somewhere, it keeps you while you're getting there. The farther the distance . . . the cheaper your cost of living."

How far had they come now from trees that were cathedral spires and clouds that were palaces and castles! They were talking about the cost of living on the earth. Or was it to be at sea?

"I'm sorry, Jim. We have no money," Gerry said. "You have Mother's power of attorney. You know that better than anyone else."

"It can be arranged."

"By whom, Jim? By you?"

"I can intercede with the bank. I had news over the air to-night. Everard, their pastoral inspector, is on his way here. He'll see for himself there's considerable future in this season alone for Yandoo."

If it was possible Gerry's heart dropped lower. The pastoral inspector was coming. Was it possible Jim wanted to get rid of the last Meredith from Yandoo before the inspector came? And probably the manager who was with him?

Was this why he had brought her out here? Was this all there was to it? And he had talked it over with Lulu. Why should Lulu want her to go except that Lulu would agree with anything that pleased Jim Conrad?

Gerry stopped and looked at him. This time it was his face that was framed in the moonlight. Only his eyes were dark and inscrutable. The rest of his face was cold as ice in that white light.

"Jim," she said, "you want me to go, don't you? You want me to leave Yandoo?"

His voice was very steady but again there was that curious deep note in it. The expression on his face was set hard as if by some conscious effort.

"Yes, Gerry. I think it is better that you join your mother for the time being."

They stood, immobile, looking at one another. Gerry half lifted her hand, then dropped it to her side. She turned as if to walk on. They were within sight of the homestead gate now.

"I know you think I do not care deeply enough about my

mother," she said, forcing her voice to a calmness that for all her effort still sounded strained in her own ears. "Waiting at the billabong while the doctor saw her . . . and staying here while she went to hospital. But there is a reason, Jim. I just can't explain it to you. There is a reason. I must stay here."

"Must?" His voice was cold and hard.

"Yes," Gerry said, suddenly angry. "*Must*."

They walked on towards the wicket gate. Jim opened it for her and she passed through. He closed it between them.

"We'll see about that in the morning," he said. "Good night, Gerry."

She turned away and walked up the path towards the veranda. She felt as if she was walking away from the world of dreams into the world of hard reality.

Yet that "Good night, Gerry," had a subtly different quality about it from his "We'll see about that in the morning." The words seemed to linger reluctantly on the air like an echo.

CHAPTER SEVENTEEN

THE NEXT MORNING at an hour when the homestead seemed safe from the invasion of men Gerry broached the subject of her suggested departure with Lulu. They had made their morning tea in the kitchen and each carried her cup and saucer to the shaded corner of the west veranda.

They sat in the deep chairs, sipping the tea.

"Jim Conrad thinks I ought to go and join Mother," Gerry said. "He thinks you agree, Lulu."

Lulu reached for a cigarette from the red lacquer box she had brought out from the living-room.

"Well, why not?" she asked lightly. "A trip to Sydney ought to be inviting enough without the prospect of going further afield."

"Does he think that Mother needs me?" Gerry asked. "He can't really know how close Mother and Aunt Sally are . . . and he must know how near the brink Yandoo has been and that I owed it to Mother to stay here."

"Oh, all that's past now," Lulu said airily. "Jim and I can look after everything here. I certainly think you ought to go, Gerry. There's nothing for you here."

Gerry flinched. She knew very well that while Lulu had been a wonderful help on the book-keeping side she had had no interest in the homestead itself. It was Gerry who had spring-cleaned it and brought about the gloss and shine that was on everything from the windows to the polished floors. And a house didn't stay that way unless someone kept at it with the duster and the polishing cloth. Lulu with her elaborate ideas of meals and menus kept Jeannie and Mary tied to the kitchen.

"I'm sorry," Gerry said slowly, "but I don't want to go. Not yet anyway . . ."

Lulu looked at her sharply.

"What's keeping you? Simon can look after himself, you know. He did right up until he met you. We'll promise to keep a running supply of raspberry sponges for him."

"What's keeping me is Yandoo," Gerry said doggedly. "And Simon's not the only person round the homestead I might care about. I mean care that they are well looked after. There's David for instance . . ."

"My dear girl, David's not a bit interested in you, so get that out of your head," Lulu astonished her by saying. "David is an opportunist and he'll look in the direction where he makes the greatest gain. Yandoo doesn't mean anything but a few months' experience to him."

"Lulu!" Gerry said. "I had no idea you thought about people that way."

"Why not?" said Lulu, blowing a smoke ring. "I'm an opportunist myself, didn't you know?"

"I quite frankly don't understand you. But in case you think David and I are anything more than friends I can assure you . . ."

"You don't have to assure me. I know. So you see there is nothing to keep you on Yandoo."

Gerry was silent for a long minute.

"You know, I don't think Aunt Sally would let you stay here alone," she said slowly. "Do you want to go away too, Lulu?"

Lulu frowned now and shook the ash from her cigarette with a sudden flicking movement of her hand.

"I'm not quite ready to go *yet*," she said. "Everything depends on how things turn out when our visitors come."

"What do you mean by visitors, Lulu? Do you mean the pastoral inspector from the bank and . . ."

"Yes. And the surveyor from the air company and his offsider. Then there's another man coming with them. Everything really depends on *him*."

So Lulu also knew that Jim's position on Yandoo would be very much in the balance when the manager came. Jim was silent on his affairs with Gerry but obviously he had talked them over with Lulu. And possibly she had gained much inside information from doing the correspondence. The mail had more than once had letters for Jim marked with the imprint of the Northern Bank Ltd.

"When are they coming?" Gerry asked.

"Probably before the end of the week. Ruloo will relay any message to us on the session either to-night or to-morrow night."

Gerry thought it would be childish to complain that nobody had told her of these things but she felt an odd mixture of anger and hurt. After all, it was her mother's station. Jim and Lulu both acted as if it was theirs. And both of them wanted her to go.

"I think perhaps I might go to Sydney to see Mother," Gerry said at length. "But I won't go until after the visit is over. The men will have to be put up in the homestead to begin with and you'll need my help, Lulu. Besides that, it will give us time to get in touch with both Mother and Aunt Sally."

Lulu's manner changed.

"Perhaps you're right. Mother just might make a fuss. I'll tell Jim when he comes in to-night. We can wait until the men leave to arrange air bookings from Sydney for you."

Gerry again had that longing to go and lay her troubles at Bill Seddon's feet. The thing she had minded most about spending the greater part of her time in or around the homestead was that it had cut her off from the faithful old stockman. She didn't even know on what part of the station he was now working. He hadn't been in for several days so he must be out camping at one of the bores or the outstation.

Simon was in with the first bunch of stockmen that night. It was not yet sundown and the day had been very hot. Gerry asked Simon if he would like a swim before dinner.

"You bet," he said. "I'll see you down the creek in ten minutes."

Gerry had taken Mandy for a short gallop and had not

yet unsaddled. She went inside and put on the old shirt and the short shorts in which she generally went swimming, and swinging up again on Mandy's back she trotted down to the creek. Below the swimming pool she unsaddled Mandy and let her take a mud bath in the shallows.

By the time she had finished giving the mare some sound advice about how to swim, and put the saddle back, Simon came down the track with David.

"No leaving me out," said David. "I saw this young tyke heading for the track with only his shorts on and I guessed he had an assignment, with whom, and where."

"Golly, he talks like an encyclopædia," Simon said.

"That's one thing you can't copy, monster," said David. "You haven't the education and *ipso facto* you haven't the required vocabulary."

"I bet I can copy you in that water, anyhow," said Simon. "I can't beat you yet but one day I will. You watch my over-arm stroke now . . . and the six-beat patter. I've been practising."

Gerry and David stood on the bank and watched Simon.

"So help me!" said David. "That kid's got a perfect crawl stroke. Did I teach him all that?"

"Nobody has to teach Simon anything. He just copies," Gerry said. "All the same, you were the perfect example, David."

"Then let's in and after him. I'll show him a thing or two about spot-diving."

Gerry and David dived into the water and in a few minutes were at the other end of the pool.

Gerry put up her hand and clung to a tree root and watched while David put Simon through his paces at diving for mud from a position in the water.

David dived deep and swam some distance under water. He came up and shook the wet hair out of his eyes.

"Just stay still for a while and let the mud settle," he said. "Then dive when I dive and I'll show you something you can't do, young Simon." He called to Gerry, "There's a wonderland down there amongst those old tree roots. Dive when I dive . . . and watch. Ready? One two three! *Down!*"

Gerry was not very keen about swimming in the fresh creek water with her eyes open but she felt David specially wanted to show her something so she dived when he and Simon did.

It was in truth a wonderland. The big old red gum on the

bank must have sent down those giant roots hundreds of years ago. Now they were submerged by water and they made avenues and arches through which David swam with a beautiful gliding leg movement. It was beautiful to see the ease and grace with which he turned, swimming beneath one on his face, rolling smoothly over and gliding through the next on his back and then turning sideways and in an effortless way shouldering his way between two roots that left a passage too narrow for the whole width of his shoulders, then shooting up to the surface to refill his lungs with air.

Gerry and Simon had already had to return to the upper world for air and dive again to see his performance finish.

"Oh David, that was beautiful," Gerry said, treading water. "I wish I could swim like you. And underwater too."

"I wish I could ride like you. And on hurdlers too."

They both laughed.

"You could if you tried," they both said simultaneously.

Then amidst showers of laughter each sent a spray of water with the palm of the hand over the other.

Simon had clambered on the bank and was examining the huge roots of the gum tree that showed above the water.

"Come on, let's out," shouted David across the water. "I've a job to do for Jim before dinner." He was on the bank now. "Time's flown and the boss'll be rampaging if he has to wait too long."

Gerry was on the opposite bank.

She waved her hand.

"Okay," she called. "You go on. Simon and I'll walk."

She stood, hands on hips, the water streaming from her and making little rivulets down her legs and across the sand on which she stood. Jim would be in a rampaging mood anyway, she thought, watching David go up the track. Lulu would have given him her, Gerry's, decision by now. He wouldn't be pleased by her decision to go to Sydney *after* the bank man had been and the manager had arrived. Dinner wouldn't be much fun to-night, Gerry thought.

She heard Simon's splash as he dived back into the water but she was deep in thought, a little frown between her brows. What would she do if Jim *ordered* her to go? Would he do that? And would she have the courage to stand out against him?

But this was silly thinking. Neither Jim nor anyone else could order her away from her own home.

She turned impatiently to call to Simon. He was not in sight.

"Simon! Simon!"

Suddenly she felt panic. He had dived. She was sure he had dived. She hadn't exactly seen him, though something going into the water had crossed the outside edge of her vision. And she had heard a splash.

Almost instantly she knew what he had done. He had dived down amongst those roots. He had *copied* David. But he should have been up by now.

Gerry drew in a deep breath.

"Please God, help me," she prayed. She wasn't very clever in the water herself.

She waited that one important moment that was necessary to calm herself. Then she breathed out and filled her lungs again. Then she dived.

Simon was caught in the last of the roots, the ones David had had to turn sideways to shoulder his way through.

Gerry was still saying a prayer. Carefully she swam round the whole nest of roots. To try and follow him through would be disastrous. She was utterly calm and knew that some outside agency was helping her. It must be God because she wasn't good enough for that herself.

Her lungs felt like bursting when she caught Simon's hair and began to pull. She moved him a little. She had to let go and come up for air. It would be easier now . . . he was just under her.

She filled her lungs again and dived. This time she caught his whole head and pulled, kicking backwards with her legs. He was moving . . . moving. Suddenly his body was freed and it shot up to the surface without any effort on her part. One stroke with her arm and she had caught one of the surface roots. She held Simon's head with her free hand.

"Breathe deeply now. Breathe deeply. One, two, three." Was she talking to herself or Simon?

He was alive. He was gasping. She had to hold him there because there wasn't much of her and she wasn't strong enough to land him up on top of the big overhanging roots. And she wasn't strong enough to pull him safely across to the landing bank. She clung with one hand stretched high above her to the root and with the other to Simon's head until both arms ached. Water was running from his nose and mouth. He retched and gasped again. In a minute when his lungs got full of air maybe he wouldn't be so heavy to hold.

171

Gerry pulled him closer to her. Presently she changed her one-handed grip of him. She had her arm around his shoulders now, pressing him against her, so his chin was levered up against her shoulder. If he could only breathe voluntarily and not in those spasmodic jerks! She ought to get him to land and lay him on his stomach and press backwards and forwards like she'd seen them do in life-saving exhibitions on Bondi beach.

But she couldn't get him to land. He was heavy and if she lost her grip and he sank . . . even for a minute . . . one of those spasmodic intakes of breath would fill his lungs with water again. Then it might be too late. If only she could get him horizontal instead of upright!

She held him pressed against her and her body swung a little in the water. Quite accidentally her toe found a hold on one of the submerged roots. It was a small root but she pressed on it and it held.

She was all right now . . . if only the arm clinging to the top root didn't ache so badly. How long could she bear that ache before her arm became numb and in its numbness her hand lost hold? Well, it wouldn't matter if Simon had enough air in his lungs by then. He'd float and she'd be able to pull him over to the other bank with one arm. Or would she? Could she swim on her back without the use of one arm and the other holding Simon?

More water ran from Simon's nose and mouth, and he gasped again. This time his whole body quivered. His face was too close to hers to see him clearly. It made her cross-eyed looking into his face but she thought his eyes flickered.

If he was coming to life, it was safer this way. The other way she might risk losing him. He wouldn't recover if he sank and filled his lungs with water a second time.

Suddenly she remembered Mandy. She whistled. A minute later Mandy could be heard walking, clod-hopping along the creek bank. Gerry whistled again. Mandy came through the trees to the edge of the bank.

"Mandy . . . Mandy . . . Mandy, darling!" Gerry called.

The mare dropped her head and looked over the bulbous overhanging roots. Her ears suddenly lay flat back against her head and she neighed. She reared back, then took a delicate frightened step forward again.

"Mandy, darling," Gerry said, "can't you throw me your reins?"

172

There were tears in her eyes because she knew Mandy would have done so if she had known how.

Gerry moved her weight on her toe where it pressed on the underwater root and it altered the angle of the arm that was holding on above. She cried out with the agonising pain.

"Mandy . . . Mandy . . ." she said and knew her voice was little more than a whispering prayer. "Do something, Mandy darling! Come in the water and pull me out . . . or go home and tell them . . ." But her voice was lost in something that was less than a whisper now because she knew that Mandy could not understand. But she went on praying to herself:

"Mandy . . . Mandy . . . Mandy, darling."

The mare jerked her head up and down again. She brought her ears forward and looked at her mistress in the water. Water poured out of Simon's mouth again and he gulped in air.

"If I stay here . . . I can save him," Gerry thought. Her arm was past hurting now. It was dead. "If I just hang on."

Mandy stepped gingerly backwards. She was out of sight now. She blew through her nose and lips and shook her bridle. Gerry could hear the jingle. Then she heard something more. Mandy was crashing through the bushes to the track. Then suddenly she was galloping away in the direction of the homestead.

Oddly enough Gerry felt sleepy now. She had to remember not to fall asleep. She might drop Simon. She wouldn't drop the arm that was holding the branch because she knew that it would be agony to bring back the blood circulating into it. Even unconscious she would never drop that arm.

She had put Mandy's saddle back after that mud-bath. A horse going home, saddled but riderless, would mean something. If someone saw her . . . Mandy wouldn't put herself in the saddling paddock. She had gone home because she had *known*. She would find someone.

It seemed hours later, except that the sun had not yet sunk, when Jim and David, both on Mandy, came back down the homestead track.

Gerry didn't know who was there. She only knew Mandy had come back. She couldn't be bothered looking up to see who had come with Mandy. Her chin was resting on Simon's head and her eyes were closed because she had to keep thinking about not going to sleep and not letting Simon go.

Whoever was there was not talking either. They were awfully quiet. Presently she knew someone was in the water beside her and someone took Simon out of the circle of her arm. That hurt too because it took some of the weight off the arm holding on and to move even by the fraction of an inch was agony to that arm.

Her body swung a little in the water and that hurt the arm too. It made her cry.

Then a minute later Jim was lying over the top roots reaching down to her.

"Don't move my arm, Jim . . . don't move my arm . . . please, Jim . . ."

"I know," he said gently. "That's why I'm getting you this way, Gerry. So you can keep your arm up. Here's David."

There was a splashing in the water and David was beside her.

"Get under her and lift her gently, David," Jim said. "I'll haul her up as you lift. Do it as slowly as you can. That arm will murder her."

David had her round the waist and he lifted. Gerry was sure it was slow and gentle but the weight of her own body on her arm was easing and she cried again with the pain.

Jim had got one hand under that arm now and he was holding it aloft. David lifted again and Jim, lying full length, the toes of his boots twisted under roots to hold him, got his other hand under her free arm.

"Now," said Jim.

With a gigantic splash of his feet kicking against water David lifted again. Jim had got her head and shoulders level with his.

"Lay that bad arm across my shoulder, Gerry. It will hurt but lay it there and we'll wait here a minute to give it time to ease a little."

Gerry's arm came down of its own accord on to Jim's shoulder and she cried again.

"It's . . . it's not the the pain, Jim. It's . . . it's just that I'm tired. I can't be bothered any more."

But it was the pain, together with the fact she couldn't be bothered feeling any more pain.

They seemed to stay there in that position a long long time. Jim's face was level with hers . . . only six or eight inches away . . . but she didn't want to look at it. Now that the pain in her arm was subsiding she was too tired to open her eyes. She supposed she looked silly: like a drowned rat, or something. Her hair was in her eyes, and it was wet.

174

David was doing an awful lot of swimming about. Funny how you can't keep a swimmer out of the water. It's a sort of mania with them . . . like yachting and bridge and golf. It sort of gets in the blood, they say.

There he was above Jim. That's what he must have been doing. Swimming along to climb up on the bank and help Jim. Well, she just hoped she wasn't too heavy. She couldn't imagine anything more undignified than having to be *lugged* heavily out of the water. And what an ugly word "lugged" was! And what an ugly sight she must be herself now that she came to think of it.

As if anything mattered, now that she didn't have to hold Simon up and hang on to that awful tree root any more.

The strange thing was she felt herself coming up out of the water and over the tree roots very lightly. It must be because Jim was so strong. How powerful he was!

She wondered if he could throw her about like a shuttlecock. Well . . . not in this bedraggled shirt and shorts anyway. To make a good shuttlecock one had to wear feathers . . .

She was lying on the ground and Jim was crouched right over her so that her bad arm was still lying on his shoulder.

Funny how he said nothing. Both he and David must be dumb. Well, he'd begin rampaging in a minute. She and Simon were silly darn fools . . .

Then she did hear his voice. Very near her face it was.

"Hold the arm at the same angle while I crawl out from under it, David. Don't lower it."

That arm again. Did she have to have some more pain in it? She opened her eyes, startled.

"Simon?" she said.

"He's all right. Bill Seddon's just come down and is with him. He's around but not exactly fighting fit at the moment. Now listen, Gerry, I'm going to lower your arm inch by inch. It will hurt as the circulation comes back into it, but not as much as before. Can you stand it?"

"No," she said. "No. Leave it there, please, Jim."

He was kneeling beside her and holding her arm out in a Nazi salute.

"You can take it, Gerry," he said. "You can take anything, you know."

Well, that was a compliment, anyway.

He lowered the arm, watching her face as he did so. She gave one short sharp cry and then clenched her teeth. She

175

didn't care any more what he thought of her. She knew her face was puckered in the agony of it. Jim's hand brushed the hair back from her forehead. Then slowly the pain began to recede like a tide going out. Presently there wasn't any more and she just felt tired. But she liked it when Jim brushed her hair back again.

She turned her head and saw Mandy standing in the bushes.

"Mandy . . ." she said. "Mandy . . . Mandy . . . Mandy . . ." Her voice trailed away into quiet . . . and then silence.

CHAPTER EIGHTEEN

GERRY'S ARM was useless for two days.

"It's in a state of protest," she explained to David. "It considers it has been hardly done by and is now in a fit of sulks. But I look interesting with it hanging down like this, don't I?"

They were sitting on the veranda.

"You're an interesting person anyway, Gerry. How the devil you hung on to that kid all that time, I just don't know."

"Well, don't you go showing off in front of him again. You said yourself he'd copy a gang of safe-breakers if he was long enough in their company."

"As a matter of fact I haven't taken my eyes off him for two days for fear he's hanging to the branch of a tree just to find out what you felt like."

At that moment Simon came round the veranda. When he saw Gerry he automatically dropped one arm helplessly down by his side and continued on his way in this manner. Gerry and David gazed after him. Then their eyes met. They burst into laughter.

"He doesn't even know he does it," Gerry said helplessly.

"He knows all right," said David. "Otherwise he'd stop for conversation. It's his way of telling you you're interesting. If you'll excuse me I'll catch him and wallop him for it."

Simon's head was back around the corner of the veranda.

"Anyhow I got through four of the roots," he said.

"And if I'd have been there instead of Gerry I'd have left you stuck in the fifth," said David.

"No, you wouldn't, because that would have been murder.

Accessory after the fact. You aren't the only one who can talk like an encyclopædia, David."

"And you're taking good care we notice, aren't you?"

"I'm taking good care that Gerry notices," said Simon. He came back round the veranda. "Gerry," he said with utmost seriousness, "I have read a whole book in two days and I'll read a whole book every week of my life . . . just for you."

"Simon, dear . . ."

"I just wanted to let you know," he said airily. "And I'll eat potatoes and damper till I'm *fat*." He dropped his arm helplessly by his side again and proceeded along the veranda to the next corner. "I just wanted to let you know," he said. Then ducked round the corner before David could catch him.

"You'll miss that kid," David said, coming back to his chair by Gerry.

"Do you mean when I go away? Or when they go away?"

"What makes you think they're going away? My guess is Jim Conrad is planted here for many a long day yet."

"The bank men come on Friday," Gerry said.

"Men?" said David. "What makes it plural? There's only one of them as far as I know. That's Everard."

"Then who is the fourth man? There's the Airways surveyor and his offsider. That's three . . ."

"Railton," said David, astonished that Gerry didn't know. "My boss. General manager of Centralia Pastoral Company. He's coming up to see what kind of a loaf I've been putting in on Yandoo."

Gerry swallowed hard. Then the manager wasn't with them after all. Wouldn't he ever come, she wondered.

"Is he going the rounds with the bank man?" Gerry asked because she had to pretend some kind of interest for David's sake.

"Yes. The company's looking for young executives that have had outback experience. I just wish it was my luck that I'd be one of them he was thinking about. You know, my best qualification is that I've had this experience watching how Jim Conrad goes about things."

"Why does everyone think so much of how Jim Conrad does things?"

"Good heavens, Gerry! You've got eyes, haven't you? He's thrashed this place alive literally overnight. And not a row or a fight over it. He's got a muster team out there working the devil out of their plant. He's got old Bill Seddon

177

practising up to be supervisor of the work gang that'll lay that airstrip and from that on he's going to take charge of the out-station. He's got Lulu almost singing as she happily signs letters and types tally sheets and composes reports. He's got you putting so much spit and polish on the homestead no one would ever recognise it."

"David, you're making a speech."

"Well, so I am. There's a lot to make a speech about. There's me. I haven't had to ride a breakneck horse but I've had a chance of seeing how each and everything works on this station. Those two natives out there are ready to lay down their lives for him and the two lubras in the kitchen nearly cry with joy every time he passes the kitchen door. The place is buzzing, and everybody's happy. What more do you want? The man's a wizard."

So he was. Everything that David had said was right. Gerry had never seen it that way before. Or had she? Hadn't she known all along what was happening?

Then why had she resisted?

First it had been because she felt she had to protect Yandoo. Then it had been because she had been trying to protect herself. Protect herself from falling a victim of Jim's powerful personality.

Those letters to the manager! They had been a kind of substitute. She had had to make a feeling for someone else to save herself from having too much feeling for Jim Conrad.

But didn't he know what he did to Lulu and herself? What right had he to make *both* of them unhappy? No. Lulu wasn't unhappy. As David said, she had changed beyond recognition, almost like the station itself. And she all but sang as she worked.

Lulu was happy. That must very much be because of Jim Conrad.

Gerry pushed her chair back and stood up.

"With a silly arm like mine, David," she said, "I'll have to have some help with those beds. Do you think the General Manager of Centralia Pastoral Company will mind sharing a dressing-room with a bank official and sleeping on a veranda?"

"Those fellows sleep in palaces when they're home; and quite often in bush humpies when they're not," David said cheerfully. "Don't you worry, Gerry girl. Old man Railton has had his crack of bushwhacking days. That's why we chaps in the city end get sent out to have a go on the stations. He reckons, and quite rightly, we can't understand the pastoralists' problems if we haven't suffered a few of the problems ourselves."

It was sundown on Friday when the party arrived by car from Ruloo Station.

Jim had not spoken to Gerry again about the prospects of her going to join her mother in Sydney. He had been wonderfully kind to her in the trip in the utility up to the homestead after her adventures in the creek with Simon. First he had seen that Simon was safely stowed away in the back with Bill Seddon and then he'd packed Gerry in the front seat between himself and David.

"You drive, David," he said.

He turned round now and again to look through the canopy to see if Simon was all right. Half-way up to the homestead he had done this and when turning his head back had caught Gerry's eyes. She knew she looked bedraggled and she supposed she looked tired.

"Do you want a shoulder to lean on, Gerry?" he asked.

She found it hard to believe that Jim Conrad could sound so gentle. She shook her head.

"I'm all right," she said.

As a matter of fact she would have liked a shoulder but because it was Jim Conrad's she couldn't use it.

If she forgot that he had wanted her to leave Yandoo she might have wanted to stay on that shoulder for ever. She might have wanted to do what David had done that time they drove home from the out-station. David had turned his face into her neck and quietly and peacefully gone to sleep.

Remembering Jim wanted to send her away from Yandoo, there would have been no peace in resting her head on his shoulder. She knew he offered it out of gallantry because she had held Simon up in the water.

She had shaken her head and said, "I'm all right, thank you."

Now, days later, as she stood with Lulu on the front veranda and watched the huge overlanding car come up the track by the paddock fence she knew that all her worries would be over one way or the other. Ever since Jim Conrad had ridden in, things had been moving towards some hidden climax. This week-end would bring all the threads together in that climax.

She no longer hid the real truth about Yandoo from herself. Her mother, together with the handful of outside shareholders, held the lease and the title deeds to all installations. But there their real ownership ended. The overdraft, after the drought and fire, had grown long past the danger point. The bank could have foreclosed them. It didn't. Instead it had appointed a manager to see what could be salvaged.

Every time Gerry had said "Mother is the owner of Yandoo" she had not been looking facts in the eye. Mrs. Meredith owned it theoretically. For all practical purposes the bank owned it.

Jim Conrad had intervened and done something miraculous to the station. This week-end would settle what the bank would do about that. And about Jim Conrad.

This week-end would settle now who owned Yandoo. Had Jim Conrad got his bite? Had the bank a control over the remaining shareholders who had contributed to the station when her father had turned it into a company? That had been to provide the capital to sink bores as an addition to the natural water supplies.

When Gerry's father was dying she was fourteen. He had said to her:

"Your Aunt Sally and your mother were always attached to one another, Gerry. They will have each other. But Yandoo's got no one but you. Look after it. And one day pay back that money to the outside shareholders. Make Yandoo all Meredith again."

That was what she had never been able to tell Jim, or her mother, or Aunt Sally. Not even could she tell Bill Seddon who had worked with her father and known her grandfather on Yandoo.

That was why she had gone down to the billabong the day the doctor came to see her mother. Aunt Sally would look after her mother but who would look after Yandoo? And her father had said . . .

Her father had told her to do it.

The big car was at the garden gate now. It had swung round and braked to a stop and men were getting out of it.

For Gerry this would be the beginning or the end. She had no idea which.

Jim Conrad was out of the car first. He was opening the door for Mr. Everard to get out. Jim had ridden down to the creek crossing to meet them. Well, they'd know all about Jim by now. Mr. Everard was the inspector the bank had sent out all those months ago and it had been on his report the bank had decided to put in a manager.

He'd notice a difference now, that was certain.

The other three men were out too, and David who had just come up from shaving and bathing down at the storehouse was having his hand wrung by a big stout man. He looked pleased to see David.

Well, that was one issue settled. Evidently David wasn't going to have any difficulty with Mr. Railton.

The other two men were the Airways men. They were both lean wiry sunburnt men, one older than the other. They probably spent their life surveying airstrips on outback stations.

Dinny and Johnny had both appeared on the scene and had opened the boot of the car and were piling out cases and surveying-rods.

Gerry could hear Jeannie and Mary giggling from round the corner. They too had to be in the excitement.

The men were all talking, their voices loud and cheerful.

Gerry glanced at Lulu. Then she felt something of a shock. Gerry hadn't realised that she herself had been standing behind the veranda balustrade looking over it and between the creepers at the arrivals. It was Lulu who was standing at the head of the steps.

Gerry looked at her again.

Lulu had on a beautiful blue linen dress. Very straight and slim she looked. She carried her head beautifully too. She looked proud, and elegant, and completely at ease. Gerry remembered David's words . . . "Lulu was born to stand at the head of a staircase."

With a slight sense of shock Gerry realised this was not only true but that Lulu knew it. Lulu was in her element.

Mr. Everard was leading the way now. Jim Conrad had stepped back to speak to the natives, telling them probably where to put everything.

Mr. Everard had stood quite still looking at the garden and then at the homestead. Then he came on up the path. As he came to the steps Gerry could see that he was both surprised and pleased. As he mounted the steps he held out his hand to Lulu.

"I think we've met, Miss Meredith," he said. "If only in a letter."

Lulu took his hand but she smiled graciously and shook her

head. "I'm Lulu Sylvester," she said. "Gerry's cousin. This is Gerry."

"I beg your pardon," Mr. Everard began. Then he held out his hand to Gerry. "It's you I've met. Now tell me . . . have you a sister? I seem to remember a young stripling of a girl cantering around the place on a horse when I was here last. It took me about two days to discover she was a girl."

"It was me," Gerry said shyly. "I'm not on a horse now. And I'm in a dress . . ."

Like Lulu she wore a linen dress but hers was a rose pink where Lulu's was blue.

"She looks best in a dress," Simon said.

Gerry hadn't known he was there. He had come up from behind very silently.

"Thank you, Simon," Gerry said. "But I'd like to look best either way . . . for me, that is . . ."

"I certainly was very intrigued with your horsemanship," Mr. Everard said.

The other men were on the veranda now and Lulu had shaken hands with them all, explaining who she was and then handing them on to Gerry. Jim and David were both standing a little aside watching the small reception scene.

"You know what, Conrad?" Mr. Everard said, turning to Jim and then back to Gerry. "I would never have believed this was the same girl. You seem to be taller, Miss Meredith, or is that rather tactless of me? Girls really do stop growing when they leave school, don't they?"

"I think it's my shoes," Gerry said with a smile.

She glanced down at the pretty pointed toes and their whittle heels. They still gave her the same pleasure as they had when Aunt Sally had first sent them. She looked up quickly with that same pleasure suddenly shining shyly in her eyes. She was aware that not only Mr. Everard was looking at her but that Jim Conrad was too. And there was something very odd in Jim's eyes. There was a smile at the corner of his mouth too, and it actually reached his eyes.

"Gerry likes her new shoes," Simon said. "She's got another pair too, with buckles."

"This young man seems to have a personal claim on your interests, Miss Meredith," Mr. Everard said, still smiling.

"Oh, he has," said Gerry. "He has a personal claim on me altogether. Mostly in the region of the heart. Now would you like to come and have a brush up after your drive. Then we can have a drink and some savouries. I don't think it will be dinner for quite a while."

It was Mr. Railton Lulu was lavishing most of her attention on. She seemed to think he was much more important than the bank man. She was now leading the way along the passage to show Mr. Railton where the dressing-room was.

"David will show you the bathroom and the shower-house," she said. "The beds are on the veranda outside your french window."

David was very much doing the honours of the occasion and Gerry was surprised to find Jim sitting alone on the front veranda.

"Would you like a drink now, Jim?" she asked. "Or will you wait till the others come?"

"I think I'll have one now," he said, getting up. "And it's going to be a good stiff whisky."

Gerry sat down and accepted something very much milder for herself.

"You sounded as if you need fortifying," she said, looking at him curiously.

She had been surprised to see how friendly he and Mr. Everard had seemed. Almost as if they knew one another. Or perhaps it was that in the short drive up from the crossing Jim had been able to tell him something of what had been done on the station. And Mr. Everard had been pleased.

On the other hand Mr. Everard's pleasant manner could be just a business man's way of hiding what he really thought. Whether he was pleased or not at the role Jim Conrad had played he couldn't help but be satisfied with the results.

"Everard is a man who asks a lot of questions very fast," said Jim. "I'm not fortifying. I'm relaxing."

"Did he say anything about the manager . . . when he is coming?"

Jim put his glass down on the small table. He said nothing for a minute and then turned to Gerry. His mouth was set rather grimly.

"I hope you'll be good enough not to mention that subject for the week-end, Gerry," he said. "It's something right outside our line of discussions for the time being and I don't want Everard distracted from the main purpose of his visit."

This was the old Jim Conrad, the man who had reprimanded her for over-riding the team the day of the first muster.

She bit her lip, and said nothing.

No. The manager was not a subject Jim would want to be discussed . . . until he was ready to do it his own way.

At that moment Lulu and David came back on to the veranda. David was rubbing his hands together in an exaggerated gesture.

"Railton says he's got something up his sleeve for me. Jim, did you put in a good word?"

Jim had picked up his glass but he was looking from under scowling brows across the darkening garden.

"He asked something or other. I've forgotten what. It looks to me as if they've got a nice job upstairs for you, David. I expect you want to go back to Sydney, don't you?" He looked up at David with a quick flicking glance.

David spread his hands as if he would like to say something but couldn't quite find the right words. Then he dropped them and went to the table and poured himself out a drink. He walked back to Jim and lifted the glass in a half toast.

"Thanks, old man," he said.

Lulu had walked to the corner to speak to Jeannie and as she came back towards them Jim got up and poured a drink for her.

"Your eyes are looking bright, Lulu," he said with a half smile as he handed her glass to her.

"I'm very happy, Jim. That's why. It looks as if I've got what I wanted too. And . . ."

"Glad to hear it," Jim said almost as if he was embarrassed. "Now sit down, Lulu, and I'll pour the drinks for the men when they come out."

Funny, Gerry thought. It was just as David had said. The station and homestead were alive and humming with activity. And each individual person had grown in stature and found something in life he or she wanted.

Yes. Jim Conrad was a wizard.

It was at the dinner table that the bomb fell.

The conversation had been general and every time Mr. Everard sounded as if he was getting near to something Jim Conrad had organised or suggested, Jim would briefly turn the conversation back to something that would include Lulu and Gerry. Gerry got the impression he was working hard at keeping everyone talking about shrubs in the garden and the weather up country.

On two occasions when he did it Mr. Everard's eyes met his

and there was a hint of apology in the bank man's own eyes, and he quickly took his cue from Jim and discussed what Ruloo was doing about its garden this Dry.

Lulu had ordered a beautiful dinner. The best fillets of Yandoo's own prime beef. Peas and beans fresh from the garden, as was also the iced melon that had been dipped in ginger and port wine. The fruit salad was mostly out of tins, that was true, but the home-grown passionfruit and bananas, together with fresh oranges from the case, camouflaged the apricots and peaches that had travelled a thousand miles before coming to rest on the shelves of the store-house. And the ice-cream was very definitely Lulu's own recipe. It was green peppermint ice-cream with a chocolate sauce.

Lulu and Gerry each sat at an end of the table and so pleasant was the dinner and happy the spirit around the table that twice the visitors, first Mr. Everard and then Mr. Railton, toasted the two pretty members of the opposite sex who had provided such a lovely occasion for them.

It was nearly a brilliant occasion, for Gerry had brought out all her mother's silver and polished it till the lights kept catching points of it and making the whole table sparkle. The salads were served in crystal bowls and the vegetables in the old-fashioned but really lovely silver entrée dishes. Bowls of the brilliant bougainvillæa flowers around the room and on the table made a splash of daring colour.

It was at the ice-cream stage that the conversation turned to the seasonal prospects of the whole State. It was agreed the rainfall had been unusually heavy in the Wet and the grasses should be good for months to come. South of Yandoo, Mr. Everard said, the country was drying out pretty quickly but he thought it could hold its stock numbers through the season.

"We think you're a pretty smart fellow, Jim," he said jokingly, "but you've got to admit the season has helped you. When we put you in here as manager we reckoned . . ." He stopped dead.

Gerry's eyes froze on to Jim's eyes.

Had she heard right?

With a physical effort she wrenched her eyes away from Jim's face. She leaned forward and looked at the bank inspector. He too was looking at Jim.

"I'm sorry, old chap," he said dejectedly. "I knew that sooner or later I'd drop that brick. You shouldn't serve wine with dinner."

"I . . . I beg your pardon," Gerry said. "What did you say?"

Mr. Everard looked suddenly hopeful as if he thought perhaps Gerry hadn't heard correctly. He made a quick though rather forced recovery.

"I was talking about the season. The manager up there at Ruloo thinks it's the best ever. Jim Conrad always brings good luck in his train. A heavy Wet and a mild opening to the Dry. The creeks having a second late rise in level . . ."

He went on and on and presently Mr. Railton and the two surveyors joined in.

Gerry looked from face to face and then down the table at Jim Conrad. There was a touch of rue in Jim's smile as his eyes met hers. When Gerry dragged her own eyes away it was to meet David's smiling ones. He raised one eyebrow, then winked at her. David had heard too.

Jim!

Jim Conrad was the manager put in by the bank. He was the man come down from the north. He was the man she had written to, and told all about *Jim* . . . and let her feelings bubble through because she had wanted to get it all off her chest and it was easier to write to someone she didn't know than tell or write to someone she did know.

Phrases of what she had written about Jim Conrad sprang to her memory.

"*Oh no!*" she said to herself.

How she got through the last stages of that dinner Gerry never afterwards knew.

From dinner they went to coffee on the veranda. When the coffee was taken away brandy was brought out for the men in her father's lovely old balloon glasses.

Gerry was so very busy with her own thoughts she didn't notice what Jim talked about. She was conscious, though, of the respectful awe the other men, including Mr. Everard, had for him. He was really that legendary person of whom David had spoken.

It was no good trying to remember all she had put in those letters to him. She hadn't re-read them on purpose because she knew she had unlocked the floodgates and given so much of herself away. And she had been so fair to Jim Conrad she had filled up the pages with the wonderful things he had done.

No wonder Jim Conrad had wanted her to go away to Sydney before the bank man came. He had been afraid she would find out who he was. No wonder he had kept her out of all the business affairs of Yandoo. She had been so lofty with him that day he had come to Yandoo and she and Bill Seddon had been waiting at the boundary fence. She had told him there was a manager coming.

Her own voice rang in her memory.

A friend of the family . . . a very reliable man, and an excellent cattleman . . .

Then Jim's sarcastic reply.

A very paragon of the virtues!

"Oh, Jim!" her heart cried. "Oh, Jim! Why did you let me make such a *fool* of myself?"

At least he had tried to save her from knowing it. He had tried to send her to New Zealand, or the Barrier Reef—or somewhere.

And Lulu? What sort of a game had Lulu been playing?

It was no use to look at Lulu now. Lulu was lying back in her chair talking in undertones to David. She'd been doing that ever since dinner. Seasonal changes and the price for prime beef meant nothing to Lulu. She was exchanging the courtesies of after-dinner conversation with David alone.

Gerry was the hostess now. How was she ever going to get off this veranda and escape to her room while all these men sat about and talked as if they meant to talk the night through?

She would have to play out the part of being Miss Meredith of Yandoo and wait to say "good night" to each one of them. That would leave David and Jim the last to go. Perhaps Jim would go away quickly when the last of the visitors went indoors.

What if he didn't? What if he waited and wanted to explain himself?

Well, she'd go away herself. Run away. Miles and miles and miles . . .

How could she have been such a simpleton! As if that man coming from the north, from Arnhem Land, could possibly have taken so long! Even with the high rivers! Jim Conrad had crossed them months ago. But then Jim Conrad was a wizard, David had said so. Everyone else *thought* so.

Jim had come a long way and arrived long since. He had come from the north. Why hadn't she known? That day out at the boundary Johnny the native had all but said so. He had recognised the tribal type of Dinny, Jim's native.

Gerry brushed her hand over her eyes.

Jim had stopped talking now. Why wasn't he laughing at her? Laughing his head off, in fact?

187

All this time, underneath, he had known he was dealing with a simpleton!

It seemed interminable hours before the men rose to go. Then interminable minutes before they had completed their last "good nights."

Gerry looked nervously at Lulu.

"Come and help me put the glasses away, Lulu," she said. "The men had better get a good night's . . ." Her voice wavered.

Lulu said the next thing that shook her balance.

"The glasses can wait until the morning," she said. "David and I are going for a walk."

Gerry put both hands on the table.

"David and you?"

Lulu looked very arch.

"It won't be the first time," she said. "And Mr. Railton has uttered the few magic words that leave us rather a lot to say in private."

Gerry looked beyond Lulu at David. He jerked his thumb upward in a success sign.

"I guess it was the way Lulu stood at the head of those steps," he said mischievously. "I told you she had what it takes, young Gerry. The Number One always likes to have a look at what his offsider's wife is likely to be like."

Gerry drew in a deep breath.

"I'm just dull, I guess. I didn't know."

"Neither did we," said David consolingly. "Not until after that thirst trip we made to the out-station. After that Lulu took me in hand."

"Well, you'd better go and have that walk," Gerry said weakly.

"We're off," said David.

He sprang down the steps and held out his hand to Lulu. In a minute they were lost in the shadows of the garden.

Jim stood immobile and silent at the edge of the veranda.

It was no good running away, after all. Sooner or later she would have to face him.

Very slowly she turned to look at him. When the last of the footsteps died away over the grass he too turned towards Gerry.

They stood, eight yards of veranda between them, and looked at one another.

"You must have had fun, Jim," Gerry said sadly.

188

He shook his head.

"Not very much," he said. "She was such a sweet courageous girl. And she was in for such a let down. I couldn't find it in my heart . . ."

"I remember," Gerry said. "I told you about a manager coming. I said he was a friend of the family. Remember? A very reliable man."

"You were right about his being your friend, Gerry. He knew your father. We jackarooed together on one of Denman's big stations in the Northern Territory."

Still there was that desert of veranda between them.

"I . . . I didn't know that," she had to say truthfully.

Jim smiled.

"You know now."

He took a few short paces towards her and put out his hand. As if mesmerised, Gerry lifted hers. He took it. He took one more step and was very close to her. He was nearly touching her and her hand was crushed in his.

"Why did the bank put you in here as manager, Jim?" Gerry asked. Her voice had to be low because he was so very near her.

"Because I own one-third share in Yandoo. I have owned it for years." His voice too was soft. "The bank is not an ogre, Gerry. It believes in stations running at a profit. It put in the man who had a vested interest in seeing that it ran at a profit. And your mother and I hatched up the rest of the plot between us, I'm afraid."

He lifted her hand up and put it against his breast and held it there.

"I was worried about the cattle," Gerry said lamely. "I thought the bank might have a lien on that mob in the gully."

"The bank knows I was your biggest creditor, my dear. I had to pay running expenses out of pocket, not credit."

He put his other hand under her chin and tilted it up. His eyes were looking down into hers and his face was only inches away.

"Did you think I was cheating?" he asked. His eyebrows were making fun of her.

"I didn't know what to think, Jim."

She didn't know what to think now. In fact she couldn't think properly at all. She was too conscious of his nearness, of her hand feeling the strong stroke of his heart under it and his mouth which was so near hers.

"I did cheat you," Jim said quietly. "I let you go on thinking . . ."

"I know. You were sparing our pride, weren't you? We had so much pride. We made a mess of the station but we didn't want a 'manager' put in because it was a blow at our prestige. And then I said that silly thing about having a manager so you wouldn't treat me like a little girl who had just left school."

"Yet you were the most important girl I'd met in my life. Didn't you realise that, Gerry?"

Her eyes, which had dropped away from his face, flew back to meet his.

"There wasn't much of you," he said. "But you were very lovely. And you rode a horse magnificently. There were ten tiny freckles on your nose . . ."

"Eight," said Gerry.

"There were ten then. I counted them. It's the face cream that's hidden the others. Tell me, Gerry. What made you bring out the gold in your hair? And why do you like to wear your pretty shoes?"

"Are you making fun of me, Jim?"

But she knew he wasn't. A wonder, like the colour in the clouds at sundown, was spreading gently through her whole being. Jim's face was so close . . . he held her hand against his heart. His mouth was nearer, nearer hers. Was it possible?

"I . . . like to look nice," she whispered.

"I thought you looked lovely in a faded pair of jeans and a shirt with a tear in it."

His breath was on her mouth.

"Shall I put them on now, Jim?"

"No." His lips were brushing hers now. It was like thistledown blown by the wind. "I like you in a pink dress with gold in your hair and pretty shoes too. And freckles on your nose. I like you anyway, my darling, so long as I can hold you like this."

The last word was lost because his mouth was on hers and his arms enfolded her.

"Darling Gerry," he said at last. "Would you marry a friend of the family? A very reliable fellow?"

Gerry stood on her toes so that his mouth would not recede too far away.

"Is he a first-class man with all kinds of stock?" she asked, only echoing the pattern of those fateful words spoken so long ago. There were cathedrals and spires in her eyes and cloud palaces shot with rainbows under her feet.

"A very paragon of all the virtues," Jim said.

His mouth was on hers again, and she was lost in the embrace of his arms.

An astonishing concatenation of sounds coming from the side veranda startled them apart.

Still holding Gerry's hand, and taking her with him, Jim went to the corner.

Simon was on his bed, standing on his head and balancing his pillow on the soles of his feet.

"What the devil?" began Jim.

But Gerry laughed. There were starry tears in her eyes.

"I think he took a peek round the corner, Jim, and that's the best he can do to demonstrate his feelings."

"I'm just a poor crazy mixed-up kid," said Simon, from the wrong side up. "I got the wrong end of things about you two and David and Lulu. So I guess I'd better stay this way and see if the world behaves itself upside down."

"You're in a very good position," said Jim, "to get a certain part of your anatomy walloped."

Simon immediately returned to a normal sitting position on the bed.

"Gee, Gerry!" he said, astonished. "You've got tears in your eyes."

"That's because I'm so happy."

Simon looked imploringly at his uncle.

"Aren't girls funny?" he asked.

Jim looked at Gerry. His voice softened again.

"Let's go and find that log," he said.

"You mean the clean one on the edge of the timber?"

"Yes, darling. The clean one. We can sit on it. Remember?"

Without another word they went across the veranda, down the steps, and out into the moonlight.

Simon did a cartwheel on the floor beside his bed before he decided to get under the sheet and go to sleep.

Jim and Gerry never got to that log. Somewhere near the garden gate they stopped.

"Jim," Gerry said doubtfully, "why did you want me to go away?"

"So you would go on writing those wonderful letters to me, darling. I thought you might fall in love with the manager of Yandoo . . . but never with Jim Conrad."

"Then when did you know I *would* . . ."

"Your face when old Everard dropped that brick. You minded so very much what I thought. I nearly walked round the dining-room table and kissed you then." He paused and looked down at her.

"Will you stay on Yandoo, Jim?"

"For ever and a day. My wandering days are over. I want a woman to come home to at nights . . ."

Gerry sighed.

"I want a man to come home to me at nights. That is if I'm out of the muster team for good."

"You are, darling. You'll have other things to do."

"Yes, Jim. I hope I will."

His arms were round her . . . and it was too far to walk to to that log.

THE END